D1473973

TO DIE IN BERLIN

TO DIE IN BERLIN

BY
CARLOS CERDA

TRANSLATED BY
ANDREA G. LABINGER

Latin American Literary Review Press
Series: Discoveries
1999

The Latin American Literary Review Press publishes Latin American creative writing under the series title Discoveries, and critical works under the series title Explorations.

Library of Congress Cataloging-in-Publication Data:

Cerda, Carlos
    [Morir en Berlin. English]
    To die in Berlin / by Carlos Cerda ; translated by
Andrea G. Labinger
      p. cm
    ISBN 1-891270-02-8 (alk. paper)
    I. Title.
PQ8098.13 E668M6713   1999
863--dc21   99-16678
                                  CIP

Latin American Literary Review Press
121 Edgewood Avenue
Pittsburgh, PA. 15218

ACKNOWLEDGMENTS

This project is supported in part by grants from the National Endowment for the Arts, in Washington, D.C., a federal agency, and the Commonwealth of Pennsylvania Council on the Arts.

NATIONAL
ENDOWMENT
FOR THE ARTS

The city celebrated in these pages has
long ago ceased to exist, and the events
recounted in them would now be inconceivable.

Paul Bowles, *Let It Come Down*

CHAPTER ONE

Thinking about it now from a distance, it seems that everything became clearer and more distinct and began to hurt us in a different way the day we found out Don Carlos was dying. Although the Senator was already nearly seventy and we all knew about his ailments, none of us could have imagined the reason for the *Zettel* he slipped under Mario's door that day, written in that pretentious handwriting of his which we all knew so well, inviting Mario to visit him that afternoon "after you go to the 'Cough Hall.'"

The "Cough Hall" ...

Don Carlos lives in a building in the Volkradstrasse around the corner from the Kaufhalle. Every afternoon—and into nightfall during the winter months—Don Carlos stops by the supermarket on his way home from the Bureau. He tells us that there, in the "Cough Hall," he entertains himself by looking at newspapers and labels which he can't read, bottles of liquor and cigars that they won't allow him to taste. He buys a jar of Schmelkäse—a mild cheese that we taught him to recognize by its silvery paper wrapping—some special bread that doesn't give him an acid stomach, and a bottle of Stierblut wine, which he chose on learning that Neruda had canonized it in a poem.

He arrives at his apartment around seven, with the modest dinner his gastritis has imposed upon him. Generally he doesn't receive visitors or speak with anyone until the following day, but sometimes (although only very occasionally) he invites us to his place to discuss matters that would more appropriately be dealt with at the Bureau. The nature of these matters varies considerably, since they encompass the wide range of unsatisfied demands and forbidden desires that make up the kaleidoscope of our deprivation. Although it's been determined at the Bureau that these requests must be acted upon by the Ministry, their very discussion requires a positive endorsement by Director of Controls and Staff, a post which the Senator has occupied ever since the ghetto was established, inasmuch as the administrators and the petitioners are equally reluctant to introduce any changes into their practices. The private and frequently sensitive nature of many of these matters suggests that they not be discussed in the Bureau, a place which is frequented after hours by residents who don't belong to its central structure. Perhaps that's why Don Carlos sends us these notes asking us to drop by his apartment "if you happen to be going by the Cough Hall." Besides, this way he avoids making the matter look like a peremptory summons. These emergency sessions that the Senator devotes to official matters in his apartment help to shorten his long, solitary evenings, which begin as soon as he leaves the Bureau.

Don Carlos became a widower back in Chile, when he had just turned fifty. He has a long history of conversing amicably, but fearfully, with his shadow, while he abbreviates his nights by drinking a few glasses of wine and realizes that his new companion, as permanent as his shadow but less silent, is the painful rumbling of his guts.

People have many ways of organizing their solitude, but we're convinced that the most pathetic ones were invented here. Stupidity coupled with a penchant for purpose can create hell on earth quite effectively. Don Carlos was transferred by the Rat des Bezirkes—the Municipal Council—to a one-room apartment with a small bathroom and an equally tiny kitchen, in a building where all the apartments have only one room, all have been assigned to people over sixty-five, and all the elderly people assigned to the one hundred sixty dwellings in the building share not only their advanced age, but also the circumstance of having been widowed in the last six months.

This ship of widowers runs aground next to a canal that flows indifferently past the back of the building. The afternoon sun gives life to the flowers that the widows water on their minimal terraces, as they watch the polluted water go by and see the sunglow disappear behind the blocks of recently built constructions. Every evening around seven Don Carlos takes the elevator upstairs, surrounded by old people, some of them pleasant and chatty, others engrossed in who-knows-what, and almost all of them accompanied by their dogs, those last vestiges of company which Don Carlos, despite his years, has managed to disdain.

At that hour, when the Senator returns to his apartment, he finds the presence of the dogs unbearable. At the first floor, a veritable pack of them, their presence made known by barking from inside the building, leaves the elevator like a stampede, followed by the sharp cries of the old people. The dogs who are about to enjoy their afternoon walk mingle with the many others who are returning from the streets. Don Carlos rides the elevator upstairs with them and with his neighbors, avoiding being struck by anxious tails and licked by tongues that always seem to be about to reach him. Although he has become adept at the art of eluding these effusions, he's never managed to avoid altogether the assault on his sense of smell. He so despises the smell of the doggy hordes that their very presence makes him nauseated. The only other odor that makes him similarly upset is the smell of old people, which Don Carlos always associates with the smell of death. That's why every afternoon, on his way home from the Bureau, he prefers to linger at the supermarket, sniffing packages of tobacco or fruit, thus postponing his inevitable encounter with the stench of dogs and death.

Although Mario didn't go by the Kaufhalle that afternoon, he nonetheless showed up at eight o'clock sharp at Don Carlos' apartment, convinced that the reason for the appointment was his decision to separate from Lorena. To abandon that poor woman and those little angels, according to the gossiping huddles of old ladies in the ghetto.

The unpleasant sensation that filled his dry mouth ever since he read the summons that morning had to do with his painful decision to separate, but also (as Mario later informed us) with something else he didn't dare acknowledge, for if he did, the pain of his separation would be compounded by an indefinable feeling, something closely resembling rage, but also shame, an embarrassment combining rebellion and submission within a single feeling of excitement. The *Zettel* forebode (although it didn't actually mention any of this) a serious admonishment, not only for having separated from his wife, but even more importantly for having decided to do so (and worse yet for having already moved out of his house) without first heeding "the Bureau's opinion."

Thus he assumed that his appointment with the Senator would break down into a series of not very direct questions and even more oblique answers "about the main issue." And that main issue had nothing to do with Mario's feelings, or with the bitterness that choked Lorena's sleepless nights, or with the children's suffering, but rather with something unrelated to any of them and coming from on high. Something very important that couldn't let itself be corrupted by pain or compassion, something that seemed to float above all of them like an indifferent deity who would always ignore their real problems in favor of "the unassailable issue of loyalty." But the question of loyalty had nothing to do with his faithfulness to Lorena, to their marriage of so many years' duration, to the children of that marriage. "The issue of loyalty" was, above all, connected to a "demonstration of a breach of loyalty to the Institution," and thus it was expressed, as though it were part of a *Festschrift* or the conclusion of a debate: I'd rather side with the Bureau and be wrong than oppose the Bureau and be right.

Yes, of course he would hear that neat little slogan again. And as he parked the Trabant in front of the building with its tiny balconies, Mario thought that the best approach would be not to repress the burst of laughter that always accompanied the mention of the slogan at social gatherings in the ghetto. Yes, of course. Laughing openly was better than putting on that expression of diffidence that we used to assume when we heard it at the Bureau.

However, Mario's problem was much more complicated now. Like it or not, the old man's sermons had become part of the ghetto's clever repertory of anecdotes. After so many years, practically all of us had passed through the famous little blue room—a nickname that originated in another place and at another time, both distant—and just seeing the Senator strolling along the Alexanderplatz on a Saturday morning was enough to remind us of various ingenious phrases like that one, which Don Carlos used to repeat with deep conviction in his oh-so-private meetings at the Bureau. But the current problem wasn't the Bureau's opinion of Mario's divorce, but rather an even more delicate matter, if one understands that in this case the Bureau can approve a resident's petition only with the consent of the Ministry of the Interior.

This is in no way to imply any interference in Mario's most intimate troubles on the part of the Ministry of the Interior of the First State of Laborers and Farmers on German Soil, something like permission from the Ministry for Mario to separate from his wife. Of course not. It was rather a question of the Ministry's consent to a much more delicate matter, something about which the Bureau spoke in hushed tones, behind closed doors, with a reticence even greater than that provoked by "the main issue." It was about the business of the visas, no less.

Anyone who hasn't lived in that world might think that obtaining a visa is nothing more than a minor bureaucratic inconvenience, not at all comparable to a divorce proceeding. In those days and in that place these matters weren't considered to be of equal importance. In fact, every year hundreds of thousands of subjects of the First State of Laborers and Farmworkers on German Soil annulled their marriages, while very few managed to visit relatives on the other side of the wall.

Perhaps that's why Mario harbored the secret hope that the business about his separation would be resolved favorably—following, naturally, a full and explicit acknowledgment of "the main issue"—and the most absolute certainty that the visa request would lead to a very disagreeable exchange, doubly disagreeable, to be more precise: it would be painful to present the petition to the Senator a few minutes from now, and even sadder to inform Lorena of the Senator's perfectly predictable rejection that very evening.

In the elevator, surrounded by the stench of the dogs and the old people's wobbly smiles, Mario thinks it isn't right to have the old man living here, so far from the ghetto, from those other elevators filled with familiar expressions and words. He thinks that this winter it will be even more difficult for Don Carlos to spend his nights alone, away from the after-dinner conversations on Elli-Voigt-Strasse, with homemade bread and stewed pork along with the Stierblut and the talk spinning around a repeated subject till it forms an immense spool, to which the new voices of those who have arrived without words are incorporated. The old man, for better or for worse, is an eminence at our soirees. He's always seated at the head of the table, while the women of the household slip unnoticed into the kitchen and in a flash prepare his special meals with extra care: a bit more salt this time or a teaspoonful of pepper and garlic sauce, concealed in the richness of a little chicken broth. We forty-somethings, who have heard the Senator's stories many times, would ask him questions as if we had forgotten some detail, provoking a repetition that would be the first time for some of the younger ones, their first contact with those images of the pampa that Don Carlos crossed with Neruda in the '46 campaign. Then the children's eyes would fill with antique trains and interminable stretches of saltpeter; what a strange country their parents had lost! Imagine: deserts and mountain ranges and cities that had never felt the nuptial kiss of snow.

At that time in our little world we all witnessed the loss of certain privileges and the decline of certain dignities. Don Carlos's transfer from Elli-Voigt—the bustling heart of the ghetto, eleven blocks in which a large number of the residents were concentrated—to the shadowy Volkradstrasse, was the keenest sign in a series of changes that disturbed us, not only because of their unexpectedness but also because of the extraordinary speed with which they were put into effect. Suddenly the directors' families were placed in smaller apartments, in recently-constructed communities on the outskirts, no longer on the wide avenues with their leafy swaths of lawn and heavily solemn buildings so typical of the first periods of reconstruction. The mansion that the Party used to occupy on Heinrich-Mann-Strasse, surrounded by peaceful gardens and embassies, became Bureau headquarters as the result of its transferal to one of the apartments on the selfsame Elli-Voigt-Strasse. Finally, all single, separated or widowed people were set up in one-room apartments. We all thought an exception would be made for Don Carlos and believed that the ancient Senator, who had already been decorated dozens of times by syndicalist and solidarity organizations, would spend his final days enveloped in that special warmth that is so common in divided communities. At least that's what we felt—it was the principal characteristic of Elli-Voigt. However, since there were no apartments available for single people there, he was summarily moved to a building for widowers. Although this was one of the most regrettable moves among the many changes and declines that devastated our reduced community in the early eighties, none of us dared to argue with the logic of the measure. Don Carlos belonged to the Chilean universe as much as he did to the world of widowers. Even the Senator himself (as Mario now recalls) did nothing to stop the move, not only because he never disputed any decision by the "homeowners" as he used to say, but also because by that time, quite sickly and tired, he accepted the move as the normal beginning of a stage of life in which longer, more peaceful nights would be desirable.

Don Carlos's apartment is at the end of the hall. There's a long row of doors through which Mario hears the sounds of loneliness: the opera; a soccer game; some coughing; silence; the voice of an old woman conversing with her dog; more silence; other pale imitations of life through the squalid walls and doors. From the apartment next door to the Senator's there is no sound at all, but Mario notices that there's a note tacked to the door.

The ceiling of the corridor is lower than that of the apartments, and its white color has faded to a dirty ochre, even darker in the corners. The walls, on the other hand, have been recently painted. Their light green hue remains unstained, and one can still smell the paint.

As he nears the end of the hallway, Mario tries to silence his steps. Now he's standing in front of the white door, yellowish like the ceiling, about to knock. Would discussing the visas make any sense? How can he dare ask for them, as his in-laws' arrival is only hours away? What has the Bureau decided about his divorce? One thing is clear: don't let yourself get carried away by panic and just try to achieve your main goal. Because if the Bureau rejects the divorce, how will you get an apartment? No petition will be considered by the Municipal Council without proper endorsement by the Bureau. He remembered the sheet of paper on the wall behind the old man's desk, as unassailable as time, like the yellow color acquired by all the Bureau's announcements, like the color of the door now staring Mario in the face. He was about to retrace his steps, thinking that the best thing would be to go back to Lorena and tell her straight out that she was the one who should be handling the visas; after all they were her parents and he had enough to do what with the separation, something that fell entirely on his own shoulders, since Lorena wouldn't take a single step to speed up a procedure that she didn't want. However, he didn't budge from the door: quite the contrary, he bent his head forward until he touched the cold wood with his equally cold ear and listened. He could barely distinguish the old man's slow clattering and the brush of his slippers against the floor, a dull, tired sound that Mario imagined to be an acoustical portrait of the Senator. His presence was shrinking, his former corpulence turning into something light, strangely resembling transparency. We felt he had less need of space. And nevertheless, that presence, already so embedded in death, was one on which our lives still depended.

At last Mario rang the bell, resigned to face the situation, come what might. He realized that, unlike his last visit, when he sought out Don Carlos on his own initiative to present a problem, he was there now because he had received a summons, and all summonses are peremptory, even when the paper that Don Carlos slipped under his apartment door that morning said, "Come and see me today if you're passing by the Cough Hall."

"Did you do your shopping already, comrade?"

He greeted him with a friendly smile and Mario felt a certain anxiety in his handshake.

Those of us who have ever been in the Senator's apartment felt sorry for the old man's unavoidable loneliness, but somehow we also felt seduced by that complete freedom that those who live alone seem to enjoy. In his apartment one had the impression of being in a hotel room, everything in its exact place, temporary objects, no strings, nothing that might suggest permanence.

"Something warm to drink? A cup of tea?"

"Don't go to any trouble, Don Carlos."

"Or how about a little wine?"

"All right, some wine."

Don Carlos crossed the narrow space of his living room to the even narrower space of the kitchen. Then Mario noticed two enormous packages on the desk, elaborately wrapped in gift paper. It seemed strange to him in that place, where everything was rather sad and old, that there could be such a happy display of packages with their prodigious, streamer-like ribbons. It was then that he felt he had been caught in a trap, appearing on stage at the wrong time.

Is that why the old man asked him to come? It was an invitation, then. A party. And he was the first to arrive—and empty-handed! Of course! The old man's birthday! He'd been there last year on this date, too, and he remembered the snowstorm. They had a hard time getting the Trabant out of the snowdrift; he had to leave Lorena at the wheel while several people pushed, transforming the uproar in the street into the last revelry of the evening.

"A cup of tea or some red wine? You have to drink something in this rotten weather. Have to give the body a boost, don't you think? Sit down, comrade. Make yourself comfortable."

But the festivities had ended almost as soon as they departed. They left their small group of friends behind, huddled together in the snowstorm, taking the last puffs of their cigarettes. They didn't speak on the way back. They hadn't been speaking for several days. Yes, several, because now he remembers that after that party, after dropping Lorena off at the apartment, he went to Eva's house. One month earlier Mario had spent his first night at Eva's, and a few weeks later Lorena knew everything there was to know. That's why they hadn't spoken that night on the way back home. And it's as though he were seeing Lorena's profile at this very moment, her defeat and at the same time her wounded dignity, her gaze fixed on the windshield, on the snow that swirled about illuminated by the headlights, as silent and as sadly vulnerable as Lorena, nearly extinguished but still blanketing everything. A whole year had passed since then. Another year!

"Aren't you going to sit down? Make yourself comfortable."

Make yourself comfortable. So, this was a party and soon the others would arrive. Surely Lorena had been invited too. He thought it wouldn't make sense to offer any excuses.

"Fine, as you like, Don Carlos."

"Are you in a big hurry?"

The old man brought the first sip of wine to his lips.

"No, no. What makes you think that?"

Of course. He was the first one, the forgetful one, the big airhead, a hopeless case. Surely one of those gifts was from the United German Socialist Party. The huge one, delivered very early by the boys from the Ministry. The other one was probably from the Bureau. And now new gestures of friendship toward the old man would be arriving, smaller, but sincere nonetheless. Everyone but him! Same old dimwit. The same guy who called the old man every afternoon, asking him to speed up his petition. The same guy who showed up that very evening…for what? To congratulate the old man on what could be his last birthday? No, of course not. The irresponsible lout came to ask a favor…another favor!

Don Carlos stood next to the window, watching the snow fall on the balcony.

"I wanted to talk to you about a personal matter," he said.

Of course. That's why he had arranged everything so Mario would be the first to arrive. Mario felt his throat dry up and he swallowed some wine. He felt this was the moment just before everything would collapse. His empty hands, the two gifts smiling through the wide mouths of their ribbons and Don Carlos not looking at him, saying in a somber tone (too somber) that he wanted to talk to him about a personal matter.

"Yes, of course." Mario put his glass down on the table and lit a cigarette. "Anything new?"

"I spoke to the doctor today," said Don Carlos, walking away from the window.

With the doctor? That's why he called him, then.

"What did the doctor tell you?"

"It will be necessary to operate."

"Necessary to operate on what?"

What does he mean, "necessary?" They have to operate on him?

"They told me they had the results of the biopsy."

"Is it a tumor?"

The old man hesitated. The question cut the fragile link to his last hope. He twirled his glass around on the table and Mario observed that he had his glance fixed on the door. He was surely looking at the scratches in the wood, the infinite lines and ridges in the painting that some other owner's dog had left there as a sign of his own anguish.

"It's just a little spot. I swear, it's no bigger than an olive."

The old man momentarily seized on the possibility of self-deception, but then he once again fixed his gaze on the door and remained silent. Maybe he's looking at those scratches differently now, thought Mario; maybe he hears the howling, or he's scratching at another door, knowing he can no longer escape.

"And what did they tell you about the biopsy, Don Carlos?"

"Just what I told you, that I need an operation. And I wanted to know your opinion."

Mario deliberately stubbed out his cigarette while he tried to formulate an answer. He immediately intuited that Don Carlos didn't want medical advice, much less the truth. He wanted support, a credible lie; he wanted to go on living.

Mario's silence became painfully long.

"Who has the test results?"

"Your doctor, Wagemann. That's why I called you."

"Okay, I'll talk to him tomorrow."

"As far as your matter is concerned," Don Carlos then said, "as far as that's concerned, I can assure you that I've done everything possible. I informed them that you've already made a decision. I suppose it's serious and you've considered everything that a separation involves, especially if the spouse is a comrade who's still in the Party. I think there'll be a decision this month. Before the end of the year, as I said," and bringing his glass to his lips, he added, trying to speak calmly about his illness, "I suppose by that time I'll already have had my operation."

"Excuse me, Don Carlos, but that means you already reported it ..." (he wanted to say "favorably" but he didn't dare and said "personally" instead). "You reported it personally?"

"I turned in the paperwork, comrade. The Secretariat discusses it and decides."

"Yes, but you're part of the Secretariat, Don Carlos."

"Just a part of it, Mario. Be patient."

Patience. He'd spent years storing up patience. The old man doesn't want to tell me how he reported on my case. If his report had been positive, what reason could he have for hiding it from me, especially now, when he's dying of fright? The most likely explanation is that he requested...No. Nothing is for sure, Mario told himself. It's impossible to know who's determining your life. It's always the Secretariat, the Bureau, the Controls Commission...Never anyone with a human name, never some comrade from the ghetto. Never one of those people who invite you to their house and offer you a swallow of the last bottle of *pisco* somebody brought from Santiago, and let's wet our whistles and talk about last night's Radio Moscow broadcast, or an article from a

Chilean journal that just arrived but which was published over there two months ago. Never someone who organizes a casual soccer game or a volunteer job on the weekends, an idea that arises spontaneously when Don Carlos arrives a little late and the owner of the house greets him reverently and without asking she goes into the kitchen and in a second she's made him some chicken soup or angel hair pasta, they say the poor man's so sick...No. It's never one of them, flesh and blood people, people who have to eat chicken soup because they know the worst is yet to come, so how can you not run to the kitchen and give him a special meal, some support, a helping hand, something that makes the tough spots less difficult. It's always one of them, sure. But transformed. Participating in the impersonal nature of structure. Yes. Transformed into "part" of the Holy Trinity of the Secretariat, into "part" of the Controls Commission, into "part" of the Bureau.

Mario took another swallow. He knew the old man was already half dead and in a few months would die altogether and forever. Nevertheless, he was absolutely certain that at that very moment he hated him and wanted to say something to him about his illness that would be as miserably vague as the reply the old man had just given him. Yes, something vague and cowardly, something ambiguous and discouraging, something like: "Wagemann thinks it's more serious than he originally imagined, but we must never lose hope ..." making sure he would lose it...and how!—Just as Mario was losing his at that moment, because Don Carlos wouldn't say, "Yes, I supported your petition and the decision has already been made." Because that was also true: not only did he conceal his own opinion, but in essence he also hid something that had already been decided.

The night lagged on; the enormous gifts were the only cheerful guests at that party which seemed like it would never begin. The two men continued their conversation, interrupted by painful pauses that the glasses of Hungarian wine could scarcely mitigate. Mario believed that the old man was hiding a decision that had already been made. And the old man thought that Mario surely knew that at his age, cancer and death were the most likely outcomes. However, Mario clung to a remote hope, a hope that was bolstered by the intransigence with which the old man exercised both his defects and his loyalties. Don Carlos would never do anything (of this Mario had no doubt) that wasn't in accordance with the statutes of the Bureau. All agreements of our higher institutions are collective decisions. Such agreements, once adopted, admit neither minority nor majority dissent. Decisions shall be made public at the earliest opportunity, but the discussions leading to these decisions are never to be disclosed. Even if the old man had supported Mario's petition, he wouldn't be allowed to say so. And if the Bureau's decision regarding his petition were favorable, Don Carlos would never inform him ahead of time. Mario regarded the old man as he would have looked at his own father, had he not been so far away, as he would look at a person to whom his absolute lack of connection was at the same time an excuse for forgiveness and affection.

For his part, the Senator, shrewd with age and artifice, knew perfectly well that at that moment Mario hated him. But that hatred bothered him less than a pebble in his shoe. It sufficed to stop, take off the shoe, and remove the pebble. It would suffice to alter the truth slightly, to tell a merciful lie, or commit a venial transgression against the Bureau's rules to turn Mario's hatred into instant affection, even if it involved complicity. But that small alteration was precisely what Don Carlos could not allow himself to make.

Just as Mario was beginning to think that the other guests were really late, he heard some music coming from the apartment next door.

"At least your neighbor has good taste, Don Carlos. Too bad we can't hear it better."

"When I go to bed, with my head against the wall, it's very clear. I've been hearing it for days."

"Well, you're lucky to hear only that kind of music."

Don Carlos looked at Mario without understand what he was saying. Mario thought about the equally muffled coughs, the groans, the labored breathing of the old people he had overheard that evening all through the hallway. He looked at the scratches in the door and remembered the barking, the breath, the smell of the pack of dogs, and the old woman's voice, conversing with the weak howls of her dog.

"You know what that's called, of course?" Don Carlos phrased it as a question, despite his affirmative tone.

"I'm not sure. It's an opera, in any case."

"An opera? But they're not singing."

"It's the overture. I think it's *The Flying Dutchman*."

"And whose is it, if I may ask?"

"Wagner, Don Carlos." Mario's modest reply struck him as a tiny bit pedantic.

Mario had decided not to say a word about the visa business. And his decision wasn't just a calculated propriety, but rather was based on his firm belief that the inquiry would be completely useless. It was very difficult to get a visa for West Berlin and it was absolutely impossible to get one in forty-eight hours. If you compounded this with his situation as a man whose divorce was in question and the fact that he hadn't yet received a judgment from the Bureau, it became evident that showing up that evening to discuss the visa business, especially since Don Carlos had invited him to his birthday celebration, would be entirely useless and in bad taste.

No. He didn't want to talk to him about the visas. Later he'd figure out a way to explain things to Lorena.

He then took refuge in concentrating on the faint call of those notes that offered something different and distant from the other side of the wall. Now the silence and pauses were bearable at least, and the old man allowed the glasses to be refilled without looking for excuses or repeating useless words.

After a long while, when they finally began to think that the moment to say something was at hand, despite the music, someone knocked at the door. They were faint knocks, instead of the doorbell. The old man put his glass down and stood up, a bit surprised. When he opened the door, the light from the hall filled the room and Mario could see the silhouette of a slim girl at the same time he heard a delicate voice.

"Good evening. Sorry to bother you, but I got this note. I think someone left a package for me."

Mario noticed the old man's confusion and went to the door to assist him. With an anguished expression Don Carlos implored him to translate those unintelligible words, and Mario did. Immediately Don Carlos invited her in, and when the girl was in the middle of the room, Mario offered her a seat. But she refused and remained standing. She didn't want to bother them; she came just to pick up her packages.

Then the Senator showed her the two gift-wrapped boxes and asked Mario to translate.

"Your father left these for you," he said, handing her the packages.

The girl took them with difficulty. She nestled the profusion of colored ribbons in her arms, resting the boxes against her body.

"What time did he come?" she asked with an accent that revealed her Saxon origin.

"She wants to know what time the person who brought the packages arrived," Mario translated.

"This morning. Around ten."

"Oh, I was at the opera house," the girl said, and Mario didn't think it necessary to translate.

The girl was beautiful. She had a dancer's fine physique, and her long, straight black hair completely covered her back. She wore corduroy pants and a loose white pullover with rolled-up sleeves. Her arms were very thin, barely reaching around the enormous packages.

When she noticed the music that filtered through the wall, she said, a bit confused, "I didn't think my exercises would bother you."

"Tell her, please, that it doesn't bother me the least little bit," Don Carlos asked Mario.

"He's the one who lives here and he says it doesn't bother him one bit," Mario said.

"Tell her I enjoy falling asleep to that music," Don Carlos added, anxious for the girl to understand that message. She was the first person in the building ever to enter his house, and she was different, unreal but at the same time familiar; she was like a magnificent figurehead on the prow of the wandering widowers' ship.

Mario hesitated. The girl looked at him, waiting to hear his words.

"He likes that music," Mario repeated quickly. "Are you studying an instrument?"

"No, I'm a dancer. I dance in the opera ballet company," the girl told Mario, and then added, looking at Don Carlos, "I promise to lower the volume on my record player."

"No, no. It's true he likes to listen to your music."

"All right." After a pause she added, "Please ask him what he was like."

"Who?" the old man asked.

"The person who left these gifts."

"I already told her. It was her dad," the old man replied.

"Well,…It was your dad," Mario translated.

The girl's face revealed a fleeting uneasiness, a slight trace of barely distinguishable annoyance. Before heading for the door, she cast a sideways glance at the note that she held in her fingers somewhat clumsily, as she bore away the two enormous packages.

Don Carlos walked her to the door.

"What's your name?" Mario asked as the dancer turned to take her leave.

"Leni."

"*Gute Nacht*, Leni," Don Carlos said, turning red as a beet.

It happened every time he tried to utter two words of German.

We were sinners.

We arrived in the ghetto with the original stain marked on our foreheads: we were exiles. We had abandoned the struggle at its peak, and although we were glad to have survived, after the first report was issued, there was a growing conviction that we were all guilty. The report they demanded of us had to respond to two specific questions:

1- State under what conditions, through what contacts and in which embassy you sought asylum.

2- State if it was imperative for you to do so, and why.

We arrived in Paradise with Original Sin tucked under our arms, in the folder containing the answers we were to turn in to the Bureau. The purpose of this interrogation was never made clear, but it made us feel that sin existed, that with this sin we would begin our new lives, and that for the Bureau, the sin had a name: renunciation. We had to go on living in order to prove that we hadn't renounced our loyalties or our principles. We could continue being who we were if there was no renunciation. Somehow our lost innocence could be recovered, albeit with certain limitations, for although all of us felt guilty, guilt itself demanded a vindication of our differences. We hadn't all done it under the same conditions. One person sinned because he had no other options; another thought that by saving himself he would avoid causing further harm to the Bureau; many others whispered that this one or that one had panicked and made a hasty decision out of fear. They probably had a term for this last group that was never explicitly stated. We heard expressions like hasty, unjustified, incomprehensible, unacceptable. We never heard the word treason. But that unpronounced word hung in the air, in our recurring nightmares, in our secret regrets. We were all guilty to some degree. The only innocent ones were still over there. They were the martyrs. And finally, just as our recognition of guilt grew, so grew our worship of the martyrs.

When, in the ceremonies called to raise up our fallen wings, they spoke ardently of the victims and martyrs, we listened mutely. It was like a refrain that hissed in our ears, a sentence that no one formulated, but all of us thought we heard: you are the antithesis of a martyr; you are guilty.

Of course, there were degrees of guilt. But as nothing was explicit, each one of us had to decide our own degree and then our guilt feelings were even more internalized.

That initial feeling, absolutely generalized, gradually gave way to a kind of accusation, based not on manner or form, but rather on the very origin of the sin itself. Seeking asylum was a show of weakness, and weakness was a petit-bourgeois trait. The proletarian cadres were sinners by exception. There were fewer of them, and within that reduced group there were even some who had done it in order to continue the struggle, while others—the exceptions—had been tempted by behavior alien to their social class, resulting in turn from their nefarious contacts with the non-proletarian world, by their ties to diplomatic circles, their access to spheres of influence. Having duly resolved the question of the exceptional cases, that great, aggrieved tide which filled embassies, planes, small hotel rooms and ultimately the apartment blocks of some ghetto, it became necessary to deal with them in an instructive way. One had to combat the petit-bourgeois spirit. And so it was that the most humble and honorable manifestations of that spirit were finally defeated.

We weren't just guilty. We were guilty on account of our social condition. Sin was lodged in our being. And for that reason it was prior to and independent of our actions. Over there, one had to suspect those who had not yet displayed a likelihood of renunciation, while over here one had to anticipate new renunciations among the initiated.

And just as we ended up believing in this original sin, we also ended up forgetting our true origins.

CHAPTER TWO

Dear Leni:
I'm here in Berlin right now. Tomorrow I'm going back to Frank-
furt. I'd like to see you. I left something for you with your neighbor in
apartment 136.

-Your Father
PS: I'll stop by early tomorrow. I hope I can see you.

Back in her apartment, Leni placed the packages on the bed and now, sitting next to them, she reread the note she had found tacked to her door when she returned home from rehearsal.

It was Monday, the day she usually got home early because there was no performance in the Staatsoper. It's the only day when she can find signs of life in Unter den Linden when she goes out into the street after rehearsal, movement and voices that make the cheerful avenue even more lively, brightened by the radiance of the snow. The street lamps project yellow circles of light onto the whiteness covering the pavement, but one couldn't really say they light up the snow. The snow is the true mistress of light, the source of luminosity. That Monday, Leni had walked with her best friend, Anna, from the front of the Opera house to the Alexanderplatz, which was white as well, like a recently fallen moon, and as they breathed the clean air with its fragrance of suspended, pristine water, they cracked a few final jokes about that afternoon's occurrences. A nice afternoon, really. Especially now since they could take the S-Bahn to Marzahn, say good-bye at Frankfurter Tor with one last quip, a quick, disguised caress that might take the form of a little pat on the cheek or even a kiss, and then Anna was already on the other side of the train window, her farewell gesture lost amid the crowd that advanced along the platform towards the exit stairs, and when the last step of Leni's boots disappeared up the last few steps and the only trace of Anna was the warm moist spot on her cheek, Leni kept remembering the minutiae of the afternoon's events, thinking of her friend and feeling that at last she was no longer alone.

The move from Dresden to Berlin had been hard for Leni. After a demanding competition for the few spaces available that season in the Staatsoper, she had to live for a while longer with her classmates, now transformed into involuntary rivals who couldn't help contrasting Leni's success with their own shattered expectations. And since Leni suffered terribly in any situation that forced her to compete, she had new worries when, on arriving in Berlin, she had to solve her housing problem. After four months, a period that seemed quite short to her colleagues considering conditions in Berlin, she had once again overtaken her competitors, supplanting more than a score of contenders for the apartment at 8 Volkradstrasse who had already been chosen by the Rat des Bezirkes prior to her arrival. A decision made by the Ministry of Culture superseded any previously made assignments, and that was why Leni—not yet twenty-two years old—received a place in the ship of the condemned: one room with kitchen and bath on the thirteenth floor of a building in which only the elderly await their final days on the banks of the canal.

But nonetheless she's happy. She's finally in Berlin, where she wanted to be, where she'd dreamed of being ever since she was a child. She has a good friend now, and as both of them just arrived at the Staatsoper, they'll stay in the *corps de ballet* for a while without facing any hateful situation that might turn them into competitors. Her life in the building at 8 Volkradstrasse turned out to be less dismal in the long run than what she'd initially thought. In any case it was much less tense than staying on at her mother's house, which she would have had to share with her stepfather, a good, simple man who was incapable of understanding that it was better to diet in order to devote herself to dancing than to give up dancing in order to eat until she was stuffed.

Yes, everything was fine. Almost perfect, until the moment she found that note pinned like an insect to her apartment door.

Leni left her father's note on the bed and went over to the packages. She opened the larger one, carefully undoing the rose that crowned the knot; she removed the wrapping paper, opening up a blue box on which the name of a boutique was repeated. First she took a linen blouse out of the box, then a flowered skirt with deep pockets, and finally some pale blue jeans. The three items were all size 42: two sizes larger than her own. The second package, wrapped in bright yellow paper printed with bouquets and bells, contained two cartons of American cigarettes, a bottle of whisky, a jar of Nescafe, and some chocolate bars.

Disheartened, Leni modeled in front of the mirror. The white blouse was lovely, but if she wanted to wear it she'd have to remodel it. It would be better to give it away. The skirt could be taken in, but then the pockets would be disproportionately large. She planned to wash the jeans in the hope that they'd shrink. She put the gifts back in their boxes, took a pack of cigarettes from one of the cartons, and lit up. She bent down next to the record player and saw her elderly neighbor's face, saying words she couldn't understand, staring intently at her, asking her for something that apparently (as she now imagines) has to do with that music that begins to play again, at the usual hour, when Don Carlos climbs into bed and presses his head to the wall, although now the overture's *allegro con brio* is accompanied by her father's papers, ribbons and gifts, abandoned at the bottom of the boxes. She also has that note, which she's read a thousand times, to keep her company, and which, like the gifts, is two sizes too big, something that doesn't fit what she would have wanted, nor with what she was able to face at that moment.

Leni lay down in the bed and stared at her father's letter for a long time.

The first thing she saw the next morning when she awoke was the gift on the table, and next to the boxes, the paper and colored ribbons, and she felt pleased that it was her birthday. She washed her hair, lingering in the shower longer than usual, and then she meticulously prepared her breakfast: Nescafe (one heaping teaspoonful) with milk and a tablespoon of cream, which she allowed herself, with the promise that she wouldn't cheat on her diet again. Bearing that promise in mind, she put three chocolates wrapped in silver paper on a little plate and decided that those excesses would be partially compensated for if she skipped her toast that morning. She read until nine thirty, waiting for her father to arrive, but as she had to be at rehearsal by ten, she wrote a note which she slipped into a crack by the lock as she went out:

Dear Papa,
Excuse me, I couldn't wait for you. Let's meet at the Opera Cafe at two PM. Thanks for your lovely gifts. I'm glad you're here.
Your Leni

Since her friends wanted to celebrate with a glass of champagne after rehearsal, Leni arrived at the cafe a little after two thirty. She saw that all the tables were occupied, but she also noticed that at a corner table next to the window, there was a man waiting by himself. The suspicion that it was her father was quicker and stronger than any certainty. She went over to the table, realizing that the man didn't recognize her either, but his uneasy smile betrayed the same suspicion.

"Leni?" the man asked, standing up hesitantly.

"Yes,…papa."

The man approached the girl and kissed her on the cheek. Then, embarrassed, he extended his hand but immediately withdrew it, placing it delicately on her shoulder without daring to hug her. He pointed to the empty seat.

"Sit down, Leni."

The father sat down next to his daughter and kept gazing at her. He observed her carefully made-up face, her cascading black hair arranged in a braid, her delicate ballerina's figure. Leni was sure he had envisioned her differently, and slowly she began to recognize her father's thick body, his enormous hands that played nervously with a cigarette lighter, his strangely familiar face and his clothes, in ostentatiously bad taste.

"What do you want to eat?" the man asked solicitously.

Leni took the menu, although she knew what she could eat. She took the menu so she could look at something other than her father's eyes.

"I want some beef broth," she said after a while, laying the menu down on the table.

"Wonderful! And what else?"

"Nothing else. Just the soup," Leni said, smiling.

"You have to eat something else. That's why you're so skinny."

Leni laughed nervously.

"I mustn't eat too much. I have to stay slim."

Her father shrugged his shoulders, smiling. When the waiter approached he asked Leni what she wanted to drink.

"Some juice," said Leni, looking at the waiter.

"Then we'll have two beef broths, a *Schweinesteak*, a glass of juice, and two cognacs," the father said. When the waiter walked away, he put his hand on Leni's shoulder and, looking into her eyes, he said, his voice still uncertain, "In that regard you haven't changed. Even as a child you didn't like to eat. Every bowl of soup was a battle."

Leni smiled, lowering her gaze. Her father's glance made her blush and feel uncomfortable. But the hand on her shoulder was giving her chills. For that reason, with a careful movement, she turned around to reach her purse and remove a handkerchief.

Her father poured himself the rest of the cognac and lit a cigarette.

"May I?" asked Leni, pointing to the pack.

"Sure," said her father, offering it to her. "Do you smoke a lot?"

"Not too much."

"If you smoke a lot and you don't eat, you'll get sick." After an even more uncomfortable pause, he persisted, "Tell me what you do. That way we can start a conversation, don't you think? Listen, you know? I think you look so nice! You're different from what I had imagined. I didn't think you'd be so pretty, that's the truth. But tell me, what do you do? That's it! Let's start with that! Tell me what you do."

"I'm a dancer."

"But…a dancer…what kind? The father looked for a word that he didn't want to pronounce in order to ask a question he didn't want to ask. "A dancer…you mean, like the ones who work in cabarets?"

"I don't understand what you're trying to ask me. I dance ballet. I work in the Komische Oper."

"Ballet!" the father exclaimed and whistled. "Listen, but…how is it you know how to dance? I mean, how did you learn?"

"Well, I went to dancing school in Dresden. I studied for nine years and I finished. That's how." She said it as if she were explaining how to break an egg.

"Nine years!" He whistled again. "Nine years learning to dance!"

"Nine, or even more," Leni repeated, laughing. "And then I spent two years in Leipzig, and now I'm here."

"Listen, tell me…Your mama? Do you see her?"

"Sometimes, when she comes to Berlin. I can't travel. I have performances or rehearsals almost every day."

"And you live alone?"

"Yes, I live alone."

"And…isn't it hard for you to live alone? Couldn't you live with a girlfriend?"

"No, papa. I want to live alone. I like it like that."

The waiter came by with a tray and put the two cognacs and the juice on the table. The father took a glass of cognac and handed it to Leni. Then he raised his own glass and toasted: "To your birthday."

Leni smiled at him, looked at her glass, and said in a small voice: "To our getting together."

"You're toasting, but you're not drinking," the father said, noticing that Leni barely brought the glass to her lips.

"I can't. Not now. Tonight I will."

"Listen, tell me, what kind of job is this? You can't eat, you can't drink a glass of cognac. What is it? Tell me. Couldn't you find anything better? Or do they pay you so well? Of course, they must pay you very well."

"I like what I do," Leni said, staring at her glass. Then she stubbed out her cigarette in the ashtray. "And you? What do you do? I know you live in Cologne."

"Lived. Now I'm in Frankfurt. I do the same thing I used to do here. You know. I drive trucks."

"And do you like your work?"

The man shrugged his shoulders, then shook his head.

"What does that mean, 'do I like it?'" You have to do something, right? I've spent almost thirty years stuck in the cab of a truck. Look!" And he quickly thrust out his hands, showing her his palms. "Touch them! Touch here!"

Leni hesitated, then with great effort extended her hand and barely brushed her father's palms.

"No, here. You have to touch it here. Hard, huh? Press harder—I can't feel anything. Don't be afraid—touch me. You could put the flame of your lighter against my palm and I'd hardly feel it. Don't believe me? You want me to show you?" And with a determined gesture he reached for the lighter.

"No, no, I believe you," Leni said hurriedly, looking at the couple who was watching them from the next table. "Put that out, please."

"Thirty years driving! But that's how time goes. I don't feel too old. Do you think I look old?"

"No, Leni said. "You look very well. How old are you, papa?"

"Fifty-four. I'm still young, don't you think? What about you? You're twenty-two today, aren't you? That's why I'm here. Cheers!" And he chugged down the rest of the cognac.

"But tell me something. Does your mama ever talk to you about me?"

"No."

"Never?"

"No."

"But she must have told you something sometime."

"No."

"She never told you why I had to leave?"

"Papa, please!"

"She never explained it to you?"

"She never said anything bad about you."

"What could she have said? Tell me! You think she could have said anything bad about me? I, on the other hand, ..."

"May I?" Leni asked, taking the pack of cigarettes.

"Sure, sure. Those packs are for you. Here," he said, pulling another one out of his pocket. "They're American. You don't get those around here."

"We have them, papa."

"But they're expensive."

"Yes, they are expensive."

"Listen, tell me something. Did you like my presents? You haven't said a word about them. That's stuff you don't find around here."

"Yes, papa. I liked them. A lot."

"I don't know your size. But I imagine they fit you."

"Yes, papa. They're my size. They fit fine."

The waiter brought the glasses. The man asked for a piece of bread, another cognac and a beer. When the waiter returned with the order, the man started tossing pieces of bread into his soup bowl.

"That's life," he said, pouring himself a drink. Everything's got its disadvantages. *You* can't eat, and *I* have to spend my whole life on the road. This trip to Berlin was unexpected. I travel a lot to Amsterdam, to Brussels. But they never authorized me to go Berlin before. Imagine how happy I was when they gave me the visa. A week ago I called your mother and asked for your address. She gave it to me and then she hung up on me. *Alte Ziege!* How is…? Well, anyway. Does she live alone?"

"No."

"She's got a guy?"

"She has a husband. It's been seven years."

The man said nothing. He concentrated on his soup, into which he kept tossing pieces of bread, sulking. All the while he avoided looking at Leni and continued to look away after he placed his spoon in the bowl and lit a cigarette.

"And you?" Leni asked. "Do you live alone?"

"Yes and no. I didn't remarry. So you could say I live alone. In this line of work you're always kind of alone." He drank the rest of the cognac. "See how strange things are—I live alone, you live alone, but the *Alte Ziege* found someone for herself. Don't get married, Leni. If you want some good advice from a good father. Don't get married," he said solemnly, adding: "Or at least don't get married yet. Got a boyfriend?"

"No."

"That's good! Work, save your money. Save all the money you can, and then no one will ever put you down. Listen, aren't you going to eat anything?" he asked when the waiter came to take away the soup bowls. "Don't you want some dessert? A piece of cake?"

"I want a coffee," Leni said, lighting another cigarette.

The man called the waiter over and ordered a coffee and a cognac.

"Don't think I drink like this all the time. When I'm working I can't. *If you drink, don't drive; if you drive, don't drink.* Ever see those signs on the highway?"

"Yes, papa."

"Listen, tell me something. Are you sad?"

"No, papa. Why?"

"I don't know. You look a little sad to me. Maybe I'm ruining your birthday. You probably wanted to do something else. We could go for a walk, if you like."

"I can't." Leni looked at her watch. "I have rehearsal at four."

"And what time will you be finished?"

"Eleven."

"Eleven!" He whistled.

"Our performance is at seven-thirty. I was thinking if you'd like to come ..."

"Sure. But tell me—you dance there, right?"

"Yes. That's why I'm inviting you."

"I'd love to. I'd really love to. But I don't know if I can...like this...I think people go to these things in tuxedos and long dresses. Of course this jacket is new ..."

Leni laughed. She found her father's gesture touchingly funny. Without blushing, she stared at the boldly checkered jacket, the green shirt, the black tie with yellow polka dots. It was funny, and she could look at him without blushing because everything was so decidedly different from what she had imagined.

"If you think I could, then I'll buy a ticket and I'll watch you dance. That's something I would have never imagined doing!"

Leni took her purse from the back of the chair and removed her wallet, extracting one ticket for the opera. The man took it, regarded it curiously, read the name of the ballet aloud as if it were a made-up word and put away the ticket. As he was about to put his billfold in his inside jacket pocket, he stopped short and said, "But I want to pay you for the ticket."

"Papa!"

The man removed a West German one hundred Deutschmark bill from his billfold and placed it on the table.

"Put that away," Leni said nervously. "Everyone's watching us."

"Take it," her father said. "You keep it. It's yours. You can buy anything you want."

Leni took her wallet, which was still on the table, but she avoided looking at the bill. She spoke in a low, but intense voice: "Papa, please take that bill. People are looking at us. Don't you understand what could happen?"

The man started to laugh. Reaching out his arm, he grasped Leni's hand. He took the wallet that the girl was about to replace in her purse and put the bill in there. It was then he noticed some photos that Leni carried in her billfold.

"*Die Alte Ziege!*" he said, leaving a photo of her mother on the table. Then he grabbed another one in which Leni was six years old, pigtailed and playing with a china doll.

"I took that picture," the man said. "It was the last picture of you I took. Do you remember?"

"I remember. Then you went away."

The man took out a third photo and looked at it for a long time without saying anything. Then he drank down the cognac in a single gulp, lit a cigarette, looked at the photo again, and said: "The truth is, I've gotten old too."

In the dressing room Leni showed Anna the one hundred Deutschmark bill. She told her that her father had given it to her and that he'd be at the show that night. She'd told him that her part wasn't so important, that she danced in the chorus and only appeared on stage once. At the end of the second act, when a group in white leotards entered, she was the fourth from the right. He wouldn't be able to see her face because in that scene the corps wore rabbit masks. But if he counted from the right as soon as the group came on stage, he could follow her and see her dance for three minutes. Later, when the *corps de ballet* stood still at the back of the stage, posing as statues, she wouldn't be the fourth anymore, but rather the second, this time counting from the left.

They'd also agreed to eat together after the performance, and she had promised that this time she'd really eat properly and have a cognac with him, at least one. Her father had found out that the most expensive restaurant in East Berlin was the *Ermelerhaus*, on the east bank of the Spree River, and he decided that they should go there. In addition, he had decided that if there was an orchestra, they would dance until dawn, until he had to get back in the truck and return to Frankfurt.

But Leni wanted something quite different. She would have preferred to celebrate her birthday in her room, inviting her girlfriend and her favorite acquaintances, and ever since that morning she had felt happy, thinking that her father would spend the evening with them.

As she was getting ready to go on stage, her friend asked her why she seemed so nervous. Leni shrugged, although she knew it wasn't her habitual stage fright, but rather a kind of fear, an unpleasant sensation of insecurity and a strange pain, as if an old wound had reopened in her. When she finished applying her makeup, she discovered that her palms were sweaty, and she remembered her father's palms, able to withstand fire. She relived the unfamiliar sadness she had felt on touching them and the chill she could barely conceal when her father's hand caressed her shoulder.

She didn't mention a word of this to her friend. Smoking American cigarettes, they waited for their cue. They decided to have Leni's birthday celebration the following night. After the show, Leni would do what had already been decided. And since her father was leaving at dawn, in just a few hours everything would be back to normal. But deep down she knew that from now on she would have to live with that definitive paternal absence, to survive that belated miscarriage.

CHAPTER THREE

The days following Mario's departure were days of seclusion and fasting for Lorena. She couldn't eat. She could hardly breathe, and it seemed to her that at any moment the lack of air and choking feeling would paralyze her heart. In spite of all that she wasn't able to stay in one place for more than a moment. Night and day she ran around the apartment, lighting one cigarette after another, but as she couldn't abide her own interminable, erratic fluttering around every corner—in which the children's clothing and toys had piled up in dismaying disorder—she finally locked herself in the master bedroom, determined not to leave until someone took charge of her and her life, if any life was left after her confinement. Without eating, she relinquished her body to the tyranny of pain and languished tearfully, asking herself the same question over and over: Why me? Why us? Weren't we happy, then? Surrendering to that strange complacency created by suffering beyond all tolerable limits, she spent days and nights sprawled on her bed, so seemingly wide now, without raising her eyes or turning her gaze up from the floor. Her friends in the ghetto took care of the children, who didn't stop asking each other—and her—the same question each time they approached her bedroom door: Where's daddy? Isn't daddy going to come? Are you crying because daddy went away? Like it or not, that was the only advantage of the kind of promiscuity which some members of the ghetto called communal life, since thanks to their custom of sharing everything, she herself had kept other children in her house for identical or similar reasons. Different children, who nonetheless asked the same question: Why did daddy go away? So one day when she stopped hearing their voices and their sobbing from outside the bedroom door, she assumed they were being cared for, and then she was able to focus on her suffering and the mysterious voluptuousness that forages around its borders, without thinking of anything besides the same question, repeated a thousand times: Why me? Why?

Unresponsive as a stone, she heard her neighbors' questions through the door:

"Don't you want to eat something?"

"Wouldn't a little broth make you feel better?"

"Don't you want to give the children a kiss?"

And if occasionally she turned around in bed to rest her cheek on another, colder spot on the pillow, neither this shift nor the new recriminations could stanch her tears. Instead they multiplied the reasons for her pain. It was then she cried for her dear father, remembering her country and her home. And to think she left them to follow the very man who was now leaving her! How she wanted to be with them! And how far, how far away they were!

Convinced that everything would be more bearable if she weren't alone in that strange land, she decided to return to Chile immediately with the children, without waiting for Mario to reconsider his decision. Thus, after a few interminable days of tears and recriminations, a clear course of desired action emerged, and with that desire an impetus that led her from her bedroom into a long, warm bath where she recalled the Sundays of her childhood: the sunlit warmth of the steam, and the tenderness (absent, but near in her memory) of her mother's hands, spreading fragrant foam through her hair. Stimulated by this caress reconstructed in her reverie, she felt less alone and found the strength to leave her apartment, talk with her friends, and retrieve her children.

Nevertheless she needed more time before she could return to work. Not because her job at the press was unpleasant, or because her colleagues on Glinkastrasse didn't receive her warmly. It was just that telling her story there was different. Yes, it was quite different. There she really would have to tell it, dredge up past history, reveal what everyone in the ghetto kept quiet, simply because they already knew. She'd have to sit down to a cup of coffee at *Zweites Frühstück* and wait for Frau Gerlach, who had been informed of her excused absence, although not of the reasons for it (but who nonetheless was alert to her aggrieved appearance) to more or less probe her daily agenda of misfortunes under some pretext, to toss motives aside and hone in on the cause, suspended in a kind of fluttering above her open wound, distant from Lorena's private life but clearly eager to hear her confession. At last Lorena said it

all (she was convinced that was all that had occurred) in a bare statement that sounded harsher to her than anything else that had been said
during the last few days, using what she thought were the most precise
words possible: her husband had met another woman and had asked for
a separation so he could go and live with her.

"*Ist sie Chilenin?*" Frau Gerlach asked.

Just then Lorena felt that the sip of coffee stuck in her throat was
choking her; she couldn't tell if it was the coffee or the question. It must
have been the response she didn't dare give, because at that moment she
intuited that her solidarity with her friends in Elli-Voigt had something
to do with their common situation. Among that chorus of expatriates,
many of whom had been initiated in abandonment and all of whom were
potential Medeas, there was unanimous understanding of the event: an
exile's husband had chosen an authentic daughter of the realm. With
Frau Gerlach it was different, of course. More importantly: Lorena assumed that she had asked her that first question in order to establish
from the outset the degree of intimacy she might allow herself.

"*Nein, nein*," Lorena said when she felt her throat break free from
its assault by that hot, bitter, swallow. And she needed another pause, a
shorter one, which she dissimulated by looking for her handkerchief in
her purse, adding: "*Sie ist Deutsche.*"

"Mensch! Machst's dir schwierig, du!"

Lorena heard the exclamation, her gaze fixed on the now-cold coffee, that other deep well, at the bottom of the cup. She didn't have to
raise her eyes to know that that thing she felt on her hair and her forehead, in the tension in her temples and the burning of her cheeks, that
web which wrapped around her like a damp, unwanted caress, was Frau
Gerlach's long, sympathetic gaze. And that sensation of being enveloped by a viscous spiderweb added a new uneasiness, different from the
original cause of Frau Gerlach's compassion.

"Don't I know it's difficult," Lorena said, speaking now in her own
language.

Assailed by Frau Gerlach's pity, Lorena activated her time-proven
defenses. One of them was to seek refuge in familiar words which created a kind of sharp cut through their dialogue, although they kept speaking of the same things. The drawbridge was raised and the spiderweb
disappeared almost immediately. Then Lorena raised her glance as well,
the two women's eyes met, and the conversation continued on less pi-
ous, but more comradely ground, where a dialogue between equals could
be regenerated. At last Frau Gerlach could appreciate what at first glance

might have been seen as a way to establish distance. She uttered her first words in Spanish somewhat haltingly, but later she was swept into the flow of the conversation, relying less and less on habitual catch phrases, and after a few minutes she asked Lorena to make her practice her Spanish—for at least one hour a day. "Latin American Spanish" she called it, that language which since 1973 had begun to gain importance in the lives of students of Romance languages in Berlin. In Gerlach's case it acquired the utmost importance when she was hired as a reader of Latin American literature by *Volk und Welt* press, located at an old house on Glinkastrasse, one of those architectural antiques that, because of its dangerous proximity to the Wall, had been evacuated at first and later made available to the ministries or the Volkspolizei.

And Lorena remembers how that same look—that cloying spiderweb —had enveloped her completely the first day they met in that very office, several years before. And she remembers, too, that Frau Gerlach's condescending pity was evident not only in that way (in which it would later be displayed so many times!), but also in a *Pause*—there were so many breaks!—While drinking, as is customary during coffee breaks, a cup of coffee that always ended up getting cold and resembling a well at the bottom of the cup. Another well, because Lorena felt that each one of her recurring misfortunes during these coffee break conversations was a new plunge into the bottomless depths into which she seemed condemned to fall, her face submerged in Frau Gerlach's web, and her gaze in the dark, cold dregs in the cup.

On that occasion—her first day at the press—Frau Gerlach's compassionate expression became a long, silent look when Lorena told her that she had been an actress in Chile, and that, although very young, she had enjoyed considerable success, and though of course her dream was to have been able to act in Germany, that now seemed completely impossible. Yes, of course in Leipzig she had received a sort of scholarship from the *Schauspielhaus*; in the eight months she was there, she learned more than she had ever learned before—it was wonderful. Everyone told her how much she had perfected her technique, too…But despite the intensive German course, emoting from the stage without an accent was…well,…That was a serious business!

Lorena found Gerlach's compassion intolerable from the very first. That's why she tried to reassure her crestfallen hostess that finding her a job at the press seemed like the best solution. She explained that she liked literature—she'd probably read more Latin American literature than all the readers of the First Laborers' and Farmworkers' State on German

Soil combined—and finally she told her that leaving the theater for a while wasn't the worst thing that had happened to her in the last few years.

"After all we've gone through, what matters most to me is my family."

She must have been convincing, because in the days that followed Frau Gerlach replaced her compassionate expression with another, ruddy-cheeked, affectionate one, one that shouted "look how well off you are here in paradise," a look that revealed her profound satisfaction. There it was, like an indisputable truth, the evidence of the absolute superiority of a system that rarely allowed itself the immodesty of displaying its virtues. And there was the definitive proof of it, to make one believe. To believe in a different way, with more certainty and more enthusiasm, in that which she had always believed somewhat timidly and uncertainly. Something she believed in because that's what she had been taught. Those ideas, as full and as perfect as the red binding on the manuals, those panoramas of universal history in which every category functioned like clockwork, encompassing all the centuries of mankind and every man in history, without a single cell of truth in a single flesh-and-blood creature. Well, then,…all that was changing! That was the miracle! That's why Most Holy Saint Lorena had appeared, without a halo, but suffused with the radiance of her pain and misery, to illuminate the virtues of that system which had so generously welcomed her. And in order to take full advantage of Saint Lorena's beatific presence, Frau Gerlach insisted on asking her all the old familiar questions in the presence of those whose faith needed bolstering:

"And your children, could they have gone to school in Chile?"

"Yes."

"But for free, like here?"

"They could before. For free."

"Thanks to socialism, of course. But you had only three years of socialism. Before that you would have had to pay, I imagine."

"We didn't have three years of socialism, Carola. We didn't have a single day of socialism, if by 'socialism' you mean what you learned here in the *Parteischule*. And before Allende my children could have gone to school, too. And for free, as you said."

Carola Gerlach sipped her coffee without worrying about how the steam fogged her thick lenses. She remained still, staring at her own black well at the bottom of her cup, thinking. After a while, during which she tried to reconcile the *Parteischule*'s catechism with this bit of news about the strange paradise from which Santa Lorena had been expelled, she sighed deeply, raised her own drawbridge, and said, as though talking to herself, "*Ich verstehe gar nichts ...*"

"Exactly. You don't understand anything at all," Lorena wanted to say. But she kept quiet and changed the subject, since it didn't make any sense to try to make Carola understand. The only times when there was any mutual comprehension occurred on those few occasions when her references to Chile coincided with Chapter IV of the *Socialist Party's Instructive Manual for Employees of State Organizations*, dedicated to the so-called Third World countries, especially section XIV of that chapter, which was concerned specifically with the Chilean situation, slightly more than three pages.

Luckily, Lorena didn't have to tolerate these problems in communicating with Frau Gerlach for very long. A few months after beginning her job at *Volk und Welt*, the State publishing house for foreign language literature, she discovered that the work she did every day at a desk crowded with piles of books could be accomplished more comfortably and with even greater concentration in her apartment on Elli-Voigt-Strasse.

What finally restored her sanity was the arrival of a young Uruguayan by the name of Humberto Carrasco, a budding poet and recent graduate of Karl Marx University in Leipzig, who, in order to be assigned an internship in a State organization, needed to prove his effectiveness at the workplace. They managed rather easily to squeeze in another desk (really, a very small school desk) next to the women's, but after a week Frau Gerlach (whose mood was strangely affected by the Uruguayan's constant presence), half-excited and half-embarrassed, told them that the management had decided that Lorena should work at home, coming in to the office with her reviews only on Monday mornings.

From that moment on Lorena showed up at the press for only the four hours weekly required by the arrangement. The Uruguayan poet inherited her desk and she used the school desk, which they had shoved into a corner next to the bookshelf that spewed books and files from all its worn-out shelves. She handed in the reviews she had completed during the week—four to six pages about each book, and never more than two books—and the others ignored her with a very clear conscience, since the presence of a third person in that tiny office made it impossible to do real work there. On those days the mid-morning *Pause* lasted till noon, almost always spent chatting about the books they had reviewed during that week, which allowed Frau Gerlach to supplement her reports to the director with observations that revealed her broad knowledge of Latin American literature. At noon Lorena picked up her new assignment of two or three books from Carola, and after marking the titles of those books in a notebook, she left the press before lunch. She preferred to eat something quickly at the Espresso Cafe on Friedrichstrasse, surrounded by students, actors, musicians from the *Staatsoper*, people whom she never saw anywhere else. There were also young people with dyed hair and black leather jackets adorned with intimidating chains, peacefully reading the literary section of *Neues Deutschland*. In short, people unlike the stuffed-shirt bureaucrats who lunched at the press cafeteria or in the restaurants on Unter den Linden.

According to precepts established ever since Georg Wilhelm Friedrich Hegel gave his *Lessons on the History of Philosophy* around 1825, the last hour of the morning ends at 12:50. For this unavoidable reason, Mario—the fortuitous occupant of the same classroom in which the philosopher taught—always concluded his class, also the last one of the morning, at exactly 12:50. It took him seven minutes to hand in his course folder and chat as briefly and routinely as possible with his colleagues in the Sektion Romanistik; then he would run out to the street, cross Unter den Linden just as the number 57 bus reached the Staatsoper stop (at 12:59, in maniacal conformity with the schedule posted at the bus stop), continue running towards Friedrichstrasse, and, still running, punctually arrive at the door of the Espresso at exactly 1:00. Mario knew that Lorena would have been waiting for him for exactly thirteen minutes (the lunch she was escaping at the press cafeteria was served at 12:45), and so she almost always managed to grab a table before he arrived and placed her bag on the table. And that corner of the cafe, Lorena's smile, and the books that awaited him in the woman's bag all represented for Mario the punctual happiness of Mondays.

"Anything good come in?" he would ask after kissing her.

Then Lorena would take the books out of her purse, delaying her movements in order to enhance the surprise, and she would place them next to the dish of pickles. She knew that what attracted Mario about these dates wasn't the goulash or the pickled appetizers, the cafe's insipid specialties, but rather the books she had picked up from the press that week. And since she often had something very interesting in her bag, the enthusiasm she saw in Mario's eyes was part of Monday's renewed happiness for Lorena.

At that time nothing that could have predicted the catastrophe.

Lorena lived in Berlin for twelve years, the last of them by herself, without Mario.

At that time relations within our ghetto were as sharp as the edge of a knife. For some, the closeness approximated the warmth of brotherhood, while for others, there was not just increased distance, but outright antipathy. And since one tends to be more obsessive in hatred than in affection, aversions ran rampant, and the familiar intimacy between friends was the place where hostility towards the rejects became justified, nurtured and cultivated. In sum, the only things lacking on Elli-Voigt-Strasse were neutrality and tolerance. We had created another exile within our exile.

Common practices among those who had established solid, familiar bonds included taking communal vacations, revealing secrets aloud, and exchanging mail that arrived from the forbidden homeland. In those days, a letter from Lorena's parents sat on her friend Cecilia's nightstand, and Cecilia's brother's cassette containing a broadcast of the latest protest made its way to the bottom of Lorena's purse. Thus, no one was surprised that one morning Lorena posted a telegram from her friend Patricia on the building's bulletin board next to the first floor elevators, as a way of sharing her unexpected good news.

That morning as she was taking the children to school ("that morning" is just an expression; it was December and still black as night outside), Lorena saw a red circle stuck to the metal part of her mailbox, announcing the arrival of a telegram. At that moment she felt an instant certainty that the little red circle would predict a change in the direction of her life at last. As she opened the telegram, two words seized her attention: Mexico and Patricia. They seemed to be underlined in red, as bright as the circle that announced them.

The news, which would change her life completely, was related to "the matter of the visas"—to use the Bureau's ponderous jargon—or "that visa shit," as Lorena used to say, referring to the Mexican visa that, having been denied her for years, also managed to negate the most personal part of her being, preventing her from curling back into her dream like a wave, stepping out onto a stage again and turning into reality something that in Berlin was more like a recurring nightmare: she was looking at the stage from the wings, ready to make her entrance; she could feel the imminence of that moment like a leap into empty space, like a strange vertigo, only to fall into the heat of footlights and words. Yes, words. In her dream Lorena walked on stage and the actors held hands, singing to Lorca's verses:

Rosita, Rosita, to look at your toe,
if this were allowed me,
*how far would I go?**

And these simple words sounded as though they had never existed without that song, and the song was something that had never been separate from her life, and both life and the song were she herself and her own words, those words she could pronounce as though they held the flavor of a fruit in her mouth.

The news from her friend was even better than what she had been waiting for all this time. The problem of getting visas for herself and the children: resolved. Her acceptance by El Galpón Theater, a Uruguayan company that was now extending her a hand: resolved. The problem of the tickets: resolved, with the help of an international refugee organization. Another letter would be arriving soon with details.

She ran to the school, pushing her children's sled across the first snow of the winter. December had just begun. If everything turned out according to plan, in a few weeks she probably would have her exit visa and the tickets. What international organization could that be? UNHCSR? WCC? WUS? Those words, so often overheard at dinner table conversations in the ghetto, now had a different resonance because they had to do with her: in some office in some city in the world, there were three tickets waiting for her. Perhaps her name and those of her children were on a list and she'd be flying off to Mexico before the year's end. The new year would be truly new, without snow. Her dream would be fulfilled, without the Bureau. It would be a new life…without Mario.

She's approaching the square, white, flag-adorned school building. Only the last stretch still awaits her: to cross the wide esplanade of the playground, swept by a biting wind, icy moisture sticking to her face, a fluttering that seems to be singing along with her this morning…but the whistling of the wind suddenly sounds like a snake hissing. What if Mario doesn't want her to go away with the children? What does the law say? What will the Bureau have to say? She herself had done everything possible to delay a decision about the divorce for as long as she could. She was buying time, she told herself, harboring an immeasurable hope. And if he should return? And if one day we all wake up from this bad dream? Had she bought time or wasted it?

*From Federico García Lorca, *Doña Rosita the Spinster*. In *Five Plays by Lorca: Comedies and Tragedies*, trans. James Graham-Luján and Richard L. O'Connell, New Directions: New York, 1963.

She handed the children over to *Tante* Gudrun, and without being able to conceal her excitement, chaotically stuck her change of clothing in the drawers. She needed air. She wanted to be out in the street again, to be alone again. Alone? She felt a tremendous desire to do something precise and appropriate to the occasion, but she couldn't imagine what that might be. She didn't want to go back to the apartment. She wanted to talk to someone—yes, that would be better, but with whom? No, no! It would be dangerous. She couldn't make any mistakes now.

With a start, she stepped up her pace even more. Now she really knew what she had to do. The first thing was to keep her news from becoming the ghetto's shared possession. If she wanted to leave with the children, it was very important to think things out calmly and not let her plans be discovered.

Once again she crosses the esplanade that separates the school from the buildings bordering the Leninallee. It's beginning to grow light. The snow covering the pavement begins to cast off the yellowish reflections of the street lights and starts to turn blue, echoing a sky that promises to be clear from dawn on, shedding its hue on the whiteness, dipping into the sparkling yellow of the puddles. Lorena's boots have already splashed around in them several times, as she runs home without trying to avoid them. Must get home soon. Now she understands that it's a question of life or death. Yes, it is, because reading the telegram was enough to sever, with a single knife thrust, what deserves to be called life from what is indistinguishable from a gradual death, from being dead amid so many cement blocks, so many thousands of little windows and balconies that have nothing at all to do with her. She climbs up the steps of her building. Now, that *does* have something to do with her. She's lived here for twelve years and she hopes to have no more than two weeks left. Yes, life is there: in the words and melody of her dream; in her friend's constant, touching efforts; in the sun that Patricia has described so many times in her letters—that warmth in which people have always found their true home. She bumps into Frau Schulze, coming along bundled in her fake leather coat and her rabbit's fur hat; they greet each other just like every other morning; and now she's by the elevator, removing the letter from the cork bulletin board; now she's riding up; now she's sitting on her bed, telephone in hand, looking for a solution, looking for a name and number in the *Telefonbuch*, preparing for her rebirth.

Lorena watches the commotion of pedestrians on Friedrichstrasse from her table at the Espresso.

She feels she needs a break after the tumult of the past two weeks. On the little table, next to her coffee and cigarettes, is the Telex from the travel agency, an order for the three tickets she has to pick up at Interflug. She had been at Interflug that morning, where they confirmed the existence of three tickets in her name and the names of her children. The only things lacking now are the exit visas. So as soon as she received the information she now possesses—we all know in advance what the conditions for leaving are—she ran to the *Amt für Ausländerangelegenheiten* (something like the State Police Bureau for Questions Pertaining to Foreigners) knowing—also in advance—that she should have taken care of one preliminary piece of red tape, but she tries to disregard it as though that single fact might create an obstacle or an involuntary exception. It seems we all do these things, and it happens to all of us, just like Lorena. We're swept up with the soaring of the bird as it tries to reach the sky, but we crash into the window time and time again. And so Lorena crashed that morning, going from Interflug to the Volkspolizei, and from the Volkspolizei to the Ministry of the Interior, and from the Ministry of the Interior to the Chilean Antifascist Organization, and from the Chilean Antifascist Organization to the Bureau.

Yes. In the end all her flights of fancy bumped their wings against the same windowpane: the Bureau. Without the Bureau's authorization, there could be no authorization from the Ministry; without the Ministry's clearance, there could be no green light from the Volkspolizei, and without that green light, the longed-for exit visa (also a greenish color) from the GDR would never receive a water seal and the notorious stamp from the Visa Department. The efforts we always ended up making in the Bureau's waiting room should have been *initiated* at the Bureau. The Bureau was origin and beginning, judge, supreme authority, final arbitrator and indispensable requisite for any possibility of existing. We all had the impression we belonged to a world in which the Bureau was foundation and substance, the thing that supported all signs and attributes of life. The Bureau is Being, those residents who had earned their degrees in Philosophy declared, with some justification, and around the most sophisticated dinner tables, the polemic would bog down in trying to determine if the converse—Being is the Bureau—contradicted the first statement or was simply its consequence or even its complement. What do *you* think, Lorena?

Lorena drank her coffee at the Espresso, watching the sunbeam that fell on the telegram. She took heart: one must banish fear. She already had the most difficult part of it in her hands, something they couldn't take away from her—the Mexican visa, her contract with El Galpón, and the three tickets promised by the Telex she had just received that very morning, before her own soaring spirit ended up in the Ministry's basement.

Yes. She had decided that this time the last station of her *via crucis* would not be the Bureau. She had made her decision: she would settle in Mexico, reconnect with her own language, and return to the theater. She would go away with her children. Whatever Mario decided wasn't anything in which she could take part. Besides, she would do all this because it was her own personal decision, and because making it wouldn't jeopardize anyone else's freedom. That's why she would take the final step in the place the State had established for all its citizens, and that place was the Ministry of the Interior. Suddenly she understood that if she accepted the Bureau's existence, she would consequently have to accept all its baggage, including the condition of being a second-class citizen who had to submit to two codes of law and two authorities. The ghetto had been accepted, too, and after a while a door opened up allowing a double status to be established, a new relationship of power within another system of power, ultimately an exile within another exile. But why did it only become clear to her just now? Why hadn't she realized this when, so many years ago, she blindly accepted the creation of the Bureau and the fact that all her decisions, including the most personal ones, would be discussed there? Taking it all into account, the Bureau wasn't the beginning and the end of everything. In fact, in wasn't the beginning and the end of anything. The real beginning of her misfortune was having accepted the Bureau in the first place. Our first fatal error was creating the Bureau, Lorena thinks, tightly clasping the yellow envelope that contains her friend's telegram, her contract with El Galpón, the notice of approval of her Mexican visa, and the World University Service cable confirming the three tickets. She strokes the envelope and feels secure. Secure? No—she feels excited, happy, ecstatic. Does she feel free? Yes, maybe that's it. But Lorena doesn't know anymore. How does one feel when one is free? Is it the way she feels this afternoon at the Espresso? That sort of friendliness or even affection that's awakened in her by those people who aren't even looking at her, wrapped up in their own affairs, shouting or whispering, arguing or laughing? Yes, that little world she frequented for so many years without knowing anyone in it today seems warmer, more personal, more her own. And that probably has something to do with feeling free, she thinks, looking around at all the people who don't even know she's there.

CHAPTER FOUR

Three days later Lorena received a second telegram.

The night before, after putting the children to bed, she sat down at the dining room table, opened a bottle of sweet wine and a pack of cigarettes, opened the package of good writing paper she had bought that afternoon at the *Kaufhalle*, and also opened a floodgate within herself that had been closed for a long time, in order to write a letter to the Ministry of the Interior, one which she would also send to the Secretary General of the United German Socialist Party and the Director of the Bureau, asking for exit visas in order to move to Mexico and declaring in no uncertain terms that she refused to accept any discussion of the matter (which she described in the letter as "strictly personal, as personal as my relationship with my husband and my children, as personal as deciding which books to read and which wine to drink") by the petty functionaries of the Bureau.

Editing the letter, combined with the white wine (she had drunk a good portion of the bottle) led her to a state of excitement which she hadn't felt for a long time. She read the rough draft several times, walking around the apartment like a caged animal. She didn't want to be there. Or maybe she didn't want to be alone. What she really wanted was to be in Mexico already, to embrace Patricia for a long while, to begin her rehearsals at El Galpón. She'd smoked too much; she walked away from the table and the cigarettes. Stopping by the window, she saw a light in Cecilia's apartment and decided to call her to confide her secret, read her the letter, and finish off the rest of the wine together.

So it was that an hour later, after rereading the letter, Lorena and

Cecilia, stimulated by a second bottle of sweet wine, lost themselves in their thoughts, imagination and laughter. Their comments ranged from the normal interest that such an unaccustomed event would provoke to a calmer kind of reflection that harbored a glimpse of doubt over the success of the enterprise. And then came the laughter brought about just by imagining Don Carlos's face as he read the missive, or the contorted face of the Minister's secretary when he discovered that *eine chilenische Patriotin* could think that leaving the GDR was as personal a decision as choosing a wine. Their laughter increased when they imagined the secretary taking the letter to the *Stasi* functionary, holding it by the thumb and index finger, as far from his body as possible, as if his fingers held a frog, a lizard or a sewer rat.

And as certain feelings are highly contagious, they went from guffaws to a calmer, slightly sad wheezing, fearing that the possibility of all this might turn out to be more complicated than they'd thought, and finally to that mixed feeling of exaltation and sadness, complete satisfaction and dangerous anxiety which Lorena had felt before she called Cecilia, and which, understandably, they both ended up feeling once they were together.

They had no cigarettes left, and the wine was almost all gone. Cecilia suggested bundling up and going out to buy something that would allow them to continue the little party that the reading of letter had become. A while later, in Cecilia's apartment (she, too lived alone, but with just one child) they got the idea to do something even more fun. Putting on a fur coat she had bought in Moscow and a *shapka* of very white fur that made her splendid dark eyes shine even more brightly, Cecilia decided they should go out dancing.

"I think you have plenty of reasons to celebrate, don't you?"

Yes, it was true. She did have reasons to celebrate, and yet from the moment she received Patricia's telegram until this evening, so free and flighty with Cecilia, everything had been a haphazard coming and going, getting authorizations and applications, requesting papers and certificates, going from the press to the Volkspolizei and from the police to the Ministry and from the Ministry to the press again, because some piece of information was missing from the authorization, and besides she didn't have the health certificates from school and her own medical records from Charité Hospital; all that, combined with running to drop off and pick up the kids from school, turning in her reviews on Glinkastrasse, taking care of the house, and just now, practically at midnight, only three days removed from the good news, feeling that pure excitement, that nervousness streaked with fear (dark omens on her horizon, but she won't mention that to Cecilia), finally become celebration and joy.

Cecilia knew from experience that the hotels in Berlin, *Haupstadt der DDR*, have dance halls which take on a bustling, intense life after midnight, when the foreign workers who live in West Germany arrive after crossing the border. Thanks to a black market favoring the Deutschmark, they can dine lavishly, buy their eventual dance partner several bottles of champagne, and return to the other part of the city at dawn, having expended an amount of money that would scarcely have bought them a pizza and a beer on the other side, something like ten dollars. After considering various alternatives, they decided to go to the Tanzbar at the Unter den Linden Hotel. Cecilia had been there a few months earlier, at the end of a journalists' conference.

They called a taxi and took off, whispering all the way, huddled close together in the soft upholstery of the back seat. Lorena enjoys smelling Cecilia's perfume, feeling Cecilia's lips grazing her cheek, her breath mixed with the fragrance of sweet wine. "Are you sure women go there alone?" she asks. "We're *not* going alone," and it's all a great joke, Cecilia's perfume, her laughter. "Without men, I mean," Lorena whispers into her ear to keep the driver from hearing, and now Cecilia laughs even harder, "Of course women go without men. "But I don't mean going there to eat, I mean to dance." "I don't mean to eat, I mean to dance," Cecilia replies, and to stifle their laughter they have to cover their mouths with their gloved hands. The taxi's headlights shine on the light fluttering of snow, which covers up all traces of cars as it falls on the broad Karl-Marx-Allee, as white this evening as Cecilia's *shapka*. In the rear view mirror they see the taxi driver's smile, his eyes scrutinizing these women who are out looking for a party. "If you want some advice, Cafe Moscow is better for dancing than Unter den Linden." He speaks with the authority of someone who knows. "Why is it better?" "Well, they have a better band, it's less formal, and the other thing, you know?" "What other thing?" Cecilia asks, and their laughter stops. "Well, the Stasi guys. In Cafe Moscow there's less control. It's just that there are fewer foreigners," the taxi driver adds, turning his head around toward the two friends. "I'm glad to know that, but we want to go to Unter den Linden. Someone's waiting for us."

The taxi crosses Alexanderplatz, continues down Karl Liebknecht Strasse, and stops on Friedrichstrasse. Lorena realizes she's on the same corner she's passed thousands of times on her way to the press, yet she'd never heard this music flooding the street before. She looks up to the second floor because that's where the band's rhythm is coming from, but there's not a lot to see, since the windows, covered with dark curtains, reveal only a muffled play of lights and shadows. "I never thought that boring old Unter den Linden had its own bacchanal at night," she remarks to Cecilia in the ladies' room, as they open up plastic bags and take out their party shoes—Lorena's high-heeled silvery pumps, Cecilia's gold-toned flats—and stuff their muddy boots into the bags. They study themselves in the full-length mirror, look into their compact mirrors to adjust their makeup: moistened lips and round circles of rouge that adorn them for the party. They check their purses and coats at the cloakroom, stick the metal tokens into their wallets, and after buying their tickets, prepare to breach the darkness that peeks out from between the heavy curtains in the hallway, that dark space in which smoke and music are floating, where the rapid, skillful movements of the waiters seem to be floating as well.

They decided that one of the unoccupied tables was superbly located, not in an isolated corner of the ballroom, but not in the path of the lighting that illuminated the dance floor, either. Sheltered in that discreet shadow, they continued whispering; they remarked that the waiter was gorgeous, although they found him a bit distant, solemn in his funereal uniform. They ordered a bottle of Grauer Mönch, a rather dry Hungarian white wine that canceled the flavor of the earlier, sweeter one, and then they cast a critical but expectant glance at the crowd.

At that hour—already after one AM—it was obvious that alcohol was the stimulus for the bursts of laughter in various corners of the place, and at that moment, during one of the band's breaks, everything seemed to float in expectation. Fabulous-looking women walked from their tables towards the heavy curtains separating the ballroom from the toilets, while men seized the opportunity to move towards the bar in search of the companion they didn't snag in the previous round. The waiters exaggerated their rapid, professional movements, erect and ceremonious as though the musical pause were the culminating moment of the ceremony.

And so it was. Cecilia and Lorena weren't drawn to the Tanzbar because of some sudden, irrepressible passion for dancing. There's something more interesting, more mysterious, and probably darker in the expectation that's revealed in their giggling, their whispering, the nervousness that dampens their flesh, a pleasant fear that makes them lower their gaze whenever a man headed straight for the bar stops right in front of them, greets them with a smile, offers to buy them a drink. But no, they say, and then more secrets, don't you dare say yes, dummy, I'm dying, and the man, misinterpreting the whispers, explains that he's not alone, that his friend is sitting at the bar, waiting for them.

Yes, something is sought and rejected; something has been ignited in them already, though they don't want to admit it. Because after their refusal they sit, staring at the bar. There are so many people squeezed into the light which seems to emanate from the bottles; one has to search by staring. And the other guy? Wonder what he's like? Did you see him? Yeah, dummy, he looks really nice. Look, they're staring at us now.

"Don't look at him."

"Don't be ridiculous."

"Imagine what they must be thinking."

"He's looking at you."

"Forget it, I'm telling you."

"He's looking at you, Lorena."

"And how do you know that?"

"Because I'm watching him."

"Well, *I'm* not interested."

"Don't be a fool—he's terrific. They're coming over here."

"I'm leaving, Cecilia."

"You'll look ridiculous. After we say hi we can tell them we're leaving. Don't be a jerk."

"But we really *are* leaving."

"Right. Now smile. They seem nice."

"Schönen guten Abend."

"Guten Abend."

"Wollen wir zusammen etwas trinken?"

"Nein, danke. Es ist zu spät. Wir gehen schon."

But they're already seated at the table. The women, closer together. The men, blocking the sides, smiling, friendly, pleasant.

He was a *Baumaschineningenier*—a construction engineer—and his name was Klaus. He lived in Karl-Marx-Stadt and was just passing through Berlin while he took a short course at the Socialist Party School. And yet he was quite different from Frau Gerlach. He wanted to know how everything had really happened. He wanted to know what mistakes had been made and if the pre-coup Chilean situation was comparable to the GDR. Could the Chileans leave the country? Was public criticism possible? Were they comfortable here? Had they noticed any racism yet?

Yes, he was different. And his hand on her back was warm, and his breath in her ear felt affectionate when he stopped talking to concentrate on his dancing.

When she told him she was separated and she had two children, Klaus asked her what the children's names were, and when she mentioned Pablo, he cried out enthusiastically and then recited a Neruda piece in German.

"No, I don't know much Neruda. It's a poem I read once and it seemed so fantastic to me that I stuck it next to my desk calendar. But what's happening to me tonight is even more fantastic. And he asked in an amusing, but genuinely intrigued way, *"Bist du wirklich chilenin?"*

"Ja, wirklich."

Then he pushed her away a little brusquely in order to look at her, and suddenly he stopped dancing. He grabbed her hand very tightly and led her to the table where Cecilia was conversing with his friend.

"This is something to celebrate," he said and signaled the waiter to bring over another bottle of champagne. This is a special evening, Matthias. They're Chilean!"

And as they were toasting, he took out his wallet, and from the wallet he extracted a card holder that looked like a checkbook and put it on the table.

"Mein Solidaritätsbeitrag."

He explained how he paid a fee each month in support of Chilean solidarity. Lorena recalled Frau Gerlach's telling her that this forced kind of solidarity with discount tickets created resistance. But she didn't perceive any resistance at all in this man, only an ingenuous pride at the ten marks that he handed over to the *Solidaritätskonto* every month.

There it was again—that careless enthusiasm that made kindness resemble vulgarity, but now Lorena feels sad instead of annoyed, as though a profound sadness, or perhaps a form of compassion, has blended with a feeling of genuine gratitude. Despite that checkbook which he flaunted with a banker's pride, like a rather unusual person who seemed pleased to spend all his money, there was sincerity in his celebration: he believed it was a special evening because he had been making his contribution for years and this was the first time he had even spoken to a Chilean woman.

"Auf eure Freiheit," he said solemnly, holding out his glass to clink against Lorena's and Cecilia's.

"To our freedom," Cecilia repeated, clinking back.

It's obvious he's never had to deal with the ministries, Lorena thought. But later, as the others chatted and she started to surrender to Klaus's interested, friendly closeness, she imagined him involved in other kinds of deals, in order to adapt to—or to change—the ways in which others had programmed his life. She imagined that his happiness this evening was the result of his trip to Berlin, that his life in Karl-Marx-Stadt was much more limited, and that this charming, generous man had no opportunities to know the world other than these trips to Berlin or to Cottbus, and that he had no opportunity to get to know himself, either (let alone the world), because he was content with that life, and in spite of that fact (perhaps because of that fact), he poured out his warmth and his generosity to these lonely women who had lost their freedom so far away.

"I think I can confide in you," he told her later on the dance floor. And Lorena interpreted it as a confession that flowed from the most authentic part of his being and also from the embrace in which they were flying, beyond the music.

"Yes, you can," Lorena whispered in his ear.

Then, right after a pause, she heard his confession, which sounded somber, controlled: "It's not easy for us, either."

"I know."

"It's this world we have to live in. No one's perfect, I guess."

"Yes."

"But it's never been as imperfect as it is now. Here, there, everywhere."

And after a moment in which they almost abandoned themselves to the dance and the warm proximity of their bodies, he said very gently in her ear: "I mean this sincerely: if you can return to Chile, maybe someday I'll be able to get out of here. Not to leave. Just to get out. Maybe not even get out. Just to know that I *can* get out."

The music had been over for a while, and they were they only ones left in the middle of the dance floor, embracing, telling each other things that sounded as true as though they had been whispered into a single ear. It was another kind of music, a gentle sound wrapped in a nearby exhalation. And the body that warmed her without urgency was also near and true, clinging closely to hers like a caress that Lorena could accept, one in which she would have liked to rest for a long time.

Since they were no longer dancing, Lorena felt the closeness of their bodies in a different way, clinging to one another with tenderness and desire, and she thought she never could have imagined it happening so quickly, so naturally. She gave him an impulsive kiss, and the man took her hand to walk her back to the table. There he offered her another glass of champagne and asked her if her children had been to the Planetarium.

"No, I don't think so. Maybe in school ..."

When he began to explain the fantastic sights in the Planetarium, Lorena saw in Klaus's eyes the eager, surprised look of a child who hasn't died in spite of everything, while the fire in his eyes crackled along with the movement of his waving hands as he spoke to her of stars and planets, as he described the miracle, telling about it, sharing it, igniting the embers, arousing her extinguished desires.

He wanted to go there before he returned to Karl-Marx-Stadt and he invited her to go along. If she brought the children, they could go for a walk afterwards in the Weisse Flotte. If she didn't like the museum, they could at least enjoy the river crossing.

Lorena knew that was impossible.

"It's very late," she told Cecilia, when Cecilia stopped talking with Klaus's friend for a moment.

"Wait a while," Cecilia replied firmly.

"The kids are alone."

But Cecilia didn't even look at her. They were discussing the situation in South Africa, where Cecilia had been reporting for Radio Berlin International, and since her conversation partner seemed so fascinated, there was no chance of leaving. And since Lorena didn't really want to leave either, South Africa seemed like a good excuse.

There was a barely-touched bottle of champagne on the table and an almost-consumed bottle of wine. They progressed from the champagne to the fine wine, and from entwined fingers to kisses, and from kisses to Klaus's heated hands unbuttoning Lorena's blouse, and now she feels the man's tongue searching for hers, caressing it, giving her his saliva, while the intense warmth taking over her breasts now is concentrated in her nipples, and she feels how skillfully the fingers caress her, and her nipples grow hard just as her mouth is freed and searching for more tongue, more saliva, feeling it now moistening one of her nipples, probing it with a circular motion, all-encompassing, repeated, around the hard point of her nipple before he closes his lips, sucking her, biting her gently as she feels his hand down there, separating her underpants from the damp tangle, imagining its saltiness in the mouth that seeks its harbor there, its final destination, the yearned-for mooring.

Just at that moment, summoned by those atavistic impulses that always become entwined in the tangle receiving the caresses, and just when something dangerous is about to open, the *mustn't's* appear. In an instant Lorena folds up, pulls in her sails, hardens, firmly rejects the hand and closes her legs. Now she sits upright, squeezing her eyes shut because she doesn't want to see, closing herself off completely when she hears something, because she doesn't want to hear, standing up to leave, but everything is blurry, yet close by and threatening, because she doesn't want to be there, because she doesn't want to be anywhere, because she doesn't want to be.

Unlike the caresses and the plenitude of her sensations, which come on gradually, the *mustn't's* arrive suddenly and unexpectedly. It's a machete cutting through a field of sugar cane, a knife at a lamb's throat, reverse lightning that plunges everything into darkness. This time, when she felt the hand on her damp pubis, Lorena stuck her foot right into the trap, the trap opened, and she fell into a deep well, tumbling dizzily into her fear, both fear and fall precipitated by presages and incredible visions. She saw Mario's face next to hers, next to Klaus's face, each taking the place of the other. She saw him walking into the Tanzbar and even heard his voice calling her. And that was enough to summon all the rest of it, the *mustn't's* with their thousand faces twinkling in the darkness, all the voices calling her, blaming her, announcing her punishment; all the flames that had warmed her body, now concentrated in her soul, burning her. She saw her father shouting out imprecations that she couldn't manage to hear because his condemning gestures had shaken out all their words. She saw her mother shaking her head in a sign of vengeance and condemnation. She saw the children crying by her bedroom door and at the same time looking for her all through the apartment, and she heard their voices that were now coming from the bar kitchen, where the waiters went in and out, commenting on the scene. She saw Don Carlos sitting at the next table reading a yellowed copy of *El Siglo,* and although he didn't move his eyes from the paper, it was clear he had witnessed everything.

Suddenly she found herself tangled in the curtains that separated the bar from the hallway; she had drunk too much—never again. Those curtains were heavy. Black. They stank of tobacco and powder. A man's hand separated them and she could see a bit more light and the hostess's uniform, adorned with braid, at the same time she sensed Klaus's hand on her shoulder and Cecilia's voice calling her. When she realized she could support her weight on Klaus, her legs finally collapsed. They carried her toward the stairs. It was a spiral staircase that aggravated her nausea, and the first spasms of vomiting made her want to hold it in and try to stand on her own two legs, pushing away the hands that were holding her up. Then the spiral twisted on top of her, the staircase began to grow and spin faster, there was a dull thud somewhere, and that was the last thing she knew.

She feels a familiar warmth and the gentle dampness of a kiss on her cheek. She's emerging from the well, and with that kiss she finally reaches her goal and the light, but, rising to the surface, as though she were an infant being born into rejection, she needs to utter her first cry. Yes, there's something resistant, something closing up, preventing her from opening her eyes when she senses her children's frightened caresses. Both of them are there; they've climbed up into the bed and thinking she's ill, they stroke her, kiss her cheeks and her forehead, and utter tender, hushed, frightened words. Lorena replies with a groan that stretches out into a caress. She doesn't want to speak. She doesn't want to open her mouth, which feels bitter and dry. She doesn't want them to notice the vinegary smell of her hangover. She doesn't want to see them, or herself, either. She closes her eyes more tightly, repeats and draws out the groan which has become a calming response for them. She doesn't want to talk, to see. She wants to know. Who put her to bed? What's the last thing she remembers?...Klaus...Who is Klaus? With her eyes closed she has the sensation of falling into a well again. She's ashamed. Not so much for what she's done. She's frightened and ashamed of what she doesn't remember. Moving slightly to get her mouth away from her children's weak breath, she feels a sharp pain in her head, a wave of nausea that causes her to keep very still. She remembers the dance floor and a planetarium. Did they go to the Planetarium? She recalls the red circle stuck to her mailbox, announcing a telegram. But that was before, several days ago, Patricia's good news, the reason for the celebration. Now she'll have to make an effort, get up, talk to Cecilia, and then the *mustn't's* turn into a lighting bolt, with Cecilia's face scolding her, shaking her head *no*, closing her apartment door so she'll never cross the threshold again. And another vision: Tante Gudrun's harsh expression at school, *arme Kinder*, poor kids, children suffer if no one takes them to school, what kind of business is this, leaving them home alone, what kind of customs are these, when you've been given everything here? Yes, Lorena thinks, poor kids. She'll spend all day with them. Later, after she talks to Cecilia, she'll devote all her time to playing with them, poor little things. What time can it be? Can't even think of picking up a clock, even supposing it were on the nightstand. She looked over toward the window. It was a sunny day. *That radiant sun that follows snowstorms.* And it was high in the sky. She guessed it must be noon.

A long shower and a glass of cold milk that exacerbated her nausea, making her run to the bathroom to get it out of her system, finally helped her feel better, although she still had a headache. She left the children to amuse themselves in front of the television, and devoted herself to exploring the apartment in search of some evidence from the night before. Everything was the way she'd left it, though: the letter from the Ministry of the Interior on her coffee table, empty cigarette packs, two bottles of sweet wine (that awful damn cloying taste she can't get rid of!) and next to the bottles, a still-unopened telegram that brought her back for a second to the memory of the red dot stuck to her mailbox, and an early-morning scene by the elevator, and Cecilia's voice and laughter, and some men.

Suddenly she felt afraid. That telegram had arrived during the night and Cecilia had left it there for her to read at breakfast. And now she would have to open it, in spite of her fear. Could it be from Mexico? Had circumstances changed? Her heart was beating faster, but her hangover was gone. She picked up the telegram, intending only to see where it came from. In one corner, surrounded by words and numbers, she read CHIL. This didn't just make her feel better; it brought her instant joy to associate that date with the telegram—for twelve years she had received that telegram right before Christmas—but she was especially happy because her Mexico plans still stood firm and it depended on her alone (and the Ministry, of course) to make them a reality.

Relieved, Lorena opens the telegram, but reading it revives her fear. She gets up to look for a cigarette (there's got to be one somewhere—she needs a smoke!), and searching she rushes through the apartment, because she doesn't want to be near the telegram, because her happiness is over, and because the thing that now invades her is as unpleasant and dirty as her hangover.

The telegram contained more than the usual end-of-year greetings. In it her parents announced an imminent visit: *Arrive Berlin 21st. STOP. Lufthansa. STOP. Excited to meet grandchildren. STOP. Love to Mario and darlings. STOP.*

The news was burning her up, but she couldn't find cigarettes in any of the corners where she kept digging for them, desperately. She decided to borrow some from Cecilia and ask her about last night. That was one of the advantages of living in the ghetto: not having to put on a coat, boots, and a cap to go out to the Kaufhalle for small stuff, when the building was heated and you could go from one apartment to another asking for cigarettes, the newspaper, a slice of fresh-baked *kuchen*, and the next day, of course, make the same trip to return the cigarettes or the paper—or at least, there'd be some nice warm empanadas or some Chilean pepper sauce waiting for you.

"I see you're still alive," Cecilia said, opening the door and reentering her apartment so her friend could follow her inside. Like Lorena, she was still in her bathrobe, her hair uncombed, her face freshly-scrubbed and very pale.

"I'm dead."

"Sit down. It's more comfortable to die sitting."

"I need a cigarette. Urgently."

"It'll make you feel awful, but if you want, ..." and she handed her a pack from the coffee table.

"First tell me about the telegram."

"Well, when we got back you saw the notice on your mailbox and you wanted to pick it up. We found a keyring in your purse to get into the building, and we used one of the keys to open your mailbox. You started to cry. You said, 'It's all over. It's over.'"

"I thought it was from Mexico."

"So where was it from?"

"Chile. It was from my parents."

"Are they okay?"

"Fine. They're coming next Saturday."

"What?"

"Read it."

Cecilia read the telegram and the first thing she felt like doing was laughing. Anywhere else receiving a telegram like that would not only be normal, it would make you happy. In the Kingdom of the Bureau it would be laughable that someone could so magisterially ignore the rules.

"Well, it's a special case, right? I mean, about the visas."

"There's nothing so special about it. They require two weeks notice for those goddamn visas, regardless."

"Talk to Don Carlos. Tell him they've already left Chile."

"I don't want to ask the Bureau for anything."

"Oh, great! Your folks can just wait for you at the Wall till you come to your senses."

"Are you alone?"

"Why do you ask?"

"Because you seem annoyed. Are you alone, Cecilia? I'll leave, if you like..."

"You have to get the visas. That's the issue, right?"

"No. Well,...Yeah, I have to get the visas, but I've got an even worse problem. My folks don't know we're separated."

"Girl, you certainly complicate your life!"

It sounded like something Frau Gerlach had said: *"Machts dir schwierig du!"*

"What can I do, Cecilia?"

"Tell them the truth."

"They'll die!"

"What if you tell them Mario isn't in Berlin?"

"No, they'd figure it out somehow. The kids would say something, I don't know."

"Then ask Mario to stay with you for a few days. After all, you both lied to them, didn't you?"

"I lied to them. He didn't."

"He didn't know, then?"

"Yes, he knew."

"Well, ..."

Lorena took another cigarette and as she lit it she thought it didn't make sense to continue talking to Cecilia. Cecilia didn't know her parents; she hardly even knew Mario. She didn't understand anything, and besides, this afternoon (because we're already into the afternoon of the day after their night out), she was really being a pain, crazier than ever.

"What happened last night?" she asked, waiting long enough to keep the change of subject from appearing rude.

"Where did we leave off?"

"The last thing I remember is that all four of us were sitting at the table."

"Well,...all four of us is one way of putting it, I suppose. You two were all lovey-dovey, in your own world."

"Tell me, please, what happened?"

""You stood up all of a sudden and left. We thought you were going to the bathroom. We heard you scream and we went to see what was going on. You got caught in the curtain at the exit."

"Was it very obvious?"

"There was no one left in the place. We stayed with you at the door and Klaus went back to pay the bill. And then we took a taxi."

"Did you put me to bed?"

"Of course. Who else?"

"Were we alone?"

"Of course."

"And the guys?"

"They waited for me downstairs."

"What did Klaus say?"

"He wanted me to stay with you, to take care of you."

"Didn't he come upstairs?"

"No, of course not."

"And he didn't say anything else?"

"He said to call him. He left me this card ..." and she went to the sideboard to get it for her.

"Are you really annoyed at me?"

"I'm just as tired as you are, Lorena. I'm not annoyed. It happened because you're not used to it. Besides, I don't see what you've got to complain about. Klaus is very nice and he wants to see you again."

"I don't think so."

"He knows it could happen to anyone."

"I'm leaving."

"Call Klaus."

"I don't know, I don't think I will."

"It's up to you."

"Where's Marcelito?"

"In kindergarten. I dropped him off and then I went back to sleep."

Once more, the *mustn't's* appear. *Tante* Gudrun watching other children playing, her own kids getting bored, wandering around in the chaos, alone, just as they've been all day, waiting for her, as they had probably waited for her all night long.

She has to go see them right away; she hurries toward the door, asking before she leaves: "Do you really believe what you told me?"

"About what?"

"That Mario might stay with us for a few days. Do you think he'll agree?"

"Sure."

"You're completely crazy. I'm going home to the kids."

Sometimes we improvised sudden lies, and sometimes we also

planted seeds of lies that grew, lies that in time came to assume the proportions of cathedrals. These, the kind that got worse over time, were motivated by the same compassion—to avoid the painful consequences of telling the truth—but when they were found out we could no longer use the excuse that we just hadn't been thinking.

Lorena hadn't intended to lie when she wrote to her parents, a year ago now, hiding the fact that Mario's decision was categorical: he had fallen in love with another woman and he had decided to go live with her. In that letter she wrote to them about their lovely vacation in the Erzgebirge (true), about how nicely the children were growing and now both of them could write to their grandparents (also true), and of the greetings Mario sent them, as always (equally true). She didn't mention that she was writing that letter after returning from vacation and that she was already alone, or that she was writing to make her insomnia more bearable or that Mario had been living with Eva for a whole week already. Their weeks in the mountains and the happiness of those days, now condensed into a letter, seemed as real and tangible a reality to her as the fragrance of the woods, Mario's gestures, her children's laughter, and the interminable details she recalled as she was writing. The hatchet blow that felled her on the next-to-last day of their vacation now seemed like something awful, but hardly true. Making love in their bed or in the bathroom—only three nights before his pronouncement

—their walks in the snowy woods, playing with the children, or leaning close together in the little town's movie theater were so real that someone might have filmed them, and that film would have been evidence of a happy couple enjoying their vacation. The words they spoke all night long after returning from the movies and opening a bottle of wine were terrible words, but when all was said and done, they were only words. And even if they were decisions, they were full of uncertainty, shrunken with doubt, an announcement of certain actions that might occur later on, but which could still be avoided or even changed if they ever came to pass. How could she tell them all that when she hardly understood it herself? And how would she say it? When they returned to Berlin, he packed his suitcase hurriedly and then they sat down to smoke one last cigarette in silence. The unspoken words were the non-being of that being who left mutely, the shadow of a man who used to shine with words. Was that really Mario, that silent man who waited for the elevator, suitcase in hand? How could she talk about that shadow in a letter her parents would receive several days later in Santiago? And what if Mario emerged from his shadow long before that?

After a month had gone by, when her parents' reply finally arrived, with the usual greetings for Mario and the darlings—and a paragraph in which they told Mario about his Aunt Lidia's latest ailment—Lorena felt no bitterness, but instead a warm confirmation that the man belonged to her, that he was just as much a part of the house as the darlings who wandered about in circles, that he would be always and forever a part of that dismembered family, of her parents over there, of Aunt Lidia (in whatever hospital or whatever distress she might be), of her sisters in who-knows-what straits, and of him himself, his inseparable part, lost in who-knows-what depths of remorse.

It became a relief to answer right away, inventing Mario's questions about Aunt Lidia's health, asking for more details by return mail, telling them about her Sunday outing to Lake Köpenik with Mario and the kids (no longer true), or telling about the most recent opening at the Komische Oper, that marvelous version of *Bluebeard* that made Mario laugh until he cried (not true either, not anymore). She hung around until the afternoon, smoking and imagining the letter, and as the night advanced, she too advanced in her reconstruction: the wreckage was reassembled, the planks of the shipwreck came together as well, and a safe return, a mooring seemed possible. She progressed down that imaginary road so far that she finally found herself really sitting beside a laughing Mario at the Opera (and then she wanted to return and laugh that laughter again), and very late at night, completely immersed in the letter and in her delirium, she imagined him sleeping in his bed, that bed which was still, painfully, Mario's bed as far as she was concerned, and after sealing the envelope and stubbing out her last cigarette, she went back to her bedroom, feeling less alone.

The ongoing construction of the letter warmed her winter days. Lorena believed that those merciful lies would bring the real Mario back to her. Every day the letters became more necessary. She would wait for them, reply to them immediately, and if the reply was late, new visions of Mario would fall onto the paper anyway, warming the darkness, melting the frost, gathering up the pieces of lost truth, saving whatever was salvageable from the shipwreck.

The previous night, before revising her letter to the Ministry, she had written the last letter to her parents. She told them about their preparations for the new year, the Christmas presents, about New Year's Eve with fireworks in both halves of Berlin, and their upcoming winter vacation in the mountains. It had been a year—at the end of last year's vacation—since she wrote the first part of the lie. Now there was nothing to do but keep it up. She spoke of Christmas presents for Mario and the darlings, and at the end, with big, excited letters, she sent them love and kisses, asking: *How would you like to spend the holidays with us?*

Lorena wanted to forget the night before completely, wanted to erase it, to have dreamed it. To forget the shame of getting drunk, to forget Klaus, to forget the celebration in Linden-Corse, and especially the thing that now seemed to be the source of all the *mustn't's*: her incendiary letter to the Ministry. Somehow her parents' telegram was a kind of warning, a threatening finger, another sign that they were warning her of the *mustn't's* from afar.

Besides, now there was the matter of the visas, and if she wanted to try to get them, her letter to the Ministry was the first obstacle, an obstacle that differed from all the others because she had created it herself. A stupid, dangerous indulgence.

Fortunately, the letter was still there, on the sideboard, a sideboard identical to Cecilia's, purchased the same distant morning at the Centrum-Warenhaus on credit from the Ministry of the Interior. If she asked for an exception to the rules now, a gesture of clemency that represented a clear violation of protocol, what kind of consequences would standing on principle bring about? And besides, would anybody even read that letter? Some secretary, maybe, accustomed to more serious complaints? Or some functionary whose function was to carry things out to their ultimate consequences? And who would that Someone be? Not the Minister, certainly. Then who? To whom had she really written? Evidently, to no one. Yes, come to think of it, she really didn't write to anyone. And no one would read it, because whoever opened that letter, no matter who it was, was No One. Now the important thing was to get the visas, be with her parents, hide the tragedy. And if she was hoping that Mario would accept her plan, the letter to the Ministry was also an obstacle. Mario would eventually find out about her letter; he'd probably be the first to find out, even before the Bureau, even before Don Carlos, and that would cause another emotional, irresponsible, rash reaction, with no other outcome than to affect his relationship with his new family.

Suddenly Lorena thinks of her family. Her parents were well on their way now, practically flying, without the slightest suspicion of what awaited them, including the problem of not being able to cross the border. The children, who had been following her around all afternoon pulling on her bathrobe and asking her why (Why what?), and then so many more questions from the darlings (Why did you go away last night? Why doesn't Daddy come? Why do you smoke so much? Why won't you talk to us?) were no longer asking questions because they were asleep. Was that the extent of her family? What was Mario doing right now? Mario, the same Mario (that's how Lorena saw him), now across the border, far from the ghetto, on the side of the Powers-That-Be.

Yes. On the side of the Powers-That-Be. Anchored in security, in respect, in the *dachas* of the high functionaries beside lakes that looked nothing like the ones she described in her misleading letters. On the side of treason, abandonment. On the side of power. On the side of the Big Bureau and the Small Bureau, trying to secure authorization for his divorce. On Mario's side everything was possible; on hers, nothing. At most, she could ask for clemency, file applications, fill out forms, sign petitions.

In the apartment, all was quiet.

The children were sleeping. What a day! Tomorrow, *Tante* Gudrun's harsh expression, more reproaches, the *mustn't's*. Lorena walks back and forth rereading the letter. Would the Minister read it? What if it fell into his hands? What would happen if he read the thoughts of a privileged lady who furnished her ghetto apartment thanks to solidarity provided by the *Rat des Bezirkes* and the Ministry itself? Could the Minister imagine that the fire would begin at the fire station?

And what if, now when she needs the Bureau more than ever, she dares to commit an act that would shock even the most unscrupulous bureaucrat?

Lorena walks up and down with the letter; she's read it a thousand times; she's added paragraphs. It's the first time that something seemingly dead has opened up within her, surprising her, frightening her, telling her go ahead and dare, dummy, opening up with those hard, tough words in the letter that flow out of her very being like a deluge; opening much wider now as she places the deluge in the envelope and then she seals it and runs to the mailbox on the corner before she can change her mind.

CHAPTER FIVE

The Senator's decision was final. Although he wasn't in Senate chambers or in his office on Heinrich-Mann-Strasse, or even at his narrow desk at the Bureau (and although he knew he was dying), it was every bit as final.

"This is the most shameful thing that has ever happened to us."

The teakettle's whistling drifted in from the kitchen, unbearable in that small room which seemed even more denuded and less festive without the gaily adorned gift packages. The Senator paced back and forth, and in three paces covered the space between the his bed and the balcony, which couldn't be seen because the windows were fogged up from the cold and because both of them had their heads hanging down in a gesture of displeasure that bordered on recoiling.

"That letter is absolutely unacceptable. It implies we're slaves here. No, not just she—*all of us* should feel ashamed of such an atrocity," the Senator emphasized from the kitchen as he served the tea.

"I wouldn't read it that way, Don Carlos," Mario said, once again picking up the glass he had already placed on the table several times.

"It implies we don't have freedom to do anything. And the truth is that here no one has been forbidden to do anything reasonable," the Senator insisted without hiding the indignation that caused him to shout although he had already returned from the kitchen. He concentrated on stirring in the saccharine without trying to avoid the annoying clink of his teaspoon in the cup, hardly looking at Mario, but rather arguing with the real culprit, the absent one.

"I don't believe that was her intention. She says she wants to be able to decide certain things freely ..."

"Freely! Don't you see? There's an implicit accusation in that word, 'freely.' A tremendously unfair accusation."

"What Lorena wants is to process the visas without depending on the Bureau," Mario argued without great conviction. But even that weak argument fell like a bucket of benzene on the fire that fueled the Senator's crackling temper. Mario had unintentionally touched a sore spot. Lorena had gone to the Ministry to question the legitimacy of the Bureau. That was the most serious aspect of the matter, and for that very reason, the one that wasn't being mentioned. On first reading the letter, Mario noted that Lorena declared herself ready to accept socialist legalities. What she didn't accept was being made subject to dual legalities. We all felt our situation would have been considerably more tolerable if we had been treated like foreigners. The Bureau was the instrument that turned us into normal subjects of the Realm, the entity that subjected us, in reality, to a dual limitation. That's why its prerogatives seemed more irritating to us every day.

"Those visa requests for her parents weren't submitted on time," Don Carlos declared, unable to control the flood of words that ran over each other as they spilled out of his mouth, "and they were submitted without the slightest consideration for the Bureau's regulations. And it's not even as though they were requested ten or twelve days ahead of time instead of the *minimum* two weeks required by the rules. No! Certainly not! She has the audacity to ask for the visas *three days* in advance! Three days! Or am I exaggerating? Tell me if I'm exaggerating!"

Mario didn't say anything. He wanted to support Lorena, but under these conditions even the most reasonable approach made no sense. It was preferable to concede, thereby earning points for himself in the Senator's estimation. The next day the old man would hand down the final word on Lorena's life and his, too: the Bureau had to make a decision about the shocking letter, about the entry visas for Lorena's parents and the exit visas as well, about Lorena and the children, and about the no-less complicated matter of his divorce.

Spurred on by Mario's silence, Don Carlos continued to pile up reproaches: "She dares make accusations against a friendly government, which, given our status, is inappropriate ..."

"And what *is* our status?" Mario interrupted.

The old man couldn't stand being interrupted, and, besides, in this case the question was insolent. Even in his uncontrolled state, he managed to notice Mario's attempt to provoke him. He stammered a few times, red with anger, looking for that word which eluded his memory.

And finally he spat out four shots that emerged from his mouth in an explosion of saliva:

"G-g-g-guests!"

As Mario remained silent, Don Carlos continued, confident that this was the precise word to express our common condition of exiles. "We can't expect any more than what our hosts have. A reasonable exception has been made for us, and rules have been established. It's not just that she's protesting those rules! She's expects rights that no one else here has!"

The old man clamed down when he felt that his argument placed a stretch of solid ground beneath his feet. The argument was nothing new. It resorted to a kind of shared misery: the guest cannot have more rights than the host. That's why, without any pause in his pacing between the bed and the window, Don Carlos repeated, in a tone that went from open accusation and shouting—*"She expects rights that no one else here has!"*—to a measured, rhythmic, almost paternal incantation: *"She ex-pects-rights-that-no-one-else-here-has!"*

After the explosion, Mario thought the old man seemed calmer. The cause of the explosion didn't just have to do with the reprimand received from the Big Bureau (as we used to call it then), but also with the uncertainty produced by an opinion so deeply shared within our community that no one even discussed it any more. It was the collective belief that our lives would be more bearable the day the Bureau ceased to exist. The bureaucrats, however, unable to understand the generous expanse of our hope, refused to accept this: we would *all* be happier should its dissolution someday occur, and the most fortunate ones of all would be the bureaucrats themselves.

How could one reply to the old man's arguments? Mario wanted to tell him that mutual misfortune doesn't quell anyone's desire for happiness and that the fairness of a given rule is based on its content and not on the number of people it affects.

"A curfew isn't justifiable just because everyone has to endure it. If it's ever justifiable it's because of its purpose," he said, knowing this would provoke a new eruption.

The Senator, clinging to his argument, managed to contain his anger. He looked at Mario for a long time, but avoided a polemic that might derail his logic. Mario knew that the limits of his audacity had been established and he was dangerously close to those limits.

"If, like *her*,"—and the Senator said *her* in a clearly pejorative way—we expect rights that no one else here has, then the same people who extended a helping hand to us will end up hating us. There are already some who can't stand us because of the business of travel and visas. How could it *not* be annoying for these people to see that we can leave and go anywhere at all, if they can't even leave to visit their relatives! What arrogance on our part! *What kind of image are we creating?*"

"Here foreigners have permanent exit visas," Mario replied, carefully moving within the realm of objectivity to the realm of possibility.

"Who?"

"Foreign correspondents, invited scholars, officials from other parties, diplomats ..."

"And you'd like to see all five thousand Chilean exiles treated like diplomats?"

"No, I'd simply like to see us have the same basic rights *all* foreigners have. To be able to enter and leave this country just the same as any foreign colleague from my department."

"I don't believe it's exactly like that. I don't believe our Soviet colleagues can enter and leave here whenever they darn well feel like it! And what you consider a basic right is something nobody here has!"

"And do you think that's acceptable?"

"What I think has nothing to do with the matter. And what if it's not a basic right, as you see it? And what if a *more* basic right is allowing people to eat and clothe themselves and be educated, even if a small minority can't spend their summer vacations in Italy?"

"I'm not thinking about that, although I don't understand why it's a sin to spend a summer vacation in Italy. I'm thinking about Lorena, who needs to go pick up her parents. Not in Italy, Don Carlos, just in the other Berlin. Ten blocks and just a few hours from here. Her parents, whom she hasn't seen in fifteen years! I'm thinking about my colleagues, when I went to Paris last year—to a literary conference, not on vacation!—Who begged us to bring them books. And they weren't political books; they were university texts and research papers. Dr. Wagemann, Don Carlos, the very same Dr. Wagemann on whom your health now depends, gave me a list with five titles. He'd been waiting for years for a chance to order those books. When I gave them to him, the man began to cry and hugged me, he was so grateful. Over here he's a big wheel, and *finally* he was going to find out what his colleagues in other parts of the world were investigating. These are medical studies, Senator. And what's being studied in medicine ultimately has to do with people's lives. It's a crime to prevent a doctor from studying! And it's stupid to prevent a woman from crossing the Wall to go meet her parents!"

Mario's irritation grew at the mention of irritating facts. But the Senator viewed Lorena's letter as an act of effrontery. Mario, about to lose control, and Don Carlos, his indignation somewhat more under control, had marched down a path that could only lead to confrontation and recriminations. At the rim of that precipice, they would end up forgetting why Don Carlos had requested this meeting with Mario, and how enthusiastically Mario had received the veiled summons.

Climbing up to the street from the subway station, the Senator felt lost. Stretched before his eyes was an enormous expanse of snow blended with an equally white sky. He needed to take a moment to discern the pieces of a recognizable space: in the center of what must have been the plaza he thought he could make out the fountain, also covered in whiteness. Farther away, fuzzy in the mist, the still-illuminated U-Bahn sign. And against the horizon, very far off, the barely distinguishable facades of the buildings. How can one recognize a place if all its landmarks have gotten lost?

This wasn't K.; it was Don Carlos. It wasn't the surveyor in quest of the Castle; it was the Senator looking for the Chilean Consulate in West Berlin, on Friedrich-Wilhelm-Platz, hidden this morning by the snowfall. Older than K., but more hopelessly hopeful, sick, but no less diligent, Don Carlos had reinitiated the process of getting the visa that would allow him to return. We all knew that the old man wanted to have a last glimpse of what was his before he died.

The morning after Leni's first visit, Don Carlos spent just a few minutes at the Bureau. He arrived early, read a couple of applications and placed them in the appropriate files. The one containing visa applications had grown alarmingly, somewhat less so the one from people requesting transfers. He double locked the files in his desk drawer and headed for the lobby of the Secretariat's quarters—the master bedroom of the apartment—to let them know he was going to West Berlin that morning to submit a new request to leave at the Consulate. Since the door was closed, he assumed the Secretariat was probably in session. Ever since he became ill they had excused him from these meetings; he had to attend only when an application related to his Commission was being discussed. He stuck his ear against the door for quite a while: he heard some intense murmuring; they were arguing with their customary enthusiasm. That's Suárez: puffing away and making dumb remarks as usual…just blowing smoke…Gotta watch out for Suárez…But there's

Campos over there, prudent, solid as a rock...Could that hoarse voice belong to Castrito? It's obvious the dear fellow's got the flu...in this weather he'd better be careful if he doesn't want to kick the bucket...And over there's Saldana, with that singsong voice; if you don't ask him a question, he won't open his mouth...What could those fools be talking about? I wonder if there's some news from Santiago. Could it be true what they're saying about the USSR? Don Carlos can't quite make out the words, but he hears that murmur which he knows so well and which is, for him, the very music of life—there, so close by, behind that closed door ...

After a few minutes he understood the meaning behind the voices: this time the conversation was about the purchase of beef jerky for a Finance Committee dinner. Then he decided to tell Marta, the Bureau secretary, that he wouldn't be back until later that afternoon. He bundled up in his raincoat and his fur *shapka*—a gift from his last visit to Moscow ten years ago—and phoned for a taxi to take him to the Friedrichstrasse station.

Every city has a train station that gives it away, the inevitable place that reveals the very thing the city struggles to conceal. In train stations the faces of those who come to visit the city and those who are leaving become more expressive. The new arrivals openly reveal what they've come for, without embarrassment. The leave-takers, similarly, openly display their surfeit and weariness, their indifference, or their anticipated nostalgia.

Friedrichstrasse Station, the railway entry to West Berlin, is especially interesting in this regard. The meeting point not only of two great cities (in reality only one, divided), but also of two worlds, every day it receives thousands of young people who marvel at its museums and its theater productions. In order to enter this city, these young people spend hours and hours waiting at the border checkpoint at Friedrichstrasse. At the same checkpoint, on the eastern side of the Wall, thousands of old people wait as long as necessary just to get out.

This is the border pass granted to retired folks, the only East Berliners who can cross over to the western side. In addition, those who don't have a vehicle use this point to cross over. After spending an hour in line—still quite a few yards away from the police station—Don Carlos relieved his irritation by thinking about those eternal visa supplicants. He couldn't understand how those patient petitioners could try so passionately and for so long just to achieve this: a frankly intolerable experience. Simply for the sake of visiting a friend or to buy some cheap goods on sale! And the worst of it is that they always managed to get their visas somehow!

The Senator liked to walk along Friedrichstrasse, heading east from Unter den Linden, all the way to Charité Hospital. For years he had followed that route without thinking of illness; his doctor's appointments and the inevitable controls were a matter of routine. He took a break at the Metropol Café. He enjoyed stopping in the small cafe under the S-Bahn bridge to observe, from his white lacquered table, the comings and goings in the station. Life pulsated so fully on that corner; it was like a second bloodstream reviving his heart. That's why the long line of old folks waiting for taxis at the taxi stand on Bertolt-Brecht-Platz didn't surprise him. On many occasions he had seen those pensioners returning from visiting their relatives in West Berlin. As he drank his coffee, he watched them carrying their heavy suitcases and enormous boxes of detergent. The Senator almost never had to endure that long wait at the taxi stand, or the other, even slower wait, either, the one they had to face at the Volkspolizei window inside the station, in order to leave. All of that vexed him, not because the slow pace hindered some urgency on his part, but rather because it seemed that the coughing, the pallid faces, and the anguished decrepitude that awaited him here was the same as that which assailed him every day in the elevators at number 8 Volksradstrasse. It depressed him to fit so naturally into this group, but more depressing still was the realization that his identification with it was no accident. These old people had no access to the Passport for Foreigners or the Special Visa he held onto in his jacket pocket, although, like him, they shared the sad privilege that their years conferred on them, and for that reason alone they could cross over the Wall without any red tape other than a slight delay they found entirely tolerable. They had waited a lifetime to occupy a place in that line.

He thought that in some ways his situation was even worse than that of his contemporaries. Any one of them could come and go, have coffee with their son or granddaughter in a pastry shop on Kudamm, recognize familiar places from their youth, return at night to a room—probably in a building for widowers—carrying cheap goods and detergent, knowing that it would always be possible to repeat that minimal adventure: to cross a line and later be embraced at a border when it was time to set out for home.

But that was precisely what was forbidden to him: going home. The line he had to cross was very far away from that wall. If he found himself among them right now it was only to submit a new application to return home at the Consulate. How many had he submitted already? When had he submitted the last one? While he became impatient with the slowness of the line—he had the sensation of having been in the same place for a long time—he remembered each one of his efforts and arranged them in order in his memory. He thought that perhaps if he mentioned all of them he might move the Consul this morning with his persistence.

The S-Bahn terminal on Friedrichstrasse receives two types of passengers from West Berlin: those who arrive at the station in order to cross the border, and those who go there to buy alcohol, cigarettes or chocolate at incredible prices, even cheaper than at a duty-free shop in any airport. Those of us who occasionally obtained an exit visa set aside some money to buy something there before we returned home. Of course, we never saw a car full of children interested in saving on their chocolate purchases. What attracted our attention was the abject, terminal mien of the alcoholics, concentrating on counting their money, calculating whether they had enough for another bottle of wheat brandy or vodka. Broken down types, ceaselessly smoking and spitting out the detritus that their coughing brought up from their painful interiors. Livid faces, as blue as their sleepless nights, reddened only by bloody, pustulating scabs; mangy legs covered with scraps of filthy, hole-infested jeans. They arrived at Friedrichstrasse early, picked up their essential merchandise, and went back to drink it around the Zoo station, sitting in the gutters of side streets, and in winter, discovering the darkest corners of the other station, splayed out on tiles that for days remained covered with used needles piled on top of traces of blood and ancient vomit.

Something strange linked both stations together. Something sordid. Friedrichstrasse was clean, tidy in its poverty, but threatening and brutal; a guard watched from atop the tower, prodding his fiercely trained dogs to bark every so often. Zoo station, on the other hand, was open and pathetic, the place the destitute preferred because no one cared about their misery. Soldiers here, garbage there; here, guard dogs; there, empty bottles and needles thrown away in the corners. At Friedrichstrasse one saw the misery of absolute power over the people; at Zoo, the misery of people absolutely abandoned by those in power.

The Senator preferred to take the elevated train, the S-Bahn, to go to the Consulate. He believed he could make up for violating the rules by leaving a few *pfennigs* in the coffers of the Socialist treasury, and he enjoyed watching the disturbing scenery: the old, forbidden buildings near the Wall, then the upper story windows, a quick glance at that that anonymous intimacy; buildings that were less gray, some even boldly colorful, and finally that horrible station that reinforced his beliefs with each successive trip: the Zoo.

He tolerated the drunks' pathetic presence by trying to ignore them; he leaned his forehead against the window and fixed his eyes on the landscape. At the beleaguered station he walked hurriedly towards the exit, asking himself a thousand times, How can those eternal visa seekers stand all this? He had gone through the experience seven times and he hoped this time would be the last.

The night before what he imagined would be his last trip, he dreamed that the Consul handed him a diploma with permission to return. He woke up startled, and now lucid, wondered if he had been snatched from his dream by the solemn diploma or by the painful rumbling of his guts. Stimulated by the dream, he decided to leave the Bureau that morning and reinitiate the paperwork in search of his authorization. But he never imagined that the snowfall the next morning would erase the last landmarks he recognized. The Consulate building was the first thing one saw on emerging from the subway to the street, assuming that one chose the correct exit. That's why the fruit and flower kiosk next to the aristocratic building was a more reliable landmark. But it was a summer landmark. The Senator now found himself facing a vast expanse of snow. There could be no fruit and flower kiosk in this snowstorm, and the glowing letters of the subway, his two cardinal points, were as formless as a watch face without a minute hand.

The snow that morning reminded him of the desert and nitrate mines of the north. But that white immensity of his childhood had been sunny, luminous, close to the sea and the gentle sound of the waves. As an old man snow accosted him; a frozen stepmother who dissipated into dark mud, on concrete plazas and in narrow, tiled alleyways. He thought it must be like the sands of his youth, but after the fall, the descent of his white warmth into night.

Who the hell made him believe that dream? The dream was a lie, a deceiving temptation, a trap. That deserted plaza, those sodden, muddy shoes, those frozen feet, that sharp pain exacerbated by the cold—*that* was reality! The next reality would be the Consul's predictable cologne, his careful, cordial words, his diplomatic indifference. On account of that stupid dream, he failed to show up at the Bureau that morning. All day, really, because it was already around noon, and he still hadn't filed his petition, even presupposing that he could do it at all. There was also the possibility the Consul might be running late; there could be an even

longer line now at the border—it grew longer as nightfall approached—
and for that reason it might be even more difficult to find a taxi at the
stand on Friedrichstrasse. Now he would be one more in that line, and it
was as though he were watching himself from one of the lacquered tables
at Cafe Metropol. Just one more at the end of the day, colder, guiltier,
and in more pain. He'd promised to return to the Bureau in the afternoon, and those plans were going up in smoke, plain and simple; they
were disappearing, the whole day was escaping, while piles of applications piled up on his desk. And all that, just to give needless importance
to a strictly personal matter. When the hell did he allow himself to be
deceived by that dream! Hitting his head once more against the same
wall! No visa! No decree! No forgiveness! The goal grows distant and
the road grows shorter.

After running around in the puddles and the frost, his nose and even
his ears all frozen despite the *shapka*, at the fourth corner and after a
half hour, he found the building. Finally some warm air behind the screen
door and dry, shiny marble beneath his feet. He climbed the broad staircase to the third floor. He didn't trust those old, narrow elevators with
their grated doors that were so hard to pull closed, almost always black-
ened with a grease that hardly muffled the rattling. He heard some violin chords coming through a door at the first landing and then when he
stopped, out of breath, at the second, strange moans and something like
delicate barking. At last he stood before the door on the third floor, having fulfilled part of the mission of this uncomfortable journey, but still
with unpleasant traces of guilt; he didn't think it was right to make a trip
on his own behalf that he had to deny to so many applicants. But his
self-doubt melted like snow as soon as he entered the Consulate. He
liked the welcoming warmth, a squalid imitation of what he had lost:
high-pitched voices answering the phones, familiar-sounding accents,
sunny landscapes decorating the walls. Smiling pleasantly, the secretary
immediately let him into the Consul's office.

Once inside, sinking into a comfortable black leather armchair, he
felt himself also sinking into a frightening sensation of insecurity and
discouragement, and after a few moments he knew it made no sense to
wait any longer. The journey had been useless. The longed-for resolution of this last effort was a pathetic joke, a macabre delusion, an illu-
sion made of the same deceptive fabric as dreams. Despite the Consul's
friendly greeting—as always, he looked as if he'd just emerged from the
shower—what was happening there was definitely different from what
he had dreamed the night before.

The Senator thought the Consul smelled frightfully like lavender that morning. He had always thought it dangerous to be close to a perfumed woman, and even more so to a fragrant man. He remembered how he used to inhale that effeminate affectation some men left in their wake in the Senate corridors, the reading room, the dining rooms, everywhere. On previous occasions he had also inhaled a suspicious little scent in the Consul's office. He began to tremble. Once again he felt the assault of an old ulcer. Did the Consul's cologne provoke that irritation? Or was it, rather, the crab's claws devastating his poor, miserable intestines? The Consul refused to take refuge behind his desk. He brought a chair over to the one Don Carlos occupied and attempted to make friendly conversation, as unofficial as possible. But his proximity was also the proximity of his cologne, and Don Carlos's irritation found its target in this smiling man—horribly fragrant, but also frighteningly healthy—on whom his petition depended.

The smell of lavender occupied a special place in the Senator's scale of values. And this scale was based on an archetypal triangle whose apex was occupied, not by the Platonic ideal of Good, but rather by the equally incorruptible figure of the Worldwide Proletariat, a figure inspired by an image that had impressed him when he was young, during one of his Friday nights out.

One night, at the conclusion of a meal at the Budapest Restaurant on Karl-Marx-Allee, stirred by the violin music and wrapped up in who-knows-what memories, Don Carlos told us about a monument that revolved slowly above the screen of the syndicate's precarious movie theater. Unlike Metro-Goldwyn's long-haired lion, erected atop a pedestal that was as imposing as the bulk of an iceberg, stood a pair of bodies forged from metal: the Worker and the *Kolhoznika*, the Collective Farm Woman. They were the protagonists of this mythical construct, the original inhabitants of a future paradise, captured at last in full flight and firmly planted on the earth. "The sculptor has placed them at such an inhuman height that they ultimately suggest the existence of heaven," argued Rosales, who had seen that monument in Moscow; but no, that was unthinkable, and a discussion ensued that led us to imagine that it *was* possible, yes, and if it was, then which heaven could it be? In the sculpture, according to Don Carlos's description, the Worker was Adam, with broad pectorals and strong arms, and she was an Eve with sturdy legs who resisted the assault of the gusts of wind against the flowing skirt of her full dress. Both of them had one arm raised: she, with a sickle in her hand, he, with a hammer, and those arms crossed one another on high, at the apex of the triangular figure, thereby constructing an emblem of perpetual happiness. "They had a rather impersonal expression, a distant look," remarked Mario and Lorena, who had seen the same spectacular image in a movie theater in Cartagena. "Maybe that's because at that height there was nothing for them to see," someone said. "Nothing human," we countered. But the Senator had insisted: those enormous beings turning above the screen were the ideal image of the new man and woman. And that expression, lost in space, symbolized a vision of the future. The most likely explanation is that Don Carlos found them so magnificent because that muscular, metallic composition and that gaze into infinity made them seem alien to pain. How different they were from pale Rosales, who looked greenish under the best of circumstances, unable to pluck the cigarette from his mouth. His idea of a new society grew up around those symbols, which, in combination with his old prejudices, ended up determining the values he assigned to everything he thought he knew.

At this point we return to the subject of fragrance. It's obvious that this hedonistic, decadent pretension, this cult to the ethereal and transitory, was incompatible with that of those demiurges, forged of such hard metal that they suggested eternity. The Senator associated the splendid figure of those sculpted proletarians not also with the absence of pain, but also with absolute absence of odor. For that reason he was bothered by the aroma—fresh, healthy, fragrant, direct from the shower—that flooded the office the moment he entered to conduct his business. And although he took the Consul for an agreeable man (for better or for worse, he was a career diplomat and he believed the high regard was mutual), that morning the Senator decided he couldn't confide in him. In spite of the measures taken by the Consul on behalf of the exiles, that strong, faggoty odor made the Senator think that his long wait at the border had been completely useless.

"How about some coffee, Don Carlos?"

"No, thanks."

"If I can help you with anything ..."

"Something you haven't been able to help me with up till now. I'm going to die, and I'd like to do it in my own house. I think that's about where it stands."

"Are you ill?"

"Very ill."

The Consul momentarily remembered the ex-Senator's seven previous applications and at that very moment decided that this "illness" must be a new strategy.

"Well,...I'm so sorry," he said in a rather formal tone. "I imagine you want to file a new application."

As he had to attend a reception at noon, the Consul sneaked a look at his watch. He still had time, and he thought this time it would be better to explain how things worked in his office.

"Let me suggest that we think over the steps we need to take very carefully. You understand that any imprudent action might overturn everything once again. I have to tell you that your next-to-last application was analyzed just as they were about to grant permission, but the letter you attached, instead of helping, made them overturn the favorable decision that had ..."

"The letter from the Nobel Prize winner in Physics?"

"No, the letter from the Bishop."

"Then that wasn't the next-to-last one, it was the fifth application. After that one came the letter from the physicist, and with the last one I attached a letter from my sister who still lives in Parral."

"The business with your sister couldn't possibly bother anyone, and as far as the Nobel Prize winner is concerned, all well and good; these things don't enter into the realm of political pressures. But when a Bishop's miter sticks out of the mess ...!"

"In this case, it's my doctor's smock that's sticking out, at the very most."

"Or a surgeon's scalpel...and that might be the unkindest cut of all. That's why I advise caution and adequate information. Caution is a natural quality in mature people. That's why I can ask you to exercise some, Don Carlos. *I'll* provide the necessary information."

Having said this, he stood up, but instead of walking toward his desk, he chose to walk back and forth between the door and the large window while unfolding his arguments, just as Don Carlos himself did at the Bureau, or in the incomparably smaller space of his widower's apartment, whenever he wanted to express a complex idea, thus allowing the rhythm of his steps to articulate the solid chain of his reasoning more methodically.

"I want you to know they're about to approve an amnesty law that will include exiles ..."

The Senator interrupted him immediately. Overcoming the pain that emanated from his insides and the nausea that the fragrance provoked, he issued a single utterance, but he pronounced it slowly, giving each word its proper weight, so that the enormity of the injustice and the immensity of the offense would weigh on the Consul's conscience:

"That law can hardly do me any good. I've never committed a crime, and I've never been convicted."

"It doesn't matter," the Consul replied, not noticing the effort with which Don Carlos tried to reclaim his wounded dignity. "As soon as this law is passed, all restrictions against those who have left the country will automatically be lifted, and we won't be deluged with letters and applications any more. From that moment on, we'll start giving out passports without the "L." Or perhaps, to avoid the inconvenience and the expense, the same law could change the meaning of the "L," so it would no longer stand for Limited, but, say for example, Legalized or Legitimate. The "L" might also stand for Licensed, or Long-Term, since the passport is good for five years. I suppose the most important concern for you, my dear Senator, is to return home. What difference does it make to comply with a mere formality? The problem is that the amnesty has enemies within the government itself," he said, drawing his perfumed presence closer in a clandestine gesture. "They're the same old hardheads. They claim that an amnesty allowing the exiles to return home will be interpreted as a sign of weakness, or even defeat. They've informed me—unofficially, of course,—that the amnesty supporters are calling for an appreciable reduction in the number of applications. That would allow them to promote the law without jeopardizing the appearance of power."

"Are you trying to convince me that the best thing would be not to submit a new application this time?"

"Not exactly. I'm just asking that we think the matter over carefully."

"You're trying to convince me that the fewer applications there are, the sooner they'll let us return?"

"No. I'm not trying to convince you of anything. I only want to help you with a bit of advice and some information. The more evidence they have of a concerted effort to apply pressure, the more rigid their official position will be. Is it convenient to have mountains of applications piling up in our consulates? It's undeniable that they produce some minor housekeeping inconveniences in our consular work, but the truth is that in the majority of cases, those applications aren't even sent to the Ministry of External Relations. You understand, the Chancellery employees are also paralyzed by fear, and sometimes they choose not to send the mail along."

"Then the applications aren't processed?" the Senator asked, astonished.

"I'm not saying that's how it goes in all cases. You can be confident that yours were processed promptly. But when it comes to their diplomatic portfolios, the employees have a certain margin of personal discretion that allows them to establish priorities, and in that case, the applications can wait. It's not as if they're saying: ' No more applications will be processed!' No. But they lie around, you understand? They lie around. At first, on the Consul's desk, and after a few days, when they're starting to become an nuisance there, they go to the secretary's office, where they get mixed together with older piles of papers and also with documents that have to be processed without delay, so the Secretary's secretary puts them in order, expedites whatever's urgent and looks for a place for the things that will have to keep on lying around. In most cases the applications get sent to the archive section, and then they end up very handily in the basement."

"And they're still right here, beneath my feet? Applications from all the residents of Berlin?"

"Beneath your feet is the most elegant dog grooming salon in all Berlin, my dear friend. If your feet could hear, they'd end up crying along with the whimpering of the finest dogs in the city. And you know that a dog in Berlin is much more revered than a cow in India. To talk about pedigreed dogs around here is to talk about something really important. No, Don Carlos, we have no basement here. On the second floor we have dogs, and on the first floor there's a private music conservatory. Barking and music. Around here there's no basement filled with forgotten applications."

"And when all is said and done, what does it matter?" the Senator said to himself, but clearly and in a loud voice. "The Chancellery has nice, large basements, too. What difference does it make where our applications have gone to await the Judgment of the Righteous?" And, fixing his gaze on the Consul, he barked out the question, "And why should we believe that this consulate is any exception?"

The Consul, who had sat back down next to Don Carlos, remained silent for a brief moment before replying, but that moment was sufficient to reveal that his pride had been wounded. "Because the Consul who tells you so is a gentleman," he responded, also giving each of his words it proper weight. Having ascertained that his answer had produced its effect on Don Carlos's temper (the Senator fell silent, lowering his gaze and diverting it to the frosty windowpanes), he added in a very different tone, as if he wanted to detract from the importance of the message:

"Besides, I've fallen into disgrace. I have nothing more to fear. I've been called to Santiago and I know they plan to send me to Mozambique."

"I'm sorry," Don Carlos stammered.

He suddenly felt it had been ridiculous to cross over the Wall and to have made that pilgrimage in the snow, just to end up consoling the Consul. To get rid of that feeling of futility, he repeated in a very soft, almost embarrassed voice, "Believe me, I'm so sorry."

But immediately he realized that the sentence and the involuntary tone that surrounded it simply emphasized the grotesquery of the situation. Then, pointing to the official photos on the walls that hung next to a culinary map of his country (enormous lobsters from Juan Fernández and golden salmon struggling upstream in some southern river), he said in a playful tone:

"I imagine all consulates are the same. You'll be able to look at those same lobsters in Mozambique."

The Consul attempted a grateful smile, but didn't abandon his attempt to explain his situation.

"I arrived at this consulate twenty years ago. My wife is a Berliner. I have three kids and four grandchildren here. If they send me elsewhere, I'd just as soon resign. You're probably thinking I should've done it sooner…But, well, we're all afraid of something. The truth is I haven't decided on anything yet."

"You're a career Consul. I imagine you could appeal."

"Yes, I can, but my appeal would meet the same fate as the applications. There are many ways to reject a petition, Don Carlos. If you think about it carefully, the rejection always precedes the petition: it's something that's been decided in advance. That's why I think these applications make no sense. My application would lie on a desk also, and then on another, and it would end up in a file somewhere, like so many others. That's how life is, I guess. There are more applications than there are ways of approving them. It's possible that the processing clerk himself has presented his own application more than once and its processing is still unresolved. And there's always some secretary whose mission is to clear the path and toss all the applications into the wastebasket. It seems there isn't enough space for all of them and we have to accept that fact, Don Carlos."

"You're a real pessimist. Life isn't just an accumulation of rejections. At least that hasn't been my experience."

"I've had to say no to you many times."

"Only seven times."

"Seven times seven, the Bible says. I suppose it's not the first time you've been told no seven times."

"You're right. And yet,…well,…don't think I don't appreciate your advice, but,…how about we fill out one more application?"

"Whatever you like. But you know it won't do any good."

"It doesn't matter. At this point it's just to bug them. We have no other choice, don't you think?"

"Now you're the pessimist, Don Carlos. Tell me: what can I do for you?"

The old man had waited for that question all morning. But now he felt confident. He answered as quickly as a contestant on a television game show:

"Three things."

"What's the first one?"

"Send that application right now."

"Agreed. It doesn't matter, after all. And the second thing?"

"A glass of milk."

"We'll order it immediately. Hot?"

"Warm."

"And the third?"

Don Carlos cleared his throat so his voice wouldn't tremble.

"That cologne…Excuse me, but does it help you tolerate all this more easily?"

"Something pleasant always helps. For me, it's like your glass of milk. Do you want to know how it feels?"

Without waiting for the Senator's reply, the Consul left his office in search of some milk and the bottle of cologne.

He was still smelling that shit as he walked down the stairs. At the first landing he heard some barking, and on the next one some music that reminded him of what he waited for every night with his ear stuck against the wall. What had inspired that curiosity? Now he was going to arrive at La Batea smelling like a common fag. The truth is that he liked the cologne, but his greatest desire was to get rid of the odor by the time he reached the street. And since the cold froze his nostrils as he took his first steps in the snow, he imagined his indiscretion would remain a secret between the poor Consul and himself. Now, without the burden of the fragrance, he guessed that the diplomat was prepared to resign because his cologne would never be tolerated in Mozambique. He tried to vindicate himself by recalling the little joke he allowed himself to make as he left: "We have a large Regional Committee in Mozambique. You can get even by sending applications to the Chancellery."

La Batea was a favorite Chilean gathering place frequented with nostalgic fervor by those of us exiles who were also divided by the Wall. Those on the other side could sit down at its bar every night; we—actually, only those few of us who had exit visas—used to make a quick stop there before returning to the Wall. The exchange rate allowed us to have only a few drinks, hardly ever to eat anything, but at night we used to count on the assistance of those two generous, dedicated hosts from the First Laborers' and Farmworkers' State on German Soil—Douglas and the Celsa girl. At those times the anticipated drink would be on the house, thus leaving us enough to pay for the second one, all the while chatting away. La Batea was much more important to us than the Consulate; there we could carry out business without any red tape, from buying a used car to sending mail that might endanger our families. There we exchanged magazines ("just arrived from the interior") which passed from hand to hand for months. There someone might hire you to be an extra for a film shot in Berlin but set in some exotic place requiring proud, dreadlocked aborigines. At La Batea you could listen to music, dance, and even start a romance: many blonde hearts were smitten by dark manes, numbed by nostalgia. La Batea was the place for distant memories. On its walls, instead of those insipid lobsters, hung portraits that followed us, joining us through some strange sort of mysticism to our children, who also adored them: Neruda, Violeta, Víctor Jara. Discolored photographs of the pampas and the glaciers, of Santiago neighborhoods and the Puerto hills, had different affective resonances for different people, but at the same time helped construct the difficult union of our collective memory.

Don Carlos arrived at La Batea around two. When they offered him something to eat on the house, he said he had already eaten, and quite well, too. For a while now he had been skipping lunch in order to avoid that acid stomach which got worse in the afternoon. Sitting in the bar, after his second glass of a bitter liquid that had the virtue of controlling his pain, he spoke in a reserved voice with the Party Secretary, a tall, wan young man who listened attentively as he dried glasses behind the bar.

"I want to ask a favor of you, comrade."

"Name it, Don Carlos."

"But this must remain strictly between us. Do it discreetly, and without saying anything."

"*Natürlich.*" The word emerged spontaneously; for better or for worse he spoke the language he had learned playing in the schoolyard.

"We have to meet two people who are arriving from the interior."

"Understood," the boy said.

"But this time they aren't comrades."

The boy put the glass and napkin down on the bar and got ready to hear something completely new.

"I want you to help me out for a girl who can't go pick up her parents."

During his conversation with the Consul, during a particularly anguished moment, perhaps when the bureaucrat was telling him about the piles of applications in the basement of the Ministry, Don Carlos had a clear vision that pained him like his open wound: Lorena's parents at a long-ago wedding reception under a grape arbor at a house in Ñuñoa. He had given them a silver salt shaker, a small gift which he surreptitiously removed from his jacket pocket as Mario and Lorena were cutting the cake amid the guests' applause. As he danced with the bride, he placed the small, shiny object in her hand and closed her fist over it, telling her that what she held in the warmth of her hand was lasting happiness, that he had heard this from boyhood, sayings and images connected with salt, love, time to come for the lovers. He imagined Lorena's parents learning of the separation, casting their bovine gaze at a separated woman's apartment. And he also saw them dressed as on that wedding night, all trussed up and formal, dignified in their poverty, no longer beneath the grapevine now, but rather sinking into the snow that was piling up—like the applications—at Checkpoint Charlie. They were alone at the Volkspolizei station, waiting for someone to bring the visa without which they couldn't cross that wall.

With that image in mind he faced the frigid gusts in the plaza, descended into the underground labyrinth of the U-Bahn, walked up to the bar in La Batea, and asked the Party Secretary to solve this problem as discreetly as possible. When he arrived at the Friedrichstrasse station with his companions from the interior, the Secretary would be awaiting them with the visas.

And he still didn't lose sight of that image when, stopping by the Bureau that afternoon, the bomb exploded right in his face. The Minister's letter had arrived around four, and they had already phoned from the Big Bureau to schedule an urgent meeting. When he finished reading the Minister's letter and the copy of the letter Lorena had sent him, the painful image of the numb old folks gave way to an even more pathetic one, although it wasn't just an image, but rather the very tangible, vivid expression with which the four Directors regarded him, waiting to hear what he had to say about the outrage.

"It's the most shameful thing that's happened in all these years. What can I tell you?" the Senator repeated, pacing once more from the kitchen to the balcony, while he rehashed the same words, the same argument, the same bitter anger, for the thousandth time.

"To me it looks like a perfectly legitimate application, although it may not agree with your point of view," Mario contradicted, putting his second cup of tea down on the table.

"Your current father-in-law doesn't think so, comrade. Do you want to read the letter the Minister sent us?"

Mario detected a second source of annoyance in Don Carlos's tone of voice. Not only was he irritated by Lorena's letter, but also by the one the Minister had sent to the Bureau.

"Let's separate these two things, Don Carlos. If it's an official matter, it has nothing to do with my relationship with Eva. And whatever I may think is independent of official opinion and also of my personal relationships. Eva mustn't get involved in all this. I beg you to keep that in mind."

"It's seems like it's fashionable to talk about official opinions and divorce oneself from them."

"What do I have to do with anything the Minister might say?"

"Nothing, really. I was just remembering."

"Remembering what?"

"My official meeting with the Consul this morning. The official representative doesn't subscribe to official policy."

"If you're referring to the Minister, I'm not his official representative. I'm his daughter's partner, and she doesn't agree with this atrocity that's happening, either."

"Atrocity?"

"Yes. Throwing Lorena out of the country. This is a warning against dissidence."

In his vexation, Mario had pronounced the forbidden word. He would have liked to reverse his action, but there was no turning back.

"That's exactly the point. After so many years, a new outbreak of dissidence!"

The Senator was referring to a previous crisis: the famous strike we organized in Leuna, the copper mine where all exiles "of bourgeois extraction" were sent, a score of intellectuals—most of them academics—actors, journalists, former diplomats—with the very noble goal of "proletarianizing" us.

"Discontent," said Mario, knowing he had lost.

"But you said dissidence," the Senator emphasized, as he served another cup of tea.

CHAPTER SIX

> *Jason: What more fortunate solution*
> *could I have found than to marry*
> *the king's daughter, exile that I am?*

> *Euripides,* Medea

*A*lthough I search and search, I can't find the words to express your evil and cowardice. Because it's an evil act to suggest that my fate depends on the generous efforts of the person who has done me the greatest harm in my entire life.

When did you both decide that she could intercede on my behalf with her father, the very person who signed my expulsion decree? Was it before or after making love? Was it the moon, or your caresses, or the wine you've no doubt taught her to enjoy in bed that inspired your touching gesture of compassion?

Or is it that this new punishment you've announced for me won't let the two of you sleep in peace? Have I become an unbearable ghost for you? Do we share our sleepless nights, then, tossing and turning in the same sheets?

Now it's your turn to hear me out.

I was faithful. Everyone who left along with us knows that, all those who remained with me and with your children aboard this ship that no longer carries us anywhere.

For you, I was—as you told me so many times—a beam of salvation. But this light of mine that lit your way is the same one I stole from my parents' house. My parents, who are so lonely now, so deep in the shadows because of me. *If only you knew how much I yearn to be with them! If only you knew how I long to be with my sisters, to hug them, kiss them, kiss each one of their children whom I've never met!*

How I'd love to be in my childhood home, Sunday lunchtime, beneath the grape arbor! I can picture myself sitting at the table surrounded by all those who truly love me. And among them are my sisters' husbands, who don't know me, but who respect me more than you do, who love me more than you do, who are prepared—I know it!—To sacrifice for me what you never sacrificed. How I'd love to meet my dear sisters' husbands!

That's how it is: I left my nearest and dearest to follow you, because that was my duty as a wife, just as yours was not to abandon me so far from my people. I always fulfilled my obligations to you, even though it hurt my family. Just as you did. Faithful to the woman who shared your unhappiness, and faithful to the children born of that fidelity.

I look at my right hand, which rested happily in yours so many times, and with my other hand I caress my knees, as you used to do. It's a sad thing, this nostalgia my body feels. How sad my body is. It's not just blood, it's time that flows through my veins.

Is that why you did this crazy thing? Does the Generous One remind you of how my young girl's body once looked? My young knees locked around your sides, caressing you in bed? My firm breasts, about to explode on the highest part of the prow?

How well I understand you! I've just discovered what I can feel alongside a younger man. And yet I'd never abandon my children for that. And I wouldn't abandon you, either, because your age isn't your fault. Nor would I let myself swim against the current of my own flowing time.

Your boundless kindness really moves me: agreeing to stay with me while my parents are here, even though you emphasize that this generous offer will hold only if their visit is a short one. Yes, it's short. Don't you realize, paragon of sensitivity that you are, that it will always be too short for me? And don't you believe that it will be short for your children, who've been dreaming of your return all this time? Or do you want to hear that it's a long visit, so you can get out of your own decision? Well, yes, I might also tell you that it's long. Long, if I have to spend each hour pretending, at the threshold of my pain, pretending that I still have what I've already lost; happy to be close to you, knowing it's a sham; giving my dear ones a peace of mind that's just the product of deceit. Short or long? It depends. It depends on what you think is still alive, on whatever remnant of life still courses through your veins.

The key in the lock.

Mario is about to enter the apartment on Karl-Liebknecht-Strasse. Suddenly he recalls a distant gesture, a distant sound: in his house on Seminario Street, you had to turn the key ever so slightly to the right after inserting it all the way into the lock, and then pull it out a little and lift it upwards; after you heard the metallic creak you could turn the key easily and then the door would open. Why is he remembering this now? Why does he seem to hear the creaking of the door and his father repeating: "No, no. You have to pull it out a little after you push it all the way in, then lift it up and—presto! That's it." For years the lock retained its slight idiosyncrasy, to which others were added here and there: that broken roof tile, three slightly loose bricks in the grape arbor, the stone in the grotto that comes out once in a while and falls, although someone always picks it up and replaces it in its hole, where the cement is missing, and it remains there for a few days, as if nothing had happened. Who's taking care of those little defects these days? Who climbs up on the roof? Who pushes the old man's wheelchair outside so he can enjoy the sun at noon? He suddenly realized something he had never considered before: the lock had had that defect for years and no one ever called a locksmith. Everyone in the family learned the little trick—because it's just a little trick, the old man used to say—and even the maids, one after another, learned how to do it, and the gardener, too, and the gardener's assistant, when the main gardener stopped coming around; and he recalls that he himself taught Aunt Lidia the trick, when she came to take care of papa after his stroke: "You have to pull it out a little after it goes all the way in, and then lift it, but don't force it—don't break the key, Auntie, see how easy it is?" And so for Mario the precarious balance between the lock's growing deterioration and the collective skill they all developed to hide its defect became the family's most obvious point of cohesion. During the last few years they all scattered for different—or perhaps the same—reasons. Mario got married and left the seminary. His brothers did the same thing during the next three years. They lived in different houses—different doors, different locks. They thought differently and argued more bitterly all the time, and so their customary Sunday lunches became unpleasant. He chose to visit his parents on Saturday. He and Lorena would arrive around one. The metallic creak of the lock became the preamble to those rather boring lunches. They felt burdened by this life sentence, believing that those Saturday lunches would go on forever. Then he remembers: a few nights ago he dreamed that he was standing at that door once again, only a yard away from that imperfect lock. His suitcase on the ground beside him; the old man, on the other side, smiled cunningly at him as if to catch him while he inserted the key: "Do you remember the little trick?"

The door and the smile quickly evaporated. He woke up. He was drenched, but shivering, and his head throbbed. He watched Eva sleeping. He imagined her sailing within her own dream, a dream he couldn't imagine. He sat up in bed. He had just heard the same metallic creaking of the lock. And fifteen years had gone by!

Why did he recall that just now? Why did he forget it in the second dream which followed that initial surprise? Now he has the key in the lock and he's about to enter his house over here. But this isn't his house, really; it's Eva's apartment at 9 Karl-Liebknecht-Strasse, facing Alexanderplatz. It was here that his house appeared to him in a nightmare two weeks ago.

Eva pays 114 marks a month for this apartment, ten percent of her salary from Humboldt University, just as the law prescribes. It's a nice apartment, with two bedrooms, a living-dining room combination, and a fairly spacious terrace. But the truth is that it's not Eva's apartment, either: it's the place Eva has been given by the State, where she can live indefinitely, unless a serious mistake forces the State to deprive her of that privilege.

The terrace faces the stone facade of Marienkirche, a thirteenth century church whose outline looks clearer against the snow that has covered the broad expanse of the plaza for days now. The first time Mario saw the church from there—a year ago, exactly one year—he thought of a painting he'd seen somewhere. It was midnight. Christiane and Gunter had left after the second bottle of vodka and he was on that terrace with Eva for the first time, resisting the cold and the gusts of wind, facing that landscape which she presented to him as the most beautiful thing she had ever seen in her life, happy to think that this beauty coincidentally faced her terrace. In the landscape Mario had before his eyes and in the painting his memory vaguely recalled, he was dazzled by the contrast between the sky's darkness and the saltlike appearance of the snow, softened by the warm light of the street lamps and the other, cold blue light of the rounded moon beside the stylized point of the belltower. For a long time he contemplated that vast whiteness, the other white disk in the sky, the church and the golden light of the street lamps, which lent the stone its somber, millenarian air, endowing it with immediacy and closeness at the same time, like a miracle. All that was part of a toast made long ago on that unexpected night. Mario regards the landscape from the terrace. He tries to recall the painting that came before and intuits that the forgotten painting conceals some of the night's mystery. He feels Eva beside him, listens to the light rhythm of her breathing, turns her face toward him so he can look at her. He sees that she's looking at the landscape, too, and he realizes that they're feeling the same thing. And through Eva's half-opened mouth, he watches her breath fly alongside his own toward the night-heart of the magic.

In mid-November—*Im traurigen Monat November war's*—Mario received some news whose absolutely unforeseeable consequences were to add yet another mutation to those which had already determined the course of his life. It didn't come announced by a red circle on his mailbox or in the classic form of a telegram. It was a simple phone call. Its lack of drama, however, was compensated for by the magnitude of the announcement. He interpreted the news—a possible screenplay commission—as a somewhat belated recognition of his talent and the possibility of getting out of his present situation once and for all. His situation, actually, was considered to be one of the most favorable—if not the most favorable—of all those who discussed such things around dinner tables in the ghetto, since we understood that although Mario earned a living practicing his profession (quite an uncommon phenomenon in our community), it wasn't exactly the profession by which he wanted to earn that living. But we also understood that Mario had spent his life trying to get out of situations in which he voluntarily became involved. We had never met anyone so desperately determined to climb out of his own skin.

The call Mario received at the end of last winter was from a translator whom he had met a few years earlier at a solidarity meeting of the first batch of arrivals. She asked him to write a screenplay for a young director who was very enthused about his recently published book of short stories. Following the law of natural progression, the young director—just forty years old—had the goal of completing a full-length film, if he could find an interesting project. He thought a story about exiles might have a greater chance of being approved. Mario would also benefit from this sort of natural progression: after the favorable critical reaction to his first volume of short stories, something like this was inevitable, and so he went to the meeting, bolstered by his self-esteem and already dreaming of the stardom that invariably accompanies premieres.

Then he imagined himself as the protagonist of a lecture, the sudden recognition of his cleverness, and finally a signed contract, for a sum that would finally permit him to live from his writing. The signing, of course, would be preceded by a glass—or several—of champagne, and after affixing his signature, he would announce that he planned to donate part of his money to the Chilean solidarity movement. What he couldn't imagine is that there would be no contract. It was simply a project, after all, and we all knew how long the *via crucis* of projects could be and we also knew that they almost always ended up crowned with thorns and deceptions. There was, however, the pleasantness of the meeting, the champagne, betting on a happy ending (although Gunter thought happy endings were a drag), the young director's enthusiasm, and an unexpected surprise, something Mario couldn't have imagined when he received the phone call, a cat leaping into the next chair from the most unlikely place: Eva's unanticipated presence, almost like something that had been invented to prowl around in nearby nooks and crannies: at first on the sofa, then next to him at the table, and finally in his bed.

Before going inside, before making up his mind to turn the key in the lock, Mario once more asks himself what he's been ruminating about all afternoon: Should he tell her right now, or would it be better to wait until tomorrow? To tell her now might mean an all-night session, without being able to sleep a wink. Besides, if it gets ugly, if she asks him to pack his suitcase right away and leave…where would he go? He doesn't have the right to register in a hotel in Berlin because on his *Ausweis* it says very clearly that he resides in Berlin: *Jawohl*! He'd have to go to Potsdam, as he'd done once before, and spend a few days commuting for an hour-and-a-half in the morning and again in the afternoon, which wasn't such a big deal when you thought about it, especially if there's no other alternative. Yes, Potsdam is the nearest place where a Berliner can hope to get a hotel room…if by chance there's a vacancy. Fucking life. Should he tell her now? Seems like it might be better to wait till tomorrow.

Mario's and Eva's habits coincided, and that was good, and better yet was the fact that they had managed to coincide in such a short time. In effect, they had accepted one another from the very first night. When evening fell—in Berlin in winter it was already quite dark out—Eva would enter the bathtub like a peacock in a beauty salon. It's not that Eva was pretentious. She simply liked the no-excuses solitude of her bath, the water's warmth as it filled the tub, and the profusion of bath salts, colognes, and creams which delayed her subsequent entrance on stage, when Mario had already set the table with Hungarian wine and slices of sturgeon that mysteriously appeared in the house—or rather in the refrigerator—every time her parents came to visit. He usually returned home punctually from the university around seven, after his customary stroll along the bridges on the Spree. At that hour Eva was almost always in the bath while he devoted himself to organizing the dinner delights. He was meticulous with the candles, with the cheese—which had to be at room temperature, like the wine—and with the culinary surprise of the evening, sometimes a piece of pickled fish or those slices of beef tongue which he marinated in almond sauce. It was also their custom to get together to inform each other of the day's events. Mario would enter the steamy bathroom and kneel down beside the tub. Their kiss was a warm moistness, slippery, different, and then he would gaze at Eva's body, her rounded beauty beneath the transparent warmth of the water, that calm closeness telling him about her day. Eva was tiny; she was lovely in the water, a fish floating free in her natural habitat, and when she turned to take the glass of vodka (opaque in its iciness) that Mario placed within her reach—that small offering to enter into her intimacy—her legs stirred the water, her breasts seemed to grow with the little swell, and her arm rose up dripping off the excess, the gift of her slippery perfection, that shining initial toast of the evening. But the offering Mario made in order to penetrate the intimacy of Eva's bath wasn't just some vodka in a glass straight from the freezer. There was also the ritual of the gifts: Mario arrived each afternoon with something unexpected, although the frequency made it increasingly difficult to surprise her with something new. An antique salt shaker, a book about to be published, a piece of cake, a flower, a minimalist poem written on the subway, some bath salts: modest offerings in the moist, warm intimacy of the bath.

Eva's incorporation into our evenings—we learned to call her *Effa,* the lovely Effa, our Effa of tenderness, our Effa of dreams, our Effa of the Sorrows of not possessing her, our Enormously Enviable Effa (for some, anyway)—and the tales she told us and the comments that multiplied during sessions that would have seemed more appropriate among men in barrooms, reconstructed the personal story of her father, the Minister Hermann Grünberg and the vicissitudes of a love story which became the legend of Hermann and Paula. According to all indications, the dramatic events of that long-ago time justified the romantic aura that made that story so dear to the hearts of our downhearted community.

When Hermann chose to seek adventure—in Germany in 1934—

only a single first step was necessary before he found himself completely submerged in it. When he took that first step, it was likely he knew, or at least could predict, that he had set in motion a chain of unmanageable events to which he would have to submit from the very moment he tackled its first link. That first step was apparently much less a product of his free will (less independent, we thought) than Hermann imagined. One night he confided to Mario that the most important and least difficult decision of his life had been to leave his first wife the day after their wedding and go to Spain to join the forces of the Republican government. Prior to this, of course, he had exercised equally important acts of abandonment. In '33, when he entered the military academy, he was a German citizen carrying out his civic duty. One year later, having been expelled from the academy, he was a Jew who also bore the burden of being a communist. Tension was growing every day in Berlin, as well as the assault troops' aggression. Hermann was arrested in a dispute that lasted until the coming of the Reichstag. It was then that he experienced imprisonment for the first time, as well as uncertainty, fear, and the happy ending of being rescued. His father's intervention with a friend of the Minister of the Interior (or his equivalent in that power structure) allowed him to exchange his prison term for an exile that appeared to be voluntary. One afternoon the Minister told Mario about this episode in his personal life—he, who always avoided useless references to any event that wasn't part of the "long and tortured objective process of the class struggle that defines universal history," as he was heard to say many times, adhering to the Parteischule's definition. And Mario couldn't avoid a certain memory: he imagined the prison cell of that young Berlin communist as identical to the one he knew in Santiago, before his eighteenth birthday. He evoked the same feelings of uncertainty; he thought he recognized that fear. He was in a prison cell. At any moment he expected that simple arrest to turn into a something more dangerous. He imagined tortures that only happened in far-off places in those days. He remembers how he clung to a single emotion and an image held close in time and in his soul, in order to conquer his fear. He thought about Lorena, whom he had met the afternoon before at a strike and with whom he had marched through the Alameda to Estado Street, where they were arrested. He remembered her white scarf hanging like a banner at the top of that slim body squeezed into a blue school uniform. He remembered the previous afternoon, when, bearing an announcement of the strike, he arrived at the Indianapolis Cafe, where Lorena was sitting with her acquaintances from the theater, next to her girlfriend Patricia. That new presence in the cafe and at the Institute dazzled him, that pretty girl who was rehearsing a García Lorca play, who was reading Sartre and who had a copy of *La Nausée*, a beret and some apples on the table beside her. Mario evoked that image in order to overcome his fear, and he also recalled Lorena's wide eyes as he told her about that other demonstration which had given rise to the one in which they were becoming acquainted on that barely sunny April morning: the coal workers' march from Lota to Santiago, to fight for their wages and their jobs. He recalled her girlish smile when she spoke to him about Tolstoy; she had read *Resurrection* and now she wanted to read *The Death of Ivan Illich*. They kept discussing books; they drew closer together like two recently ignited flames—and talking about books was a way to make those flames grow—when the soldiers' arrival produced a general dispersal in the Alameda. He watched them arrest Lorena, too, and all night long in the cell he thought sadly of her parallel suffering, and with unbridled joy he thought about the fact that they continued to share the same experience in different locations. The next afternoon, when the Senator arrived to set him free, Lorena was waiting for him in the reception room of the police station. He remembers now that the Senator was still young then, and he recalls that Lorena found him charming, even attractive. They left the police station behind, along with the sharp heel clicking with which the guard saluted authority for the second time, and they walked along toward the Alameda until they reached the Indianapolis. The Senator bought them coffee; they talked about the march, the strike, and a bit of news that was causing consternation in those days: the construction of the Berlin Wall. Lorena wanted to hear the Senator's opinion. Mario remembers her question as being abrupt, almost rude. And now, looking at the Minister's severe face and sentimental eyes, Mario recalls how that afternoon the Senator assured them that the communists' *raison d'être* was to fight for a world without limitations, without barriers, without walls. Then he spoke to them about Gagarin and Mario feels as though he's hearing the Senator's voice: "The only man who's ever known total freedom is a Soviet. He's conquered natural laws and has managed to see the earth from space, a little sphere without boundaries, spinning around the same way for everyone." But an hour later, when he walked Lorena back home, she said, standing next to a tree in La Cañada: "Only while he's in the air. As soon as he returns to earth, he returns to borders and controls. That same man who saw the tiny little earth from high in the cosmos has never been able to leave his own country." As he didn't want to become involved in that discussion, Mario pressed Lorena's body against his in the shadow of the tree. Later, saying good-bye at her door, Lorena told him that while they were kissing, she saw a shooting star through the foliage. Yes. There was a first prison cell in his story, too, and a first love, and a first kiss.

But let's return to the Minister's story. At the advice of his most loyal friends, but mostly because of what anyone could observe in the streets every day, the future Minister, at that point just a young man who had recently left the military academy, exchanged his prison sentence for exile. Before reaching his nineteenth birthday he rented a room in a *pension* in Zurich. When he heard the story, Mario couldn't help making a comparison, a second analogy: he had arrived at the Government Workers' Hotel on the banks of the Spree the eve of his twenty-ninth birthday. This difference somehow separated their identities, and Hermann's subsequent story definitively canceled out any similarities. Nevertheless, during their chats in the Minister's garden, in their rocking chairs in the shade, contemplating the awakening buds and the enduring perfection of the greenery, they discovered another coincidence: both had gone to Zurich as exiles, Hermann in '34 and Mario in '74. And even more importantly, Lenin too had endured exile in Zurich.

We were dazzled by this image of the three exiles exhausting themselves on interminable walks, harboring the same dream at different times. If by some quirk of fate they had coincided in time and place, they would never have recognized one another. And if by the same quirk of fate they could have done so, they would never have understood one another, as they spoke different languages. Zurich, cloaked in the mist that falls over the river in the afternoon, is a small, peaceful Babel, with its expatriates conspiring to save what belongs to them or perhaps just to get out of there as quickly as possible. The fact is that there's no place on earth . less suited to a revolutionary's soul than precise, boring, predictable Zurich; yet nevertheless everyone ends up there somehow. This became a more than sufficient motive for astonishment, closeness and perhaps bursts of laughter after a few drinks: Zurich, crowded with unfortunate revolutionaries. This paradox was the subject of our after-dinner conversations for a long time, and the comments made about it, half humorous and half sentimental, bore the irreverent mark of something that was ours.

The Minister finally issued them an official invitation to the opening of *Danton's Death* at the Deutsches Theater. For days Eva and Mario had done the impossible to make the old man decide not to attend and thus be able to appropriate his tickets. Anyone would think that a Minister is precisely the kind of person who could get all the tickets he wants for an official opening. This is true. But it's not true in Eva's father's case. He never asked for anything that wasn't coming to him in accordance with rules and protocol, and this time, so no exceptions would be made, he scheduled a visit to Halle—the motive or pretext was an international conference on Händel's work—and duly announced that his daughter would attend the opening on his behalf. The show was magnificent and the applause so sustained that few of the actors could recall an opening with so many curtain calls. Following the customary party at the theater bar—especially festive and ebullient given the performance's success and the applause—Eva and Mario returned to the apartment, uncorked some Moldavian brandy and discussed the play until dawn. It was like remembering their first night together without having to say so, the most difficult kiss, the conversation about Büchner, their true meeting. First light found them naked with the distant fragrance of the brandy lingering in the prolonged contact of their kisses. They made love and slept long enough to realize very quickly that they were still together, and then Eva disappeared into the shower, into her cup of coffee back in the kitchen, behind the door that she closed noiselessly in order not to awaken him. The moment the door closed, Mario jumped out of bed to tread in Eva's footsteps; the bathroom, traces of her in the bar of soap, in her comb; and then in the kitchen, in the same cup, which he preferred to use because of that other trace, scarlet; the trace of Eva which his mouth captured in that belated, solitary kiss, so much like the aroma of bread and coffee.

That morning—which he could devote to his writing, since he had no University classes on Thursdays —Mario thought everything would be easier, and when Eva returned he'd be able to surprise her with three of four pages of the story which she had praised from the very first reading.

But that morning Mario didn't write a single line. What did he do, then, if he was so motivated by that tender conversation at dawn? This is what he did: he spent hours and hours painfully thinking about Büchner. With genuine, gut-wrenching pain. But the cause of his anguish wasn't the poet's premature death—at age 24 from the same typhus that Mario had contracted at age 15 without serious consequences—but rather the fact that he would turn 42 in a few weeks. Büchner had written a brilliant work before he was 24. Dead by 1837, he seemed younger and more contemporary today, and his vision even more heartrending and disturbing. His writing had endured and would be appreciated for decades, probably even centuries, to come. How could he have written *Danton's Death* at 21? Mario lights his fourth cigarette that morning, puts aside the rough draft of his story to look at the cold sun which is beginning to take over the cloudy sky, and wonders: How did he manage to learn so much about the French Revolution? And how at that age could he already have acquired such free, keen judgment, and a spirit that was so indifferent to the need for harmony? He returns to the table, picks up the program from last night's performance— a handsome leaflet on shiny paper that seems to ridicule his clumsy rough draft—and reads the biographical notes. Like all aspiring writers, Mario has a tendency to self-destruction: he tends to compare himself with peers who aren't; he measures himself with the most lofty yardstick, with what he most admires. And so he opens up a wound through which he suffers and bleeds: his old ulcer, irritated this afternoon by an overwhelming piece of evidence. If Büchner wrote this marvel at 21, did it make sense to attempt something at 42 that would be imperfect anyway? A few pathetic pages that would never be even remotely comparable with what Büchner wrote when he was hardly more than a boy? Did it make any sense to write badly what was already well written? Eva returned at three, running and rather harried. Her *Parteigruppe* was meeting at four. She stopped at the Markthalle, bought potato salad and a few *Bratwurst* which she popped on the grill the minute she got in.

"How's the story going?" she asked him from the bathroom, drying her hands.

"It's not," Mario said, setting the table.

"You know it never goes anywhere in the morning, especially when we've hardly slept. After a nap it'll work out for you, darling. As usual. Did anyone call?"

Now Mario listens to the meat crackling and the crystalline announcement of the salt and pepper shaker being placed on the table. *Should I tell her now? When should I tell her? How can I protect her from this pain?*

Though it was hard for us to believe, Effa and Mario never seriously considered the possibility of marriage. It was calamity enough that the

Minister's daughter was separated, and even worse that she was living with a foreigner now. Legalizing ties with *Chilenische Patrioten* bordered dangerously on another frontier: the question of marriage to foreigners. This was a favorite strategy used to obtain (although not without difficulty) an exit visa, which would allow residents of the First Laborers' and Farmworkers' State on German Soil to cross the border and emigrate—or exile themselves—to the spouse's country. Out of respect for her father's position, and probably because she never imagined she'd end up (on the informal gossip lists) belonging to the category of those who married foreigners, Eva never spoke of marriage, not even as a remote possibility.

Yet although this matter was never mentioned, there were constant allusions on Eva's part to the sluggishness with which the Bureau was handling Mario's divorce. Not to plan a wedding was one thing; Mario's remaining married to Lorena while living with Eva was quite another. He did everything possible to speed up his divorce proceedings, moved more by a desire for peace and normalcy in his new relationship than by any urge to turn Eva into an obvious blot on the Minister's public and private record. He wanted the proceedings to be expedited since he believed that the Bureau's favorable judgment would serve to confirm an evident fact, and it would do Lorena good to receive a clear sign of that evidence. Even clearer than what it already is? we thought. Doesn't he mean an *official* sign, a *bureaucratic* sign?

As a perennial, sarcastic critic of the Bureau, Mario needed those signs from the Bureau. And for her part, Lorena, just as critical or even more so of the Bureau's intolerable invasion of her private domain, needed a postponement, a delay, the notorious complications of bureaucratic red tape, because in some way—and perhaps she wasn't entirely conscious of this—the Bureau's indecision kept things in the past, and for her, freezing her past with Mario continued to be the true reality.

Up until this moment (Mario lurks around the bathtub which is chilling Eva's desolate nudity, holding his glass of vodka on the rocks) the facts, not any legal decisions, have mattered the most.

Mario was still married to Lorena, but he had already been living with Eva for a year now. There was no doubt about his having fallen out of love (Mario no longer loves Lorena), nor of his new love (he's finally found enduring lifetime happiness with Eva). And since the most powerful proof of that love could be seen in the facts, any change in those facts would destroy the only foundation that apparently sustained them. In truth, what made them happy was loving each other and enjoying each moment together. But Eva saw this happiness as tangible only if Mario was prepared to remain eternally by her side. For that reason, when Mario intimated and later confirmed his decision (involuntarily, really) to spend a few days at Lorena's house, Eva felt that the only valid and desired link (Mario in her house, lurking around her bathtub, preparing dinner, warming her bed and her body every night) was breaking in a way that was not only a shock, but also a lie. Anything that contradicted Mario's daily and nightly promises was a lie. The fact is, for a whole year she didn't even regard them as promises; for her they were solid, definite declarations. And her belief in them allowed her to hurt whomever she might hurt and risk anything she thought worth risking.

Lorena believed that having Mario by her side was sufficient proof of his love, and for that reason she never demanded more. That year, without realizing it, she imagined that she couldn't demand less, either. Their daily coexistence was the reality of that love. And she felt that any change in that reality would represent another decline, a falling out of love, because when she became aware that she'd fallen out of love with Franz, she'd told him she needed to be alone for a few days, and now she realized that Mario wanted to spend a few days without her. Even worse. Not just without her. Say what he might, Mario would be living with Lorena again.

Each argument with Mario reminded her, almost verbatim, of the excuses she had used with Franz. She couldn't erase her own voice from her memory, or Mario's voice from her ears: that voice and those words which predicted what would become a terrible reminder.

Because of the symmetry of their shared habits, Eva, in the bathtub, realizes that Mario is on the balcony, watching the hazy lights on Alexanderplatz through the fog, with Marienkirche illuminated by the golden light of the street lamps. And she knows he's wondering: *Why did I tell her? Why?* Shrouded in silence—a pause in Mario's uneasy pacing—Eva climbs out of the tub, removes the bottle of vodka from the refrigerator, and after lighting another cigarette, climbs back into the tub again, shivering now, submerged in the cold water that's numbing her, turning her skin blue, freezing her soul, like a second, unnecessary punishment.

Almost from the start our community knew that Mario's new partner suffered from severe depression. The first time he rescued her, frozen, from the bath was during the initial weeks of their relationship—that is, one year ago. It was the result of a surprise, violent visit by Franz, who burst into the apartment on the pretext of picking up his suits and shoes. Maybe it wasn't a pretext, either, because winter was growing more bitter and he had a couple of overcoats there, some very heavy jackets and two or three pair of boots. But beyond the painful recovery of his clothing—which by this time had gotten mixed up in the same closet with Mario's jackets and shoes—there were attacks, recriminations, a letter to their daughter which Eva wanted to read and which Franz adamantly opposed, sealing it with a special tape, demanding the right to privacy with his own daughter in that home which had been invaded by a stranger.

While all this was occurring, Mario was taking notes at the University library. He was researching a short story whose protagonist was an actor who insisted on building his characters—of secondary importance, ultimately, given his growing alcoholism—on exalted historical and literary models, which made his directors increasingly angry. Pleased at having discovered a clue in the prologue to the original German edition of Casanova's *Memoirs* which would explain Burke's final madness, when he had formerly been a brilliant interpreter, Mario returned to Eva's apartment happier and more excited than ever. Eva was already submerged in the tub. She had locked the door, and after a great deal of pounding and pleading, she emerged from the tub like a lost soul, shivering and ghostly pale; and after opening the bathroom door to let Mario in, she plunged back into the water again. Mario felt her icy kiss on his lips, which were warm with enthusiasm. He stuck his hands into the water, discovering the cause of that bluish paleness and the chattering of her teeth behind her frozen lips.

But that happened only once, quite a while ago, and was therefore a forgotten episode. If it was happening again now, it wasn't simply a repetition: it was something quite different. That's what Mario thought. For better or for worse, on that first occasion, he hadn't been the cause of Eva's suicidal withdrawal into the freezing bathtub. Now, on the other hand, he, his own decision, was the cause. It was different, too, because then Eva awaited his arrival to rescue her from her own withdrawal, and it was he who removed her from the frigid water and then wrapped her up in all the available towels, rubbed her with desperate, rough caresses until her skin turned red, and then carried her to the bed and covered her, first with blankets and bed linen, and later, after consolation and kisses, with his own body, grown warmer from tenderly saving hers. Now, on the other hand, the bathroom door was double locked; he begged her to open up, told her nothing had changed, came back again and again, knocking and demanding, kicking and imploring, promising everything, because he knew the half-empty bottle of vodka bespoke her tension, the long stretch—two or three hours, perhaps—in that cold tub, where she's freezing, he thinks, where she's killing herself, as he hears Eva's first sneezes mixed with a weak, continuous sobbing, and then he begs her to open up, he loves her more than anyone else, please forgive him, get out of that cold water because you're going to die; he thinks about calling the Volkspolizei to break the door down, swears he adores her, he'll call Lorena right now and explain that it was a foolish idea, he'll never leave her, and what he'd planned regarding Lorena's parents' arrival simply won't work out.

CHAPTER SEVEN

The Senator received an invitation to the premiere of a Soviet film about agricultural collectivization, loosely based on Sholokhov's *The Soil Upturned.* This type of invitation was rather frequent, the frequency depending on the film's popularity with the paying public. Generally — even more so in winter — Don Carlos avoided these invitations, and when he ended up receiving them anyway, he usually gave them to Martita Alvarado, the secretary, or to Frau Richter, the woman who cleaned the Bureau offices, the homes of some of its employees, and Don Carlos's apartment as well, ever since he'd been living on Volksradstrasse. Frau Richter arrived there punctually on Tuesdays and Thursdays at two; she cleaned, prepared an apple *Kuchen* (on Tuesdays) and some cherry jam (on Thursdays), leaving a custard dessert in the oven for the Senator to devour that same evening. She made the floor of his tiny dwelling shine like a mirror; she washed and ironed his shirts. In time Frau Richter also became *Tante Ilse* for Don Carlos.

The *Tantes* were an institution: the foundation of cleanliness and neatness in family homes, in public offices, in movie houses and theaters, in parks, in train stations and in the subway stations. They were elderly ladies whose miserable pensions condemned them to work at the most brutal jobs till their dying day. One could see them everywhere, dragging mops and pushing brooms, filling up wastepaper baskets and garbage cans, those heavy drums with wheels that were used for street cleaning. In some remote past, many of them had belonged to bourgeois families who lost everything in the war or in the revolution. These *Tantes* usually were exemplary, indefatigable Teutons, strong and sturdy; they had survived bombings, concentration camps, and rape; they were good for a laugh or an off-color joke, cheerful as only they could be, and possessing enough Teutonic strength to clean an office and even three apartments in a single day.

The Senator thought that *Tante* Ilse had earned herself enough credit to receive his unwanted invitation. He left the tickets on top of the refrigerator, next to her monthly tip, for it was well known that the Bureau's employees' salaries were paid by the United German Socialist Party — *Jawohl!*

However, the next day, when he went to make breakfast and found the two tickets in the same place, he imagined the old woman must have been as afraid of the icy streets as he was, so he decided to give them to Martita. But Martita already had her own, which complicated matters seriously, since anything that resembled waste irritated the Senator and gave him stomach cramps. He then locked himself in his cubicle at the Bureau and started to think of the most appropriate beneficiary. It was also Don Carlos's idiosyncrasy to identify gifts with rewards, a gesture combining kindness with motivation, favor with merit. Which one of those jerks deserved this reward? He was thinking all this without noticing that *Tante* Ilse had placed a tray with his glass of medication and a sugar bowl down on the desk.

"You seem worried. Are you having some kind of problem?" the old woman inquired directly.

"Well, since you rejected my tickets ..."

"I'm not going to make myself sick just to avoid causing you a problem with those tickets, mein Herr. Besides, what good does it do you to invite an old lady?"

"I didn't intend to go with you. I just thought you might like to invite someone."

"I suggest you use them to invite some pretty young girl. Hasn't anyone ever told you that our young ladies prefer more experienced men?"

"I'll think about your suggestion," the Senator said, prolonging the joke. "Don't you have an eligible granddaughter?"

"Unfortunately not. All my granddaughters have been married and separated. They're hunting for a second husband, because, as you know, man is the only animal that trips over the same stone twice. But I have something much nicer for you."

"You don't say!"

"She's a lovely girl ..."

"And what makes you think this lovely girl would accept my invitation, Mrs. Richter?" Don Carlos asked, suspecting that the joke was becoming serious.

"Because yesterday she came looking for you at your apartment. And she asked what time you'd be back. I told her I didn't have information about your private life, *mein Herr.*"

"I imagine you're talking about my neighbor."

"Neighbor? I didn't know there were any young girls in your building. It seems strange."

"She's the only one. It's a temporary exception. The Ministry of Culture has to find lodging for her, but for now ..."

"So you have lady artist friends, *Mein Herr.*"

"She's a dancer."

"And what's your dancer's name?"

"Leni."

"Well, go to the movies with your dancer. I'm sure she'll be happy to accept your invitation."

"Are you serious, Frau Richter?"

"What do *you* think, *Herr Senator*?"

Once more—for the second time in relation to Leni—the Senator turned as red as a beet, although this time he hadn't said a single word in German.

Frau Richter gave a deep, exaggerated sigh and walked out of Don Carlos's cubicle, scarcely hiding a meaningful little smile.

"Oh, *mein Gott!*" Don Carlos heard her exclaim just before *Tante* Ilse closed the door.

Leni told him she'd come to pick him up at seven, but it's past seven thirty already and the premiere begins at eight sharp. If she gets here in the next five minutes—and if by chance they can find a taxi at the stand in front of the *Kaufhalle*—they might still arrive on time.

Will she come? Won't she come?

When the radio signal announced eight o'clock, the old man took off his tie, replaced the envelope in which the Bureau's gilded letterhead gleamed on the coffee table, and prepared to wait for who-knows-what. A nice cup of tea—that would relieve the pain. The worst part is that the pain that hurts the most isn't coming from his stomach. Another wound has opened up. Now his life hurts, in a different way. And what with the tea and whatever's wrong with him, let's see what happens if he turns on Radio Moscow in Spanish, because it's already nine o'clock, time for the news, and then on top of everything the ulcer's acting up again, he goes to get another aspirin, why can't he just sit down? and he marches back and forth between the bed and the balcony as if they'd just locked him up in this cage! It was the tea, surely. Yes, he decides it was the tea. He's been told: he has to give up tea, also, especially after seven. It doesn't let you sleep well; it causes uneasiness; that's what he gets for drinking tea. Now he'll have a glass of Stierblut, and then to bed, hit the hay, as that irresponsible Mario says, who hasn't come to visit him in two days. Right, hit the hay, and none of this business about hurt feelings. If she didn't show up it's because she had an extra rehearsal or she had to fill in for someone else tonight. Surely when she arrives he'll hear the music, as usual, and then she'll come over with an explanation and say good night. Yes, he thinks the wine does him more good every day. It's the only thing that makes him feel better without stirring up that damn ulcer which hurts him so, yes, but less than that other wound, the one he didn't know about or had forgotten about a long time ago, that pain that drags him from the bed to the balcony and from the balcony to the bed, that wound which doesn't stop stinging, not even with the second or third glass of Hungarian wine.

"If you couldn't come, why didn't you figure out some way to let me know?"

Leni arrives after ten. Without making any excuses, she asks about his white shirt; she wants him to put on that shirt. They converse in that strange language composed of gestures, badly-pronounced words, Leni's quick apprenticeship and the old man's desire, even quicker, to understand her. Why that shirt? Because he has to come to her birthday party. But her birthday already took place. No, the date passed, but not the party—the party is about to begin. But the shirt is dirty; he'll have to look for a different one. This one looks suitable, but it needs to be ironed. And while Leni clears the table, abstractedly pulls out the envelope with the invitation, and places a folded sheet on the table to iron Don Carlos's shirt on, he resists her invitation. He's furious he didn't know…no, that's a lie! At that moment nothing could have infuriated him. He thinks his relief is stronger than his pain; that's what happens with those old guts of his. He would have liked to buy her a nice gift—he recalls those two enormous packages that were on the same table which she's using now to iron his shirt,—and besides, he's troubled by the idea of being in a place where he knows no one. No one? Didn't he always want to see the other half of his apartment, that exact replica of his own, that identical space repeated *ad infinitum* throughout the widowers' ship, those niches

that were a precursor of the final one? Didn't he try, during his frightened, sleepless nights, to imagine the furniture, the walls, and the corners of the place from which music emanated, always after eleven, to
lull him to sleep? And, ever since Leni first came to his room bearing the
piece of paper her father had tacked to her door, ever since he began to
hear that melody through the partition, didn't he try to imagine her walking from the bed to the balcony, alone, from the bed to the balcony,
across the three or four yards of that apartment which was identical to
his own? It was lovely to imagine. Is that why he didn't want to see it
now? Or did he?

"I don't feel good; please excuse me."

"I've never seen you looking better. And I know you're angry because I didn't come at seven," she said, pointing to her watch. "But now
you know why. I had forgotten about that party. We had a drink at the
opera house café and suddenly we decided to go to my house. All night
long I've been thinking about what we planned yesterday. I wanted to
go to the movies with you, too."

Don Carlos never had children. He didn't know how to act with a
granddaughter who had let him down. Maybe he needed to show understanding, not let himself be carried away by his own pain or by his pride.
At last he accepted. He would go to the party in time to watch her blow
out the candles on her birthday cake. She'd come by to pick him up.
When Leni left, the Senator stretched out in bed with his ear against the
partition.

When we heard the story there were certain reactions within our
community — surprise, criticism, bad-mouthing, but very little understanding and no indifference whatsoever. If we were to search for the
main thread of this complicated embroidery, Mario, who visited us often, must have been the origin of the gossip. However we can't discount
an even more unlikely source of the rumors: there are those who think
that Frau Richter was the first one to mention Leni's frequent visits to
the Senator, and more paradoxically yet, to the Bureau itself, even while
Frau Richter was dusting the cubicle where Don Carlos attended to the
affairs of the Controls Commission. A third theory traces the origin of
the gossip to a plural, almost collective fount of information: many of
the Senator's evening visitors ("those eternal seekers of visas, authorizations, permissions and pardons") were astonished to find him in the
company of a pretty German girl. Too skinny, according to the men;

adorable, in the words of the older women; really strange, as described by our Medeas.

The truth is, the chain of explosions that followed the initial comments was no surprise. Without a doubt, it was quite a *cause célèbre* that a pretty girl should visit a sick, old man's room every day to make him a cup of tea, leaving her cassette player every morning so he could listen to music during the day, and dutifully coming to look for him every night around eleven. One might say this was an exaggeration on our part. All right, then, but consider this, ladies and gentlemen: in our ghetto and at the height of our abandonment, such things occurred infrequently. Remember, too, that we were residents without hope; we lived in a country where an eternal sameness had been decreed. Already bored with our own history, less heroic and more domestic with each passing day, aboard that phantom ship on which no one—neither the stubborn crew nor the resigned passengers—expected the slightest change, it wasn't surprising that Leni's innocent visits to Don Carlos would become the subject of gossip and the cause of uneasiness, especially at the Bureau, because of the unpredictable consequences these events might have among our depressed, but nonetheless explosive phalanxes.

The facts can be stated omitting the shocking outcry with which they were received and amplified.

The day after her first visit—the night when she came by to pick up her father's presents—Leni decided to thank Don Carlos for his kindness by giving him some of the chocolates from her gift package, having already distributed the rest among her friends in the ballet corps, who were less rigorous about their diets and deprivations than she was. Since the unmentionable Mario had dropped by that evening to find out about his divorce and to plead for some kind of resolution of the visa situation, he acted as interpreter once again. Leni sat down next to them and drank a glass of wine. One should also state for the record that she received an extremely cordial welcome that night because both of them foresaw that Leni's knock on the door would put an end to a discussion that promised to turn out most disagreeably. In fact, the matter under discussion was very thorny, and the question of the visas in this case was of a quadruple nature, since it dealt with two entrance visas for Lorena's parents and two for Mario and Lorena, who felt they had the right to go pick them up at Tegel and cross the border with them. And it just wasn't about four visas ("Four visas!" Don Carlos shouted. "Four!" extending his hand with this thumb folded into the palm, as though he were making a strange gesture of exorcism), but it was also about a matter of protocol that was being modified in a way that was as unheard of as the number of visas requested. "Visas will not be granted less than two weeks in advance. Visas cannot be requested on one day's notice. It's the least that can be expected in such exceptional cases. Remember that our hosts have no right to obtain visas, even if they request them a year ahead of time," Don Carlos repeated over and over, walking up and down the length of his tiny abode without looking at Mario, as though he were trying to memorize a strange code that would be completed with even stranger arguments.

They were in the middle of this when Leni knocked at the door for the second time. That night she learned a great deal of what there was to learn about Don Carlos. She learned, thanks to the kind services provided by Mario, who insisted on translating with virtuosity in order to impress the girl. The first thing that astonished Leni was finding out that Don Carlos had spent more than a year in the Chacabuco concentration camp. Then she told them that beginning when she was a young girl, she and her classmates had visited Buchenwald several times, and the teacher had told them that it would be nearly impossible for something like that to happen again. Thus, very impressed, she regarded Don Carlos with sad, but at the same time admiring eyes, and both men had the impression that in the silence following the old man's revelation, she was not just meditating or suffering, but rather searching in her imagination for something she could do for that solitary, sick man whom chance had placed on the other side of the partition of her small, temporary dwelling. Her eyes grew wide again when she found out that Don Carlos had learned to read when he was sixteen, at the syndical school, that he had worked on the docks at Antofagasta since childhood, although he was born in the countryside in the central part of the country, in Curimón, near San Felipe, and had been taken up north by his parents, who went there looking for work in Chacabuco.

"Chacabuco? Like the camp?" Leni asked.

"It's the same place."

When the Senator's parents arrived there looking for work, like thousands of other peasants, it was a nitrate mine. When the Senator returned there as a prisoner fifty years later, the old nitrate mine offices had been converted by the military into a detention camp for political prisoners. The name isn't a coincidence; it's the same place.

Then Mario remembers something that might be interesting to Leni, and he tells her about that recollection, although he knows the old man is more than bored: he's in despair because he can't understand what they're talking about.

In November 1974, a few days after his arrival in Berlin, Mario was invited to visit the Buchenwald concentration camp. The detail everyone remarked upon about this extermination camp wasn't just the brutality of the procedures used there. Auschwitz, Dachau, and Buchenwald didn't differ from one another in this regard; they shared the same painful distinction of extreme savagery. Buchenwald's special feature was its proximity to Weimar, capital of German culture. That means that the inhabitants of that beautiful city often passed by Goethe's or Schiller's houses, both now converted into museums, but from there they could also see the camp and the columns of smoke rising from the crematorium.

He recalls that on his visit to Buchenwald he was accompanied by Christiane, a young interpreter with whom he had become friends and in whose house he was to meet Eva many years later. During the trip, Christiane, whom he had just met that morning, treated him with a ghastly commiseration that made the trip to that death and annihilation factory even more dramatic. Built in 1934, Buchenwald eventually held 120,000 prisoners—it was larger than Weimar—of whom around sixty thousand died. Managed according to canons befitting the most rigorous industrial plant, its pavilions, which held its sinister stocks, were situated so as to achieve maximum productivity. These pavilions eventually stored tons of human hair, bones and skin (it's acknowledged that Hitler had *Mein Kampf* bound with human skin), and gold extracted from teeth. After being despoiled of their lives and their bodies, the prisoners were also despoiled of their belongings, if anything can be said to belong to anyone under those circumstances, so that the warehouses and patios were filled with thousands upon thousands of shoes, articles of clothing, watches, canes of varied quality, eyeglasses which were later separated into lenses and frames, thus carrying on the mania for classification that at first resulted in separating the owners from one another, if they had arrived together, and later in separating laces from shoes, belts from pants, dental plates from teeth. In order to gather all these marketable objects together, it was necessary to have a pavilion close to the beginning of the process in order to provide the raw material; that is, cadavers. And the truth is that they were produced at a very high rate and with an efficiency that deserved a nobler cause. Every few minutes the interpreter told him not to worry: she was absolutely sure that nothing like that would ever happen on earth again.

"And Chacabuco?" Mario asked her.

The interpreter was familiar with the information that had been published about the so-called prisoner of war camps in Chile, although those prisoners of war hadn't been captured in any war, but rather arrested in their own homes, homes that were their refuge, and even in the factories where they had gone to work on that morning of September 11. She also knew about Dawson, about the Chilean Stadium and the National Stadium, massive detention areas where torture and murder took place. For that reason, her gestures of solidarity toward Mario and her attempts to comfort him seemed doubly pathetic to him. They contained a measure of deliberate deceit—although it was a praiseworthy effort—and they had a painful effect from a practical standpoint, as her somewhat doctrinaire, feigned reassurance that never again on the face of the earth would there be a massive camp for kidnapping victims, or daily abuse, or forced labor and the death penalty without laws or trials—was being contradicted at that selfsame moment. Mario recalls asking Christiane if she was from Weimar and she said, no, she was a Berliner. She was born in Berlin, and her parents had died in the bombing of May 7, 1945, the last day of the war. Mario now thinks that when he asked her that question, he associated being a Weimar native with some kind of deliberate blindness with possible genetic characteristics that might be transmitted to future generations.

She didn't deny the existence of Buchenwald. In fact, she earned her living showing it to people. She denied that other places like it existed. Her faith in mankind—a confused sort of confidence—made her blind to the repeated occurrence of behaviors that belied that confidence. And so she preferred to forget, or not to see. "There are also Chileans who stroll around Weimar and avoid looking towards Buchenwald," he told Christiane.

"In Weimar? Are you referring to the Chilean exiles who live there?" Christiane asked then, in 1974, and now, twelve years later, Leni asks the same thing.

No, of course not. It was a joke, a metaphor. There are some Chileans who didn't want to know from the start, and who still resist knowing. They live there, in Chile, but it's as if they were strolling around Weimar. Chacabuco is very close to Weimar. This is the theme of deliberate blindness and pained conscience; it's Buchenwald and Weimar; it's Chacabuco and Chile; it's also an old theme in our literature: the theme of civilization and barbary.

"Chacabuco," Leni repeated with an accent, and then she was silent. All these Chilean words were strange, but they sounded nice; they sounded different.

Half asleep, he was already tired of waiting, regretting not having accepted Leni's invitation, feeling sorry for not partaking of that life which filtered through the partition, when he heard several knocks on the door. Leni, who had put on a white tunic that made her look even thinner and a pair of earrings of the same color, made up her eyes, highlighted her cheeks and accentuated her lip color, took him gaily by the hand, and saying, "Come on, everyone wants to meet you," pulled him from his room before the Senator could object.

On hearing a sudden silence descend as he entered Leni's apartment, Don Carlos understood that she had been telling her guests about him. After greeting the seven or eight people who filled the girl's small apartment, the old man cast a sharp, quick glance around all the corners. He wanted to gaze head-on at that space which he had constructed in his imagination during the past few sleepless nights. His neighbor's apartment was not just entirely different from his own but also absolutely different from how he had imagined it. Naturally, it didn't resemble a bedroom, for the bed that occupied a considerable portion of the space in the Senator's apartment was replaced here by a sofa covered with colored cushions, so that the room looked more like a little living room, with very white walls (his were an ochre that had darkened over time) on which beautiful posters of the Komische Oper and the State Ballet displayed their lively colors. There were also some smaller pictures, photos of the ballet corps rehearsing or in full production. Those white walls and the multiplication of the dancers' elegant gestures in the photos and on the posters which seemed to multiply the immediate beauty of the girls assembled there, formed a splendid frame that accentuated each detail of her decor: that Viennese chair, the chest with emblems of cities Leni would never know, the gleaming equipment from which her nocturnal music filtered through the partition. It was obvious someone lived here. It didn't look like a hotel room. Every corner held cared-for, personal belongings.

Leni, who didn't release his hand, introduced him around and invited him to sit down on the sofa. The Senator thought Leni looked even lovelier than usual tonight, although later he thought she had always seemed lovely to him; it was just that this was the first time he was sitting in her apartment and the first time she held his hand for what seemed to him an inordinately long time. But in that place everything seemed to have the right to exist in a different way, more freely and magically than anywhere else. Perhaps it was the bluish semidarkness coming from the blue lamp, the ballerinas' beautiful silhouettes or the male dancers' unconventional clothing, their brightly colored shirts adorned with strange pins, necklaces down to their waists and silk handkerchiefs worn with artful insouciance.

He had just begun to take note of those presences which so differentiated his tiny dwelling from his neighbor's apartment when the lights went out. In the darkness he saw Leni approach, illuminated by the tentative glow of the candles flickering on her birthday cake. He joined the general applause but stopped applauding when he saw, as though it were Leni's shadow, the figure of a young man who suddenly appeared against the glowing light. The young man came to life when he got accustomed to the darkness illuminated by the tiny flames, and Don Carlos thought that the candles gave a special radiance to his fine face, his long mane of hair, his partially unbuttoned denim shirt and especially the boy's hand next to Leni's neck. The glow lit up his naked dancer's torso and the affectionate arm that ended in that desired embrace, resting on his neighbor's shoulders. He saw the girl's face in that same glowing light and knew at that moment he had never before seen a more beautiful face. With a quick puff Leni extinguished the image of her own loveliness. And after a moment of darkness that was as instantaneous as the illumination of perfection on that strange night, the light bulbs accompanied the applause which continued: they were applauding the kiss, that overly long time during which Leni's mouth was overtaken by the boy's; the desired embrace, the young man's hand caressing Leni's fine, straight back. That kiss seemed eternal to him, and the applause that celebrated it was equally eternal. Why was he so annoyed? Did he recognize that his unexpected sweating was a sign of his deep displeasure? Why did that displeasure immediately activate the pain of something in his body that was dying?

As soon as the kiss and the applause ended, Leni cut the first slice of cake and headed straight for Don Carlos, who had attempted to hide among the guests. Leni placed the first piece of that wonderful confection in his hands and astonished the Senator even more by depositing a noisy kiss on his cheek, which precipitated even louder applause. But what made him even more confused about the persistence of the applause, which was now taking on a singular rhythm, was the second kiss that Leni placed, with the expertise of a nurse, between the corner of his cheek and the beginning of his lips. Don Carlos felt the dampness of the kiss landing on the dry corner of his mouth. He felt a long-forgotten— perhaps unfamiliar—tremor, and, barely recovered from the shock, continued hearing applause that was, in his opinion, the formal, obligatory degeneration of the applause that accompanied that other moist, pro-longed kiss which had sparked the young people's enthusiasm. The corner of his mouth hurt where Leni had kissed him. Wasn't it ridiculous for a young girl—she could easily be his granddaughter!— to act so boldly in front of everyone? And on top of it all, they applauded! He fell back onto the sofa, and when no one was watching him any longer (even Leni had withdrawn to a corner of the room to continue serving the cake), he tried to observe the girl's behavior. It was likely that the young man with the long mane was her boyfriend. But why, then, while Leni placed pieces of cake on plates, did he dance with an-other dancer, a stunning girl? Objectively speaking, she was even more beautiful than Leni. And why was the boy now assailing her with equal affection and even kissing her on the cheek, the forehead, the shoulders, in the middle of a dance?

The sound of the doorbell roused him from thoughts that were start-ing to become disagreeable. When Leni opened the door, he saw an older man enter—very different from all the young people he had met there—dressed in a white suit and an unbuttoned black shirt—and even grayer than Don Carlos was (his long hair was completely white), but quick and youthful in his movements, his smile, his readiness to em-brace Leni, lift her in the air and spin her around in his arms while they both kissed; quick to remove a small velvet jewelry bag which had been pinned to his lapel like a brooch and hand it to her, giving her another eternal kiss right there in the place where the Senator still felt Leni's lips.

The recent arrival—as they used to say in old-fashioned novels and as he discovered a while later—was a very famous Italian choreogra-pher who had been invited by the Staatsoper to participate in the govern-ment production of *The Flying Dutchman*, after having choreographed the Wagner opera in New York and Paris. When Leni introduced him, Don Carlos couldn't understand what she was saying, but he deduced it from the choreographer's nearly perfect Spanish, an Italian-accented Spanish which he thought would be the evening's saving grace, despite his fatigue and the sharp pain that had begun to disturb him again.

"I want to choreograph a work based on some Neruda poems. I love Neruda," he said as he sat down by his side and pulled a cigar from his white jacket pocket.

At that point Don Carlos felt that his relief came not only from understanding what was being said to him, but also from the fact that he could now speak of things with which he was familiar. The Italian was pleasant, cordial, and addressed him with special attention, as if the rest of the small retinue didn't exist.

"Leni told me you were in a concentration camp. I was very anxious to talk to you."

"I'm most grateful."

"I want to choreograph a work about humiliation," the Italian said. "I want to show the limits of what a human being can tolerate physically. And I want to show how much a torturer can stand. All of this through choreography, you understand. Leni told me you were in Chuki... Chami ..."

"Chacabuco," the Senator said enthusiastically. He never thought there could be a ballet about those sad, monotonous days.

"*Ecco*! Chacabuco!" and he lit the cigar, which had gone out. "Did they torture you in Chacabuco?"

"No. I was under arrest there for several months, but they didn't torture me."

"And how did you get out of there?"

"Thanks to the intervention of the World Council of Churches."

"If you'll excuse the question...What religion are you?"

"None."

"Then why that Council?"

"Because they intervened for all of us, believers and nonbelievers. It's a long story."

"And then you sought asylum?"

"Yes. I left Chacabuco under order of expulsion."

"And why did you seek asylum here?"

"Because that's what the Party decided."

"But they didn't torture you?"

"No."

Suddenly they heard some jazz playing. The choreographer glanced around and when his glance met Leni's smiling eyes, he stood up, went toward her, extended his arms histrionically and asked her to dance.

One of the boys—the one who from the start looked the most extravagant to Don Carlos—offered him a glass of white wine. The Senator thanked him and they toasted in silence. The wine was warm. Leni danced with the choreographer in a rather intimate way, by the Senator's standards. The long-maned boy who had planted an extensive kiss on Leni's mouth was now dancing with the most attractive girl at the party. The prettiest one, Leni, had her cheek stuck to the choreographer's and her long, wavy black hair mingled with the choreographer's completely white locks. And their bodies were moving perfectly to the rhythm of music which Don Carlos couldn't have been able to dance to, even if Leni had asked him; and they seemed so divinely suited to something of which he was completely ignorant: the mystery and insinuating language of the dance. He saw how Leni's body and the choreographer's drew closer, linked together in a game of advance and retreat that acquired rhythm and vertigo along with the music. Don Carlos thought—not even thought: intuited, knew, guessed—that if he had been in the choreographer's place, the same, identical movements would have seemed obscene.

How old was that white-haired man, dressed so differently from himself, so alien to the gray suit and standardized accessories of the Bureau? While he watched the man dance with Leni, some of the guests — perhaps the youngest ones — sat down on the floor next to him and tried to start a conversation. But Don Carlos responded to the youths' efforts with gestures that impeded any attempt at conversation. Someone removed the already empty glass from his hand and put another one in it, this one with a dark liquid that was probably cognac, which the Senator warmed up between his open palms, at the same time caressing the idea that a nice glass of cognac at the right temperature could calm the pain, which was now becoming more intense. They asked him questions he didn't understand; some looked at him curiously; others, with a certain kindness; yet others with cold, mistrustful suspicion. And his pain grew along with Leni's intimacy with the choreographer. And his weariness grew, and that other pain; the intense sorrow that flooded him like a first death, prior to the death that made itself known through his tormented intestines and which was the simple certainty that very soon everything would keep on happening: the dance and the kisses would go on, the music and the words, but he would no longer be there, not even as the silent protagonist of the simple act of seeing.

Suddenly Leni settled in a chair next to Don Carlos, took his hand and, asking the choreographer to act as translator, told him: "Forgive me. I'd like to stay at your side. Now that I know you, it makes me sad to leave this apartment. You know that I'm here just temporarily."

"It makes me sad, too, to be separated from you. Very sad. I'm the one who's here temporarily," the choreographer translated.

"Did they give you permission to go home? You finally got it?" Leni asked, her face reddened by sudden enthusiasm.

"No. That's not possible any more."

"You're moving to a larger apartment, then? Congratulations! I'd love to visit you in your new home."

"No, no one's promised me a larger apartment."

Leni was silent for a moment before asking, "Then why did you say you're here temporarily, like me?"

"Well, in a manner of speaking. I don't feel very good. Please, walk me back to my place."

"Do you need anything? A tranquilizer?"

"No, I'll take one before I go to bed. I need to sleep."

Leni and the choreographer walked him back to the door of his apartment. The old man knew he always kept his key in his right jacket pocket. When he opened the door, Leni motioned to the choreographer to go away. They entered the room together. Leni turned on the light. The Senator walked over to his bed, holding his stomach with both hands.

"I'll make you a cup of tea."

"No, thanks. I want to go to bed."

Leni held his arm delicately and helped him into bed. The old man took a relieved breath and closed his eyes.

"Forgive me," said Leni, stroking his cheek. I shouldn't have insisted that you come."

"No, no. I wanted to go. Thank you for the invitation. It was a lovely party."

"They're nice people."

The old man understood, nodded his head.

"Now I want to sleep," he said.

"Does it hurt a lot?"

He understood that also.

"No, not so much. No one dies of this pain, I suppose."

Don Carlos opened his eyes and saw her so near, so perfect in her white bridal tunic. She was a suffering bride who could barely contain her tears.

"Don't be upset. I won't die before you move away from this building."

But that was very hard for Leni to understand. Because the gestures and words she had learned from him were insufficient, Leni didn't understand what Don Carlos was saying to her. She kissed him, and after turning off the light she left him alone in his apartment.

CHAPTER EIGHT

Someone threw a pair of high black boots in Hermann's face. Who knows who threw them or where they came from: they were very old boots, and as he had no other choice, he ended up putting them on to protect his feet from the snow. On account of those boots he crashed into Paula's furious stare — well, really all of Paula — one day, for the first time. He was slowly eating his soup at the long table for refugees when the collision took place. Hermann always ate slowly, conscientiously, but no one would have assumed that his monotonous grazing and his muteness stemmed from his thinking about something else. Actually he was thinking precisely about what he was doing at that moment, the gratifying, indisputable fact that, after so many comings and goings, so much blood and heartrending devastation, the world and some men in it had worked things out so people like him could have a bowl of hot soup at noontime to warm their insides. He chewed everything with the same rapt concentration: a slice of black bread smeared with fat, an apple, a piece of dried beef jerky. That noontime, as he was slowly bringing a spoonful of vegetable soup toward his mouth, thinking about the miracle of still being able to eat, he was snatched from his concentration by Paula's wide, expressive gaze, which had been disparagingly assessing him from head to foot for quite a while without his noticing, although he did note that all the scorn contained in the gaze ultimately focused on the swaggering misery of his boots. Suddenly a gob of spit, combined with the disdain of her stare, landed like drizzle on the discolored leather, worn out at the toes, uneven and muddy at the heels. Hermann turned his face to look at the mouth that had paid such diligent, lubricious attention to his humble footwear. He turned with the same slowness with which he consumed the other modest gifts that life kept giving him, and, upon completing the gesture, he saw, atop a rather tiny body, highlighted delicately and tenuously against the slats of the shed, the most adorable face he had ever seen. Its beauty effortlessly encompassed her indignant burning eyes, the proud set of her chin, the haughty air of her broad forehead, delineated at the juncture of her black hair by the flowered kerchief the peasant women of Talitsa wore, especially when they served meals to the refugees. Forty years later, in his own garden, looking at the flowers as if his gaze were fixed in another era, Hermann told Mario that he had fallen in love with her at the very moment her saliva fell on those boots which he had taken from a Nazi officer whom he never saw and whose leftover boots he had worn as a consequence of mankind's sundry miseries: physical, because one has to cover one's feet in winter on the steppes; economic, because there was nothing left to wear and a pair of boots like those could be used by many combatants — on different sides — as others fell; and finally the miseries of chance, which led Hermann's feet, tired from traversing Europe in the battle against Hitler, to those old boots that had belonged to some Nazi officer and which aroused Paula's pain and rage.

At one of the ghetto's soirées, Effa told us the other version of this story. Aided by translation, her own gestures, and the gestures with which we all embellished the tale in order to find words that would express them, Paula's story was reconstructed, along with its prologue involving her furious glare and the insulting spitball that crushed Hermann as he silently ate his refugee lunch.

Paula lived on the outskirts of Yedenitz, in the former Bessarabia, with her parents, her four younger brothers and sisters, and her grandfather. When her village was occupied, she experienced her salvation and her misfortune in a single night. Effa first told us about her salvation: the soldiers had orders to crown the first stage of the incursion by bringing all the women who could satisfy the officers and troops over to headquarters. She was the only person in her household who fulfilled the requirements of that unfortunate command, so she was added to the involuntary offering of about fifty females who had been chosen to enliven that night, probably the only night, since the little hamlet was just one more stopping point on a route that had grander objectives. What happened there became a forgotten episode for the inhabitants over the next few days, as they were subjected to greater military demands in which the risk of defeat was already foreseen.

Later on, that thing which never became part of the fabric of re-membrance or regret—either because new crimes erase old ones from consciousness or because at the end of it all there would be a well-aimed bullet and eternal oblivion—became a memory and a nightmare that Paula would endure all her life. Separated from her parents and siblings, she was taken to the police station which the invaders had improvised in the village church, and there she was separated once more from her people—the other kidnapped women—and led into a small room which the chief officer had transformed into his private office that night. Paula was seventeen years old at the time. At that age, attained in a peaceful village, one would have every right to believe that this second separa-tion meant an immediate death sentence which she was incapable of understanding. For that reason, she found it strange that the officer treated her with a certain amount of courtesy when he indicated that she should sit down and he offered her a piece of black bread and a glass of water. She knew they couldn't offer her much more than that. The officer, with whom she didn't exchange a single word, because they couldn't under-stand one another, was actually rather formal in his gestures. He closed the door, which muffled the cries of pain coming from the plaza. Again Paula sensed that she was being separated from something that belonged to her. The officer sat down behind the desk on a leather chair with a stately backrest and waited until Paula finished eating the piece of bread; then, with another precise gesture, he ordered her to approach. When Paula was close enough, he reached out his arms, caressed her neck, and removed her woolen outer clothing, her brother's shirt, and finally her bra. He contemplated Paula's nudity for a long time, filling his gaze with her trembling breasts and her face which burned as on the after-noons she used to knit by the fire. Paula felt that the officer's gaping stare, fixed on her naked breasts, was breaking down an intimacy that the men in her family had safeguarded without her understanding what it meant. The officer pointed to his boots and gestured for her to remove them. Paula, who had bent down to allow those hands to disrobe her more easily but also to hide her nudity, finally kneeled down next to the officer's boots. She pulled them off with two efficient yanks that could hardly conceal all the hatred and fear she felt, and she waited for some-thing to happen (what, she couldn't know), in any case something terri-bly painful that she had been awaiting ever since her kidnapping. Then, after another pause, the officer made another gesture for her to put his boots on him again. When he had them on, perfect and gleaming up to his knees, he stepped down hard to adjust them, took a few steps toward the table, took a swig from his bottle of Ukrainian cognac and sat down again in the leather chair. He repeated the look that went from her breasts (firmer now) to her increasingly confused eyes, and again pointed to the boots. When she began to yank them off for a second time, Paula heard desperate cries coming from the street. The horror of the action grew worse with repetition. The cries from outside were increasingly desperate, as the instructions delivered by his finger pointed to the boots again and again, take them off, put them back on. And each time he went for the bottle a bit less steadily until he finally didn't let go of it at all and made a gesture for her to leave.

This, in brief, is the story of her salvation. The officer didn't want a woman; he wanted a slave. But at the very moment Paula felt safe, she also foresaw her misfortune. She had spent a great deal of time involved with those boots, listening to the cries. Outside everything was burning. Paula ran down the long street of her village avoiding the flames and embers, discovering sobs that were obscured by the cries. Cries and tears accompanied her until she reached the last stages of the immolation of her house. Her family's cries had been doused along with the flames. Then her own tears began, but they too would be suffocated by the fire of time, although much more slowly, with licks of flame sparking her memory in all her dreams to come.

The occupation of Yedenitz lasted only that one night. The foreigners, who had nothing to do there, continued their march; those for whom everything was there were extinguished along with the ashes. The fifty fortunate survivors—the prettiest girls in the village—buried their dead, fashioned crosses from charred sticks, reassembled abandoned wagons, gathered the horses· which had fled from the fire and emigrated to the east.

After three months they reached the Russian border. They remained there for a period of time which they were unable to calculate: maybe another month, maybe another year. At the end of that uncertain wait they were sent to Talitsa, another small village, a refugee camp.

There, a few years later, as Paula served vegetable soup at the long table of survivors, she felt the fire of that night still burning inside her. Next to the horse's hooves she saw a pair of high black boots, her house aflame, a family lost, her seventeen years writhing among the embers.

They threw a pair of high black boots in his face, and he recognized them immediately — a *Wehrmacht* officer's boots — and he also understood immediately what they represented for the Red Army commissioner who received them. Yes, he could understand that. What surpassed his powers of comprehension was the incongruity between his personal history and the kick he received from those boots being hurled practically in his face. He had left Germany prior to his imminent arrest; he had fought for the Spanish Republic by his own personal decision the day after his wedding in Switzerland, the first station of his exile; on instructions from the Republican government he had taken refuge in France at the end of the Spanish Civil War; the French collaborationist government detained him, imprisoned him and then condemned him to a year in an Algerian concentration camp, really just an ordinary prison (one night Mario showed us pictures of Hermann's cell given to him by the Minister himself), and thanks to an agreement among the governments of France, Germany, and the Soviet Union, at the end of two years he was released from there and sent to the USSR. He finally arrived in Talitsa, in its own way another sort of concentration camp, only there the prisoners mingled with different kinds of refugees, including political prisoners from Moscow and Leningrad. There, in Talitsa, with its bucolic, provincial, Chekhovian air, and the drama provided by the concentration of victims of various battles fought under different flags, four years later he would receive, as his thanks, those boots thrown directly into his face. It's true that at the time he was still under investigation by official agencies. When the judgment of those agencies turned out favorably, they enlisted him in the Red Army — a decision that aroused his pride and enthusiasm — and he left for the front at Stalingrad. He spent the first two years of that historic siege as a soldier and the last two, when it was believed that resistance was no longer possible, as an instructor for children who were learning to use weapons to defend the city where their parents lay beneath the snow. And when victory burst forth and peacetime allowed the recovery of an apparent normalcy, an imitation of the life that had been experienced by millions of those fallen who no longer sat at the head of the table or shared a bed, Hermann Grünberg was once again deployed to Talitsa. He was very probably the only German to return victorious from that long siege, happy at the auspicious defeat of the German Army. The *Wehrmacht* was beginning its retreat from that and other fronts. The Soviets who marched back with Hermann finally reached their homes. Many of them embraced their wives, their parents, or their children and began to repair the traces the war had left on the roofs of their houses or in the garbage-strewn streets. Hermann returned to the same shed where the refugees and those defeated under many flags crowded together, happy to have contributed to the victory of the only flag he had ever felt was his. In Talitsa everything remained more or less the same: the agricultural chores — now more necessary than ever — the antifascist school, the swigs of that strange alcohol that they got from potatoes, and lunch, the only meal that was served daily at the long table in the shed. It was in that refugee camp — the last stop for foreigners of dubious provenance and Nazi prisoners of war — that his face became the target of enormous aggression by the commissioner, who, on choosing those boots for him, had identified him as an enemy, or at least someone who could be suspected of being one.

When Effa told us this story, trying not to cry, we sensed that she loved us. And we sensed that she wanted to be accepted into Mario's world. But since we doubted that our world was still Mario's, we listened to her with affection, but also with great sadness. We knew that in embracing us, she felt she was embracing the world of her parents. But neither Mario nor we belonged to that world any more. And even her parents probably were no longer faithful to their own memory.

CHAPTER NINE

The Pan Am flight carrying Lorena's parents to Berlin landed at Tegel at 4:50, five minutes late. And the Secretary of the West Berlin Socialist Party—the skinny young man who tended bar at La Batea—was there right on time, holding up a yellow piece of cardboard on which he had written with green marker: *Señores Fernández.*

Although he had only held his post for two months, he knew that every so often his responsibilities would connect him with more interesting events than organizing a raffle to raise funds for the resistance or paying the rent for countrymen who were threatened with eviction. When he heard the Senator's charge ("You have to go pick up a girl's parents"), he understood that his duty was to decipher the hidden meaning in that message, and he imagined a top security mission: to meet two eminent functionaries from the interior at Tegel Airport and then bring them into West Berlin, two valiant comrades who were arriving, like harbingers of tragedy, from the heart of the battle and bearing its horrendous scars. That's why he was so surprised when two nice, harmless-looking old people responded to the call, avowing that they were Señor and Señora Fernández.

When Lorena's father, Don Arnaldo Fernández, was forced to retire, his condition didn't change as everyone had predicted. The customary routine is to go from being an active wage-earner to a passive one, with the resulting decrease in income that one might imagine. Instigated by his son-in-law, Cecilia's husband, he finally accepted the risk that would transform him from being an involuntary passive agent, that sort of honorable retiree living on the edge of ruin, into an entrepreneur entering a profitable construction business. It was a matter of investing the fifteen million pesos he received as a retirement pension into a door and window factory. His son-in-law understood all about it, as he was a civil engineer, and the expectations promised by the stock market made the investment seem minimally risky and the returns more than satisfactory. When his son-in-law had laid the foundation of the project, and after presenting the remaining specifications had received the bank's approval, Don Arnaldo experienced a series of ambivalent and somewhat distressing emotions for weeks. On the one hand he somehow felt that the product of his thirty-five years of work was being devalued. He wasn't able to explain this feeling very clearly, and was even less able to make it compatible with the arguments given by the rest of the family—with the singular exception of Doña Elvira—all of whom decisively and optimistically approved of the new business and the investment it represented: nothing less than the sum total of his retirement fund. When, at the beginning, he offered a bit of weak resistance, he pleaded his absolute ignorance of what was about to become his new field of endeavor. His son-in-law's familiarity with the subject was adequate reassurance within the family and the most solid argument everyone used to counter his objections. However, those arguments couldn't reduce the solid core of uncertainty that robbed him of sleep for the first few months and that resisted being dissolved by any argument which didn't have its roots in his own, long experience. Don Arnaldo saw it this way: for thirty-five years he had worked at Casa García, a store that had been important a couple of decades ago, but which was condemned to ruin by commercial centers and shopping malls. When this ruin finally came about, Don Arnaldo paradoxically managed to retire under better circumstances than he had hoped for. But he always thought those fifteen million pesos were the result of the effective work he had done his whole life long. He was paid for what he knew how to do and for what he did well, according to everyone. For better or for worse, he started out at the store doing menial tasks and gradually learned everything necessary until he became Director of Sales, an important post in a business where the term "manager" was never used to describe those who had a certain amount of responsibility for the functioning of the House. And then he received that retirement pension of fifteen million pesos because over many years he had learned to recognize fabrics, at first simply by touch and later just by looking at them; to order suits most efficiently, taking advantage of the lulls between seasons; to treat clients with a courtesy that never bordered on familiarity and with a formality that could never be interpreted as coldness. Many years before the end, when he was newly married, he already knew how to move about the fitting room with ease, how to inspire confidence, to spark the customer's enthusiasm for the garment he was going to buy; to point out, even before the customer mentioned it, that slight unevenness in the shoulder pads or that wrinkle in the trousers that could only be noticed after taking a few steps, and then to kneel down elegantly, marking an deft chalk line here or there, thus concluding the sale to the complete satisfaction of the regulars who always returned, asking for Señor Fernández. And after all the years he devoted to this apprenticeship and then to the virtuous practice of the familiar craft, when he was already Head of Sales, came other years which he dedicated with identical pains to teaching, to molding the many others who arrived without knowing the difference between woolen cloth and cheap wool blends, between combed cashmere and flannel, many who also ended up adept in the art of placing pins in a basting without the client's noticing, or marking a cross in the fold of a lapel with a rapid tracing of chalk. And so, as the years went by, his daughters grew; and with some saving his house in La Cañada also grew, along with the grapevines, the grotto, the iron fence that replaced the wooden one, and the wider door, because some day—especially if Lorenita started University and promised to settle down—the imaginary car would have to pass through there to get to the as-yet-unbuilt garage. So life consisted of watching his daughters grow and enlarging his house in La Cañada. And life also consisted of nine or ten hours a day on the floor and the stairs of that other house, Casa García. There the younger ones kept on arriving and trying to learn, while he, already quite worn out, had to make equally diligent efforts to keep from forgetting the details of what he was teaching them.

Fifteen million for a job well done for thirty-five years. And now the bank was going to lend him thirty more to do something he knew absolutely nothing about! Since at some point he would have to return that money, he felt completely dependent on his son-in-law's abilities, but he also felt rewarded for something he didn't possess, like a sort of parasite, a sort of speculator. And during his sleepless nights, after the third or fourth trip to the refrigerator to get another glass of water— which he later got used to mixing with some homemade wine,—he went back to bed, lit a cigarette, and thought: Why fifteen million for what I did well for thirty-five years and thirty million for what I don't know how to do and haven't ever done yet? How will this all turn out?

The next morning his son-in-law tried to calm his fears: "The bank is lending us the money because I'm a contractor, Don Arnaldo, and because I know my job. And since we've formed a corporation, you get the money—or rather we get it—because you've invested the capital. If business is good and we have a sufficient base, the bank will give us credit. They're in the money-lending business, you understand? They're not doing us any favors. Besides, they're collecting interest from us and they have the mortgage as collateral."

"And how will we pay them back?"

"With the yield from the stock."

"And when will that be?"

"That depends. As soon as possible, as far as I'm concerned. I can't sleep well either, with this debt hanging over my head. The important thing is that we're going to start producing and we have three good contracts. This thing can't fail, believe me."

"Well, if you say so. And what role am I supposed to have in all this?"

"You're my partner."

"But I don't understand anything about doors or construction."

"It's not necessary. You're the silent partner."

The silent partner boarded the Lufthansa flight at two PM on December 21, 1985. It was his first flight, and ever since takeoff the frightening noise of the motors announcing twenty hours of sitting with his feet twenty-seven thousand feet up in the air made him realize that together with the bankruptcy of Fernández Doors and Windows, Inc., this flight was the worst thing that could happen to him in his life. At his side, also trembling and disoriented, Doña Elvira tried to conceal her fear by repeating the eternal reproach: "If you had listened to me, we wouldn't be in this mess."

"Be quiet, woman. There's no talking allowed on airplanes."

As a complete silence prevailed, for the first time in a long time Doña Elvira believed her husband's radical pronouncement and directed her glance towards the clouds that surrounded the enormous wings of the device. When the plane tilted she also saw her city for the first time from a height that she had always believed was reserved for God the Father. It was an enormous expanse of brown stuff, almost shapeless, no longer revealing the outline of streets or rooftops. That strange stuff that kept moving farther away no longer seemed like the object of God's vigilance, or of anyone's. She thought that her house, her daughter's houses, the Thursday market, the gladiolas she watered every afternoon, splashing the foundation bricks in the process, were all disappearing in that magma.

"If it came crashing down, it would be much better," she said as quietly as she could. Now she knew that there was no talking on airplanes and so she said it very quietly so only he could hear her.

With his feet planted firmly on the ground, Don Arnaldo would have responded to such provocation with an insult. But it seems that fear also has a sedative effect, because he spoke to her without the slightest note of aggression and he was nicer than he had been in a long time.

"We're going to see your daughter. And you're going to meet your grandchildren. When they bring the meal, try to eat something."

"What meal?"

"The one they serve on the flight, woman. The girls already explained that to you."

"They explained it to me?"

"They explained it to you. And they asked you to eat."

"I can't swallow. Don't you understand that?" she said mutely.

"Maybe here you'll be able to swallow," Don Arnaldo said.

"Maybe," she said in another tone of voice, surprised at her husband's tender, frightened manner.

Doña Elvira stopped eating when her daughters told her all was lost and it would be better to leave, especially when things were going so well for Lorena in Germany. She didn't do it deliberately. It wasn't a conscious act of rejecting everything that had been going on around her for so long. In truth it seemed as though those misfortunes were being obliterated by time or perhaps by others whose immediacy made them seem worse. It was, in fact, on a calm, happy day, returning from an excursion to Maipo Ravine with Arnaldo, Cecilia, her son-in-law and her spoiled grandchildren, when, at her daughter's house, she found herself unable to swallow the rest of the roast they had brought back from the picnic. On the trip back she was silent, which surprised everyone and gave rise to jokes that didn't manage to shake her out of her silence. She was remembering something Cecilia said at lunch, but everyone thought she was just mesmerized by the river that disappeared into the gorge and the mountains supporting the landscape, though the mountains disappeared too; their immediate, imposing height grew distant as the car approached the vineyards on the Santiago hills: the end of the excursion, and the end of that Sunday.

"Wouldn't you like to get to know your other grandchildren, mama?"

It was the announcement of this other ending she was beginning to live at that moment: the mountains, the clouds, now gone as well.

The flight attendant helped them pull down a plastic tray from the seat back in front of them. On it she placed another, similar tray, also plastic—blue, but smaller—containing various jars of the same color plastic, in which there were pieces of chicken, some vegetables, and a few slices of bread, and which more than a meal, resembled a display of variations on the same substance.

The old man looked at his aged partner, hoping to see her pick up the fork, or even look at the plate, to make some gesture toward the tray. But he observed her indifference to that pathetic mess whose only virtue was that it had no odor whatsoever. Then he spoke to her in a friendly tone which she had forgotten:

"Eat, woman. Doesn't it make you happy to think about meeting your grandchildren?"

And she thought that, despite the turbulence, the warmth of his request didn't stem from fear.

Fernández Windows and Doors, Inc. went bankrupt because the business venture Don Arnaldo's son-in-law proposed to him would have been perfect if you didn't take real life into account, or didn't realize that real life could change, as it does more often than one would expect, with a stubbornness that almost always thwarts our desires.

It so happened that different circumstances affected the construction boom, and then the doors which had already been commissioned couldn't be purchased by the businesses that needed them. And when these, too, went under, the bankruptcy of Don Arnaldo's and his son-in-law's brand new enterprise was one more leaf in the windstorm that rocked the incipient utopia, with the resulting decline of what should have been growing along with its aborted harvest, alerting the majority of those who were involved in the debacle and those whose scruples tended to be on the weak side to the uselessness of the immense crime that had been committed. Neither the bombing of La Moneda Palace nor the executions—including those of men in uniform—nor the genocide that darkened the already somber life beyond its walls, nor the burning hatred that at first separated families because of political conflicts and later brought unity through the magnitude of horror, nor the atmosphere of a city under occupation which lasted for years, with a curfew, a declared state of siege, a state of emergency, and a state of total irrationality, seemed to have achieved their objectives. Don Arnaldo, who at first sympathized with the coup because he believed in private enterprise, wondered why Casa García had gone under, why private enterprise was now in bankruptcy, and why his own business, now that he had acceded to the position of business owner, was in the same state of ruin. His oldest daughter had to go into exile because the dictatorship threatened her life and her husband's; and now he was broke for having believed in a system which had expatriated part of his own family. And, as though all this weren't enough, in his letters to Lorena and Mario, he told them that all was smooth sailing in his business venture with Raúl.

"In spite of everything, I believe in the system," his son-in-law repeated to him every day. "The bank is right: we shouldn't sell the machinery."

"Until when?"

"Until the thing takes off again."

"And meanwhile we eat shit?"

"Yes. I'd rather eat shit than sell the business outright. Besides, there's no one to buy it now."

"If we sold the machinery at least we could pay off something."

"A chickenshit amount, which doesn't do them any good, anyway. You don't understand, Dad. The worst thing that could happen to them would be for us to declare bankruptcy."

"Why's that?"

"Because they're in bankruptcy themselves now."

" ..."

"They have to show the greatest possible number of solvent debtors. Can't you understand such a simple thing, Don Arnaldo?"

"Of course I can't. I understand fabric, suits, sales. That's what I've lived from all my life."

And since his son-in-law was right—although that reasoning was incomprehensible to Don Arnaldo's ingenuous thought processes—the bank executive had to be frank, even unequivocal, with them when he asked them to hold on to the machinery, the plant and the fictitious business name, confiding that they too were going through a momentary crisis which made it inconvenient for them to reveal their debtors' insolvency. He suggested, as compensation for the waste resulting from keeping an unproductive business alive, the advantages of a convenient debt management plan. His proposal was incomprehensible to a simple man who had lived exclusively from his work. At the height of the crisis facing Fernández Doors and Windows, Inc., the bank generously offered to convert their debt into dollars, at the current rate of 39 pesos to the dollar. A week later the rate rose to 93 pesos to the dollar and the debt increased, including interest, to more than ninety million pesos, a sum which kept fluctuating daily and accumulating daily interest. On January 13, 1983, the bank is taken over, and then a kind of second miracle takes place, a new, generous offer that Don Arnaldo is equally incapable of understanding: the refinancing of the debt in his favor on condition that Fernández Windows and Doors, Inc. stay in existence. The son-in-law thinks of this as manna from heaven. But they have to lease a place to store the machinery. The bank assures them that this expense is worthwhile, if they consider the advantages of refinancing. The little bit they take in here and there, almost always sporadic jobs and help from other family members, is consumed by renting that foul-smelling warehouse—a clandestine distillery closed three years earlier for manufacturing lethal, adulterated *pisco*—where, like buried treasure, they store, that machinery which in their madness they believe will produce those doors and windows that Don Arnaldo knows nothing about. In exchange for this act of lunacy, the bank will reward them with an even greater one: permission to sign an IOU for a sum that Don Arnaldo considers astronomical, but which according to Raúl has the advantage of a three year grace period and an equally long period in which to cancel.

"And why are they offering us this?" Don Arnaldo asks his son-in-law every day.

"You want to know where the catch is, right?"

"Yes. I think there's a catch."

"You think they're trying to pull the wool over our eyes, but what it means it that they don't want us to declare bankruptcy."

"Why not?"

"So we won't be written off as deadbeats when they're bought out."

"And why's that?"

"Because they're bankrupt too. Or don't you understand that?"

"I don't understand. Forgive me, but I can't understand it," Don Arnaldo says, half-asleep, talking in his sleep now. Something like a frightened wakefulness penetrates the surface of his apparent repose. Twenty-seven thousand feet separate him from earth. He feels the precariousness in that misleading weightlessness and the vertigo produced by his transitory residence in the air.

"It's not necessary; I've told you that already." He thinks he hears his son-in-law's voice flying overhead like a distant echo in the endless nocturnal ocean.

"You never understand anything," Doña Elvira says, also half asleep.

"Be quiet, woman; let me sleep."

"Sign the IOU, Señor Fernández. It's the best thing."

"I have to consult my son-in-law first."

"Sign it, Don Arnaldo, sign it."

"I told you not to sign it!"

"And I told you there's no talking allowed on airplanes. Eat. You're going to die if you don't eat."

"If you don't sign, the IOU becomes a cash debt, Don Arnaldo."

"What I'm going to die from is not being in my own house."

"And the IOU can't be signed without turning over the house?"

"No, it can't. Sign here."

"I used to like to wait for you when I watered the gladiolas, or when I was knitting in the grape arbor."

"I know what a house is, Señor Fernández. I'm trying to buy one myself. Sign, please, Señor Fernández."

"The time period expired. Just look how the six months flew by. I'll have to turn the house over to them, Raúl."

"Come live with us, then."

"Would you like me to raise your seat back, sir?"

"We'll manage somehow. For better or for worse I got you involved in this, Don Arnaldo."

"But I don't know if Elvira ..."

"You do know. I want to stay in my own house."

"Believe me, signing was the best thing, Señor Fernández. You have three married daughters, don't you?"

"Did you discuss this with my daughter, Raúl?"

"My God! Did you put the teakettle on, Papa?"

"I wanted to make myself a cup of tea."

"Didn't you smell something burning? Don't you see the smoke? The teakettle was empty, Papa. You're going to drive me crazy!"

"Would you like something, sir?"

"Yes, some tea. Do I have the right to have a nice cup of tea?"

"I can't stand it any more, Raúl. Luckily this time he didn't set us all on fire."

"What do you want me to do? I spend all day running back and forth, dealing with everything that comes along. You're the one who should take care of it. He's your father, isn't he?"

"Quiet! He might be listening."

"Did you notice he stopped smoking?"

"He stopped smoking? What wonderful news! I'm telling you, he locks himself up for hours in the bathroom, puffing away. The house stinks of cigarettes."

"Well, he's trying."

"If you'd like you can sit in the rear, sir. There's an empty seat in the smoking section."

"No, thanks. I'll put it out. Excuse me."

"I'm sorry, sir, but those are the rules."

"He told me he'd quit and I believed him, Cecilia. He even told me that way he could pay us back for what he spent with the credit card."

"Our duty-free shop is now open to passengers. Anyone wishing to make purchases may pay with international credit cards."

'Whisky, sir? Cigarettes? Watches? French perfume?"

"But it's such an expensive perfume, Arnaldo."

"Well, if…It's something elegant. One day, just one day…I don't know how to explain it to you. It's just that they made me retire, Elvira. But I'm going to collect fifteen million pesos!"

"My dad is driving me crazy, Raúl. Now he's gotten the idea of going to the kiosk to buy cigarettes one by one. And that's how he spends the day. He goes out every few minutes and he always leaves the door open; but then he locks himself in the bathroom. Tell him it would be better for all of us if he didn't quit smoking."

"Lorena…Lorena."

"Don't you feel well, sir? Would you like a glass of juice? A sedative? Do you want me to lean the seat back so you can sleep?"

"He never sleeps at night."

"Shall I bring you some chocolates, ma'am? Or would you like the snack you didn't touch?"

"I want to go back home."

"Do you live in Santiago?"

"Not any more."

"Do you have relatives in Berlin?"

"A daughter."

"Yes, sign it, Señor Fernández. It's the best thing."

"How could I sign that, Raúl? I'll never see even a tenth of all that money. Even if I worked another thirty-five years at another Casa García."

"Stop screwing around and go sign it tomorrow! Don't you realize

TO DIE IN BERLIN • 133

they're substituting another IOU for this one? You want them to throw you in jail? Do you think they're giving us that money as a gift? Besides, if you sign it, you can relax until 1985. Remember, the bank gave you a three year grace period."

"Berlin ..."

"Yes, sir. You're going to see your daughter in Berlin."

"Lorena."

"You should try to sleep, sir. All the other passengers are sleeping."

"That's how he is. He never understands. He never understood that he shouldn't have signed those papers. If only you could have seen those gladiolas in the spring! The children used to play on that patio."

"Would you like me to turn out the light, ma'am?"

"No, thank you. I don't want to sleep. Why is that star following us?"

"It's not a star. It's the security light on the wing, ma'am."

"But it's twinkling. I think it's a star."

"It's a light, like they told you. What star would follow *us*? Why don't you just keep quiet and try to eat something?"

"Would you like to eat, ma'am?"

"Yes. I'd like a piece of roast beef. But I want it just like the one we ate on our picnic that Sunday."

"You're finally going to eat, Elvira! The trip's done you good."

"You'd like a piece of meat, ma'am?"

"Wouldn't you like to get to know your other grandchildren, Mama?"

"No, dear. I can't swallow any more."

" ..."

"You have to swallow something, Elvira. You have to swallow. Lorena will want to see you with a little color in your cheeks."

"Don't pay any attention to him, dear. He's daydreaming."

"Would you like me to bring your husband a sedative? He's sleeping very restlessly."

"No, darling. I know him well. That's how he is. He's crazy."

CHAPTER TEN

If you take lies away from the average man,
you take away his happiness.

Henrik Ibsen, *The Wild Duck*

The Senator's awakening was calm compared to the worrisome sensations of the night before. The idea of death was washed away with his shower, sweetened by *Tante* Ilse's apple *kuchen* and his morning coffee, forgotten while looking over the accumulated misery in those files full of applications.

The night after the party disaster and Leni's kiss on his cheek, his neighbor knocked punctually on his door, and Mario arrived on time, prepared to act as translator.

Leni burst in like a hurricane, spewing her pain and anguish. She brought some leftover cake which the old man hardly dared touch, but which Mario devoured with an eagerness that attested to a different sort of anxiety. After a while, they spoke of the Senator's distant past, of what Leni asked, without Don Carlos's or Mario's comprehending the reason for her interest.

"I just started to learn to read at sixteen," Don Carlos says and Mario translates, "but I put on my first pair of shoes when I was eighteen. I bought them in Antofagasta, the day we went to her Elías Lafferte speak," and Mario explains to her, as though she were an acolyte, that Lafferte was one of the founders of the Chilean Communist Party. And he explains how the names of Recabarren and Lafferte, as well as the words union, meeting, Workers' Federation, Party, pampa, community, were sacred for the Chacabuco miners and the other offices in the nitrate mines.

"They were the religious sublimation of a paradise lost and an unfulfilled promise: the salary they never received."

Leni doesn't understand. Don Carlos notices, just as he also notices that the interest which makes him tell this tale is an inexplicable interest in him as a person.

"It was like this," he says, interrupting the dialogue between Leni and Mario as if he really were a third speaker of equal rank. "The people who came up from the south, from the country, from the haciendas of the central region, were excited about the idea of earning a salary. They'd never heard of that before. They had never experienced receiving money for their work. The farm workers were contracted...no, what nonsense! Not contracted. There wasn't any contract at all; they were given a piece of land to live on and grow enough for stew and for what they called *galleta*, a kind of peasant bread they used to supplement the little they could grow on their plots of land. That was their salary. Then when they found out that in the nitrate works the miners collected their salaries in cash and that they could leave whenever they felt like it, change from one nitrate works to another, or save some of that money to return to the south with something they never dreamed of having, they were astonished. They worked it out so they could get to the nitrate works, doing odd jobs on ships, traveling as stowaways, whatever. My father invested a little money he had received from the hacienda owner, who on his deathbed wanted to pay him back for the twenty years he had lived and worked there. He was a little more than thirty years old when he left for the north. And up there, what did they find, those people who had traveled so far? They found that the so-called salary didn't exist. The miner's pay was a voucher—salary voucher, they called it—and it was only good for buying at the company's *pulpería*."

Here Mario asks him to wait, as he has to explain what a *pulpería* was, a kind of saloon and general store, he tells Leni, where the miners could find everything they needed to buy, but at prices that were fixed by the mine owners, who also owned the railroads and everything else of any value up north.

"The owners were English," Don Carlos says, becoming excited at the memory. "Just imagine, peasants like my father left everything they owned behind, because they wanted to know what money was. They left the fields where they were born, the grazing lands, the fruit, the wine, their families—they exchanged it all for the pampa, that endless desert which at first burns your soul, and then...Well, it's so beautiful I don't know how to describe it to you. That desert is bigger than this whole country, did you know?"

"No, I didn't know, " Leni says, blinking her eyes, astonished.

"Of course. Bigger. The region called Antofagasta is bigger than the whole GDR. And the desert is even larger than Antofagasta. It's so big you can't get out of there. That's what happened to us. We could never get out again. We left behind all the greenery, the rivers, our childhood homes, in order to go up north for pay. And we all ended up trapped in the desert, collecting that salary voucher that made us owe more to the *pulpería* every day. We worked from sunup to sundown and every day we owed the Englishmen more. They made huge fortunes from nitrates; at that time they built the Casino at Viña del Mar, the Sporting Club, huge mansions in Iquique and in Santiago. The Chilean spending spree of the twenties was paid for with the money we produced, while we fell deeper in debt every day and lived like animals in company shacks."

"But why didn't you leave? Why didn't you go back to your homeland?" Leni asks.

"That's not easy to answer. There were several reasons, and I have my own theory. One reason is that we were literally very much in debt. We were hostages to our own debt. And the truth is that we hadn't lost very much when we lost what you call our "homeland." Life is tough for the poor everywhere. But my theory, what I myself experienced, is that we all stayed there because we had the feeling we'd discovered something even greater than what we were looking for. That's what happens to the miner, you know. Sometimes—rarely, but it does happen—he discovers something much greater than what he was looking for."

"And what was that?" Leni asks.

"Freedom."

"Freedom? Living the way you did? Being able to buy only at the company store? In bigger debt every day? Poorer every day?"

"Yes, of course. What we finally discovered was much greater than our famous salary. There were days when we could do whatever we wanted. And then we'd go to the city, to Antofagasta. Many people went to drink and pick up girls. But some of us went there to meet, to talk about things we couldn't discuss at the nitrate works. That was the union. It met in a room at the Workers' Federation. A room just as miserable as our huts in Chacabuco, but with a wooden floor, which was a luxury for us, and that's where we organized the Community meetings and the arrival of our comrades. I bought myself my first pair of shoes to go to one of those meetings."

"And that was freedom, in your opinion?"

"Yes, that it was. We were all hoping for something. Maybe we didn't know what it was. Many times we would walk for a whole day to get to Antofagasta because someone there was going to tell us what would change our situation. And afterwards, we would walk all night long to get back to that slavery which was the opposite of what we were hoping for. But there's always hope. That's why it was so important to have someone come every three or four months to fuel that hope."

There was a very grave pause. Mario thought he shouldn't interrupt the silence. The old man tried to dissimulate with a smile, but it was like trying to hide the sun with your hand.

"It's hard for you to understand it," Mario translated.

"No, no. I understand it very well," Leni said hurriedly, her eyes burning with enthusiasm. "I understand it perfectly, and what you're telling me is very useful to me."

"I don't see how I can be useful to you."

"You see, right now I have a small role in the chorus of *The Flying Dutchman*."

"It's an opera by Wagner," Mario told Don Carlos in a more confidential tone.

"Yes, yes! Wagner!" Leni confirmed enthusiastically.

"And that has something to do with Chacabuco?"

"A whole lot. But I can see you're both tired and so am I."

The following night Leni told them the story of the ghost ship.

The two men got together there, awaiting her with a tacit, clandestine sense of expectation that neither or them mentioned. One could have imagined that Mario never suspected how the old man suffered with each passing minute, until he finally heard the doorbell or Leni's gentle knocking at his door; similarly, Don Carlos had no right to suppose that the measured way in which Mario presented his problems or informed the Senator of the conversation he had that morning with Dr. Wagemann sprang from his need to make his departure coincide (quite naturally, at that hour of the night) with the (equally understandable) offer of one last drink. Don Carlos required the presence of his one and only interpreter, although he knew it was already quite late, and somewhere—in Eva's house? Lorena's? or both? the old man didn't know which—Mario was expected.

At 11:25, as she had done all that week, Leni knocked as softly as she could, although Don Carlos had already leaped from his chair as soon as he heard the girl's steps approaching his door. Her maniacal punctuality, which annoyed Mario, had a very simple explanation. The last U-Bahn train left Alexanderplatz at 11:04, and that's why it was normal, barring an infrequent late-night rehearsal or an unexpected engagement, for her to reach the Volkradstrasse station at 11:18. The remaining minutes were taken up in walking to her apartment, putting a tape in the tape recorder, and making a quick turn before the mirror.

Leni became increasingly dependent on these meetings, perhaps because they took place at midnight, when the old people, or at least their dogs, were sleeping, and Leni found it difficult to endure the silence coming from the apartments, the silent agony of one hundred twenty frightened elderly people and the gloomy quiet of the building that unsettled her when she got home and saw her stark shadow outlined against the storm clouds. How different the Senator's apartment was, with the music that filtered through the partition from her own tape recorder, Mario's gallant charm, his lovely beard, and such dark eyes! And above all, it was different to talk about things which could only be said there, in that atmosphere of complicity. Yes, it was better to be in that room, even if it was just one more stateroom on the widowers' ship, and even if that ship was so much like the ghost ship Leni wanted to tell them about that night.

The Berlin night was less alien to her hosts whenever Leni was there. For a moment the Senator could forget that those one hundred twenty aged folks made up his final community, and after those pleasant evenings with Leni, Mario could forget the insoluble problems that besieged him.

Leni had gathered up her voluminous black mane which sat at the topmost point of her loveliness. She looked even more slender with the bun, more womanly and approachable. She kissed them and fell, exhausted, into the armchair. She drank deeply from the glass of wine Mario handed her and reminded them that this evening she wanted to tell them about *The Flying Dutchman*.

"They called me to substitute in the chorus of *Dutchman*. But I never imagined what that job would mean to me. And I think this also has something to do with both of you. What you told me about Chacabuco, *Herr Senator*, made me understand the meaning of this opera. You both know it, right?"

"Tell us how you understand it," said Mario, who did know it, so as not to exclude the Senator.

"Well, it's the story of an exile, a sailor who's been put under a curse by the devil. According to that curse, he has to sail on a ghost ship, but terrible storms keep him from reaching the shore that all the sailors dream about. He's only allowed to come ashore once every seven years, and if he can find a love there to save him, he'll be able to find peace and live out his last days happily in that port. The condition for gaining peace and dying on dry land is that a woman has to love him with absolute faithfulness. The opera starts when the ghost ship, with its red sail, reaches a small port in Norway in the middle of a storm. Another seven years have gone by, and the Flying Dutchman has the possibility of being saved by true love. In that port he meets Daland, a sailor, who, when he hears about his story and the treasures that are stored on his ship, offers him his daughter's hand and guarantees her faithfulness. In fact, the father sells his daughter, right? And the Dutchman arrives at that small port and meets Senta, the daughter of Daland, the captain. The interesting part is that at the beginning of the second act you see all the women of the port waiting for their beloved men to return, but Senta is busy staring at a portrait that hangs in her house, where the waiting women are all spinning on their spinning wheels. It's a portrait of the Flying Dutchman. That's where I come on stage, but only as part of the *corps de ballet* that backs up the chorus. Senta, the main character, only has eyes for the Dutchman's portrait, although she hears what the women are saying about the sailors and she thinks all that is horribly vulgar, very different from what she's dreaming about. Yes, that's it: it's vulgar, its small, it's so ordinary. It's like what my father told me when he was talking about trucking and having a lot of money and all the respect you get if you have it and all that. When I told my father I was a dancer, he thought I covered my behind with feathers and wiggled around in one of those reviews they call *varietés*. I didn't tell him we don't have that kind of stupid stuff here because he wouldn't have believed it, just like he didn't believe that I didn't want to take the hundred marks in the cafe, where everyone was watching us. Anyway, Senta wants someone to come along and take her away from all that, and so she dreams about the Flying Dutchman. Because for her, he's someone who can't be found anywhere; that is, he's what she would like to be. That's right, not to be anywhere. Because Senta's afraid. She thinks that to be somewhere means to be in a place where you don't want to be. And when they finally meet and she doesn't know that her father has sold her, she thinks she's found salvation. But the wandering sailor is looking for a place where he'll be saved, where he'll find peace and recognition. He's looking for the land of salvation because he wants to die in peace. In order to die in peace, he has to be received by the land of forgiveness. She, on the other hand, wants someone to take her away from that miserable, petty, awful dump, full of people who don't understand her and who decide what she should do and what she shouldn't do, what she should say and what she shouldn't say, what she should think and what she shouldn't think. What I like about the *mise-en-scène* we're doing is that there's no pat ending. In Wagner's original version, Senta throws herself off a cliff to show the Flying Dutchman that she can put the faithfulness of her love to the test of death. What I like about our version is how it shows the paradox, how it illustrates our reality. The Dutchman finds the place where all his mistakes will be forgiven, but that's not the place where Senta wants to live, because she doesn't accept the mistakes that have ruined her life. The land of redemption where he wants to die isn't the land where she wants to live."

Leni paused, and the silence made Don Carlos's face appear more somber. He looked at Mario for the signal to continue a conversation in which he perceived Leni as strangely tense, scattered, painfully lost. But on seeing him concentrate on Leni's musings, he chose simply to lower his gaze and remain watching the girl's hands, twisting in her lap and suggesting that in her eyes (which Don Carlos and Mario preferred not to see), the first tears were already welling up.

Don Carlos had a premonition that throbbed in his heart and in his temples and shook his soul, and that made that wound which would never close again begin to hurt in a new way. He knew that Leni was talking about him, about herself, about both of them, and that her strange confession was an unusual kind of declaration of love and at the same time the announcement of a breach. What forgiveness was she talking about, exactly? And why was he portrayed as the dying man who seeks peace in forgiveness? Or did she come to tell him once and for all that she's one of those women who approach foreigners to confide that they want to escape? In the Ministry, the Volkspolizei and the officers' classes he'd been told about that custom among "some disorderly dissident elements." They even did it in order to ask for the kind of help that would allow them to solidify their intentions. But was Leni one of them?

"Yesterday when you told me about your life and Chacabuco, and about the lives of so many people who tried to get out of there without managing to do it, you said the desert was enormous and that it swallowed them up. That's right, believe me. You expressed it very well. The desert is enormous and it's swallowed us all. You, me, all of us, here and there."

"I don't understand exactly what you're trying to tell me."

"You do understand," Leni said, and copious tears began to roll down her cheeks, which looked feverish.

"Don't you feel good? Can we do something for you?" Mario asked, sitting by her side on the edge of the sofa. But Leni didn't hear him, because she was concerned only with making herself understood by Don Carlos.

"I just want you to understand me. You're a good man who's already lived his life. You lived it, no matter what it was like. I feel as though I can't live mine."

"You've been able to become a dancer here," Don Carlos said.

"That's what it seems like. But, did you know I'm never going to become a soloist?"

"Why not?" Mario asked, as soon as he had translated Leni's question.

"Because my father escaped twenty years ago. If I could progress in my career, I'd get important roles. And that's impossible, because I'll never get authorization to leave here. A prima ballerina has to go on tour, go out of the country to perfect her technique, to represent our art throughout the world. And I don't have that possibility."

"You're very young. It'll surely change," Mario argued without much conviction.

"No one here believes it's going to change."

"You're a dancer. That's what counts," Mario insisted, and to console her and make Don Carlos's silence less obvious, that muteness of his which both Leni and Mario sensed as hard, mistrustful, but at the same time full of deep pain.

"No. That's where you're wrong… You," she said, looking at Don Carlos, "you said last night: 'in the nitrate works we were hostages to our debt.' I'm not a dancer. I'm a hostage who dances. A hostage who studied at the best dance academy, who was given this apartment in just a few months' time, who meets her obligations in the mechanism of the Opera company as part of the ballet corps. A hostage who takes her bow every night, walking to the edge of the stage to acknowledge the public's applause; and they're hostages too, who forget there's a Wall by watching a ballet in the evening.

Mario considered not translating these last words that Leni spoke, building her sentences between quiet sobs. The old man noticed Mario's hesitancy when Leni brought her handkerchief to her mouth.

"What did she say now?" he asked din a tone that was even harder than his previous silences.

Mario thought that it would be too much for Don Carlos and that it would be preferable, given the old man's marked improvement during the last week, just to leave everything right there and avoid the conflict that was becoming inevitable. Yet something told him that the blood had already reached the river, that any cover-up would make things even murkier, and that all Leni wanted from life at that moment was for her message to be heard. Then he translated each one of her sentences as he watched the Senator's face grow red. And he also translated the reply, as the old man spoke with a trembling chin that Mario had never noticed before, not even in his moments of greatest indignation.

Rising from his chair, the Senator said: "I think I've made a mistake. Please, leave us now. I beg you, turn down the volume of your music. I need to sleep."

He fell into an uneasy sleep with a sensation of absolute annihilation, and was awakened a little later by the pain that no longer left his tormented insides. His mouth was dry, his tongue stiff, and he felt his lips burning. He needed a glass of water. When he got up to get one, he decided that a glass of *Stierblut* would be better, and he recalled his meetings with Neruda and the happy wine of those years. In the tiny kitchen he filled the largest glass to the rim, as he summoned up images of other places, other times. He was drinking from his glass, sitting next to the little coffee table, when he noticed for the first time in many days that the music no longer filtered through the partition. He found this silence as implacable as his pain, and just as much of a threat. Among those things that were ending forever was Leni's music, those notes to which she would dance in her rehearsal the next day and also in the months to come, in successive performances on mild, green nights, with the warmth and fragrance of different summers.

With difficulty, he moved the bed away from the wall and thought that he would cover his ears with a pillow when he went to bed. In any case, the silence was perfect. It was a fearsome silence.

He felt he was beginning to distance himself from everything. He took a sip of wine. Distant from his world, which he lost so long ago. Distant from his comrades who no longer visit him—except for that stupid Mario, who only comes to see him about his divorce or those damn visas. Distant from Leni. Yes, very distant from Leni, he confirms, bringing the glass to his lips. And somewhat distant from something that seemed nearer: that body, painfully dying. And although the thing he most fears has not yet occurred, he knows that he's definitely distant from his best days, the only ones man deserves.

CHAPTER ELEVEN

S hortly before her parents' arrival, Lorena received an envelope with the Bureau's letterhead. It was the letter in which Don Carlos relayed the Ministry's decision: this time they were expelling her from her "second homeland," according to the official rhetoric they usually adopted in friendlier situations. Strictly speaking, her motherland was neither the first one nor this second one: she had been expelled from both under similar circumstances. After recalling the terror that gave rise to her first expulsion, Lorena locked herself in her room with the letter that decided the anguishing terms of her second exile. Abandoned on her bed, that intimate place, wide in its loneliness, she wept, unleashing the enormity of her misfortune.

At one point she took the pistol she and Mario kept at the bottom of a suitcase they never finished unpacking. Then she called a taxi and went to the Senator's house, hiding the loaded pistol in her raincoat pocket. It's logical to imagine that she headed for the sender's apartment with the intention of killing him. But she didn't know that. A person can pick up a weapon, point it at the object of her hatred—or her desperation—without wanting to kill anyone. Someone can even do this if she hates the very idea of a crime. However, even within the extreme acuity of her dream, Lorena arrived at the widowers' ship that night, rode up to the thirteenth floor, walked down the hallway which even in the dream reeked of paint, and entered the Senator's tiny dwelling. She didn't have to knock or be admitted, because this was a dream, and in the dream his tiny dwelling was at once Don Carlos's apartment in the widowers' ship and the minuscule cubicle he occupied at the Bureau. The Senator, half asleep and clad in his overly long pajama pants, tried to convince her that the Bureau was already closed, that the matter of her divorce was still being discussed, and the Ministry's decision was out of his hands. Regarding the question of the visas, there were clear-cut rules and established waiting periods which everyone had to respect. As Lorena didn't reveal the slightest intention of opening her mouth, the old man asked her what she was looking for there at that hour of the night. Then Lorena pulled out the hard, definitive object that weighed heavily in her raincoat pocket, and pointing it at him hesitantly, told him that she wanted only to put a bullet in him right there, where death would come slowly but surely, because she needed the rest of the night to make him understand the harm they had caused her.

She half awoke with the letter still in her hand, as the sky began to turn blue outside her window, and the only clear image that still remained from the other side was that of the old man clad in his pajama pants, trembling in the face of death, just as she kept trembling, perhaps from the cold, perhaps from crying.

Completely awake now, her mood brightened by a long, hot shower, Lorena thought that the wave of well-being that rose to her face with the steam from the water had to do with a sudden, new vision of the previous day's events. Even the letter from the Bureau, the main reason for her nightmare, acquired a positive interpretation with this surprising reconsideration of the facts: the tapestry as seen from the right side, the opposite side of the fabric. And with that image the stimulating revelation presented itself to her: Patricia's determined and ultimately successful efforts to allow her to live and work in Mexico, the good news about the "Aztec visas," the children's willingness to accompany her on this new adventure, their first. Yes, reviewed and put in a different order, everything now had new meaning, Lorena thought, combing her hair before the mirror, which was still steamy from her shower. It wasn't all just tremendously positive, but it was also the compendium of announcements and solutions she had been awaiting for a long time, which led her to accept the possibility of happiness without Mario, or—when she became more demanding of her own image in the mirror—the idea of something resembling happiness in a world without Mario.

She was finally going to see her parents after twelve years. What did that annoying visa business matter, then! Somehow or other the Senator himself had organized Don Arnaldo's and Doña Flora's reception at Tegel and their transportation to the border at Friedrichstrasse, where she would be waiting for them this afternoon. She would finally leave Berlin, at the latest three or four days after her parents returned to Santiago. She would finally return to the theater. She had dreamed about being on stage again, rehearsals, daily performances; she had dreamed about Mexican sunshine several times. She had dreamed about a renewed closeness with her friend. And all that was a reality that would begin to come true in a few hours, when she saw her parents emerge through the foreigners' gate at Friedrichstrasse! After all the embraces, the happiness, and the tears, she would show them her family, the grandchildren they didn't know, and their son-in-law, a bit heavier, with a few gray hairs, knowing what her parents would think: That Mario didn't turn out to be such a bad guy, after all. He turned out to be the best son-in-law, in spite of everything.

And now, as she hurriedly gets dressed (don't want to miss the beauty parlor appointment), she repeats this thought on her father's behalf, and it's as though she were hearing his voice, his movements as slow and wise as his words, saying once again: "Yes, the best one, anyway. Finally reality has lined up according to the way things should be." And even if Mario did go away at one time, today is the day of his homecoming, the river's return to its course, the return home from flight."

How wonderful it was she never told them about his leaving! How wonderful to have omitted that flight from her letters, when it was always obvious that he would return to his abode! Discussing that with them would somehow have been an adulteration of reality, thinks Lorena, who now sees her intuition and her desires confirmed. Yes, it was right not to have ever written a single line about that. Reality was better than its sad appearance. Reality was Mario coming to pick her up at four to go to Friedrichstrasse; it was Mario depositing his suitcase on the bed, taking out his shirts, his underwear, his pictures of the kids. Reality was Mario in his own house. Reality was the desired course of life following the continuous writing of her letters, with no alterations.

So, then, this last letter, the one from the Bureau, was nothing more than another episode, perhaps the most ridiculous one of all, if you considered its real consequences; the saddest one of all since it involves the poor Senator, who's already dying, and a Bureau that she visited less and less, for the majority of her affairs were now being resolved directly in the *Rat des Bezirkes* or in the *Amt für Ausländerangelegenheiten*. That letter, relaying its arbitrary decision to her, had the virtue of being the last piece of writing that could inflict another injustice upon her. In a sense, it had the character of an archaeological artifact which she would display in Mexico like a medal for her own dignity and courage in not allowing herself to be humiliated or intimidated. Then Lorena laughs, seeing the letter in this light, as it lies undramatically on the nightstand, and she laughs even harder when she thinks that the Bureau functionaries already knew about her decision to leave for Mexico while they were composing it, and they even knew that she already had the visas and that the three tickets were calmly waiting on the top shelf of the closet.

What will Mario think when she shows him the letter from the Bureau? Will he see the aggrieved Eva's distant, but at the same time very direct influence on this decision by the Ministry of the Interior? Is she suffering now, just as Lorena suffered for more than a year, and for the same reason? On this point, too, the back of the tapestry, the other side, revealed shapes and colors that were different from the reverse. The back contained vague outlines, and was opaque and contorted. From that opacity it was possible to imagine Eva's spiteful gesture, her request to her father to punish Lorena for her letter to the Ministry with a drastic, moralizing resolution. However, there was a quiet spot in the tapestry for Eva, a way of seeing it which respected her pain and left no room for blame, past or present.

And on the reverse of the tapestry there was also a place for that pain Lorena felt for Don Carlos, whom she had already begun to forgive for having signed that ridiculous, inconsequential document. Now Lorena is riding down in the elevator; she's nervous; it's time; in a few hours Mario will be back home; in a few hours, the house in Santiago will somehow be the same house again. On the first floor she stares at the bulletin board where three days ago she had tacked up her parents' telegram, in order to provide immediate, shared information to the ghetto: *Arrive Berlin 21st. STOP. Lufthansa. STOP. Excited to meet grandchildren. STOP. Love to Mario and darlings. STOP.*

She removes the telegram and puts it in her purse. The sky is clear following the snowfall and the previous evening's frigid sun. No clouds. There won't be a snowstorm for the next few days. Walking towards the U-Bahn station, Lorena thinks that finally life has been fair to her and that the 400 days she survived without Mario, and the 4700 she lived without her parents, and the 5000 she lived without practically anything of her own, are somehow coming to an end this morning, so identical to all our mornings, with the icy wind whistling down the alleyways between the tall buildings and the water in the puddles still frozen, although this morning Lorena knows that the wind and the water are telling her different things: that her body is beautiful as it leans against the

gusts and that her next steps will not be the same steps, ever again ...
They hear the pealing of a lonely bell that accentuates the silence.
One o'clock! Mario remembers how one year ago that same pealing of the bells
accompanied their first kiss. Back then the bell had announced night-
time, the promise of immediate fulfillment. Now the sun lights up Eva's
pale profile and the glistening tears in her eyes and on her cheeks. The
same sunbeam alights on another pale surface, the metallic outline of
the suitcase which waits by the door at the end of the corridor. He watches
and suffers along with Eva's suffering profile, because Eva has her gaze
fixed on the suitcase, the very personification of abandonment.

"You lied to me."

"I've never lied to you."

"You tell me you not leave."

"But I'm not leaving, Effa."

"You going away. I look at suitcase. And you tell me you never go
away from me."

Eva's effort to speak to him in his own language surprised him
from the first day. At the beginning she told him she wanted to remember what her father had taught her, but both of them understood,
without saying so, that it was a larger gesture, the desire for his company. Mario was moved by Eva's mistakes and astonished at her speed
in learning the rudiments of his native tongue. Now his tenderness yielded
to a feeling of pain, of guilt. She was learning with the corrections Mario
made, with a smile, a wink, a loving look. Now he felt the pain of each
error was a tribute he had to pay for what that suitcase meant to her,
mutely screaming there by the door. And they were just like that muteness. They had been silent, smoking, looking at objects that, in their
own silent way, spoke of abandonment, with pauses that resembled in-
termissions.

"You lie. You say you not going."

"..."

"I not expecting lies."

"..."

"I no lie to you, never."

And after a longer pause, she asked: "I ever tell you lie in all these
times?"

'I'm going to do what I promised you. I'll spend every night with
you. And it's just for a week. Besides, I want to do it, Effa, believe me.
I'm not going to come every night just because you asked me to."

"The suitcase is there. Why?"

"Because I have to leave something in Lorena's apartment in order for the lie to be believable. It's as simple as that."

"In order for a lie to be...believable," Eva repeated in an ironic tone, but the pain shined up in her eyes . "And you want I should believe lie?"

"I'm not lying to you, Effa."

"You tell me you not going. And now you go."

"But I'm not going!"

Eva went to the kitchen and came back with a bigger glass of vodka than the short ones she usually had at night. Mario lit another cigarette and after a while, to cover up the silence, he went to the kitchen for a drink as well.

"I gave everything," Eva said. And she added, after a pause," I don't want no more. Go away! Go away now! *Ich bitte dich!* Lie kills everything. Lie kills the biggest thing."

"I didn't lie to you, Effa. When I told you I'd never go back to Lorena's place I didn't know about her expulsion. That's a very hard thing for anyone to take. How could I not visit her for a few hours, a few days? Believe me, nothing's changed! I want to live with you. But, understand me, sparing her and her parents this pain is the least I can do."

"And my pain?"

"I'm staying with you! It's just a week or a little more."

"You swear you be every night with me. How I can believe?"

"You *can* believe!"

"And the suitcase, then?"

Mario took a long swallow. Now the feeling of deep commiseration for the pain he was causing Eva was becoming murky with feelings of annoyance, irritation at what he considered to be Eva's stubbornness in trying to reduce everything to the stupid detail of the suitcase. If he had removed it before, she wouldn't have noticed and they wouldn't be in this situation now, nor would she be suffering this way. I'm an idiot, Mario thought, and mid-thought, Eva's question hit him like something from very far away, like something he had to mull over and so needed to have repeated several times until he understood its meaning and its consequences.

"And if Lorena stay? You still go?"

"No. But you know she has to leave."

"And if she stay?" Eva insisted.

"It would be different. I could talk to her under different circumstances and explain everything to her parents."

"And you not go?"

"No, of course not. But nothing can be done now."

"You want me talk with my papa?"

"Okay."

"And if Lorena can stay here, you stay with me?"

"I *am* with you! This is just a farce for her parents' sake!"

"It more than that for her."

And after another long pause, she added: "And for you, too."

Mario refused to answer.

"You want me talk with my papa?"

"I don't think you'll accomplish anything."

Eva went to the phone and dialed her father's private number at the Ministry. Standing in the corridor that led to the door, she waited for an answer, looking at the suitcase and then at Mario, and past Mario, at the window, and past the window, at the blue Berlin sky, filled with clouds, just like the first night, just like the meeting which all this year felt to him like the beginning of his absolute happiness, but which now seemed more like a sad memory.

While she awaited her father's voice on the telephone, and after looking at the suitcase one more time, she said, trying to keep her voice steady: "I can not to be without you. Before, I live, in spite of everything. Or I think that was living. Now I not know how to live if you not here."

Paula cast a protracted glare of hatred at Mario's suitcase. Perhaps by seeing it already by the door, she no longer regarded it as a simple suitcase containing some clothing and a couple of framed photographs, but rather as the waving tentacles of a frightful animal. Mario felt that Paula was looking at his suitcase with the same hatred that she had ostensibly dedicated to Hermann's boots forty years earlier, when she found him concentrating on his spoonfuls of soup, at the interminable refugee shelter.

Before registering the resentment in that look, Mario had witnessed the alarming movement of some Stasi boys who had occupied the block, to protect, from inside their black vehicles and with the help of portable radio equipment, the Minister's arrival at his daughter's apartment. Thus Mario was apprised of Hermann's arrival, as he once more looked at the beautiful Mariakirche on one corner of the Alexanderplatz, placed there like a gift, just opposite Eva's terrace. Then he saw that the men were stationing themselves, not just along the block, but also inside the building, guarding its doors and elevators from some invisible enemy who was about to spring into action. A few minutes before the Minister's arrival, his personal bodyguard knocked at the door to check the remaining security controls, and two young men with a rather doltish appearance and an air of self-importance entered the apartment to determine that only the Minister's daughter and her Chilean housemate were there, and that no strange elements endangered the security of their charge.

Paula's eternal and scornful glare directed at Mario's suitcase was, therefore, preceded by this farcical display, which somehow reduced its effect—or, to look at the matter in a different light—Paula had exaggerated her glaring at the suitcase so that her entry on stage would be even more noticeable than the fuss made by the security guards.

Returning her call, Eva's father told her that he'd come to see her a few minutes after two, because first he had to pick up Paula at the *Reigerungskrankenhaus*—the hospital for government and Party employees — from where she would be discharged at noon. To say that the ineffable Paula was discharged—from the *Reigerung* or any of the other sanatoriums she frequented—was just a figure of speech. And that's how Eva, the Minister, and Paula herself saw it, since, except for the burden of her extra weight, Paula looked hale and hearty, and she took these rest cures because life in the sanatorium was more entertaining than at home or in the Institute for Marxism-Leninism (Department of the History of the Antifascist Movement), where she never could quite understand her role nor why she needed to get there every morning. Besides, rest cures at these Party or government establishments brought her into contact with many comrades from all parts of the globe, where the fight for socialism had dramatic dimensions she missed in the GDR, that rather boring, humdrum place which seemed more like plains—those difficult plains Hermann recalled for her, quoting a lovely Bertolt Brecht poem— than the dangerous, lofty peaks that the rebels in the rest of the world scaled in foreign, distant places, constantly risking their lives. Besides, one should note that the company of foreigners, so natural and frequent in government sanatoriums, enabled Paula not only to be "in direct contact with the worldwide revolution," as she used to say without the slightest trace of shame, but also to avoid daily contact with the Germans. Because the consort of the Minister of the Interior of the First Laborers' and Farmworkers' State on German Soil hated Germans above all else.

And just as she explained that hatred to Hermann the very afternoon she spat on his boots after noticing they belonged to the *Wehrmacht*, she was equally direct with Mario when she saw the discomfort that her prolonged, hateful glare at his humble suitcase could produce in him.

"This isn't a good communist attitude, Comrade Mario," and then she added, glancing around the apartment, "The truth is, I don't even know if I should call you 'comrade' any more."

"Mama, *bitte*, don't make things more complicated."

"I'm not the one who's complicating things for you. You've always done that very nicely all by yourself."

"Don't start, please!" the Minister said energetically. "We didn't come here to argue; we're here to listen," and after subduing Paula with an intense, hard stare, he kissed Eva and reached out for Mario's hand, in an effort to greet him with the greatest courtesy he could muster at that moment. And since he really couldn't summon up much, he added a smile that was as cold as the sun that came in through the window.

They sat down in silence and then exercised their customary critical scrutiny of the jumble of books and papers that added warmth to the apartment's everyday plainness. Eva offered them a cup of coffee. Her father said he didn't have much time, but Paula asked for one, in a large cup.

"*Mit Sahne*," she added.

While Eva went to the kitchen to make the coffee, Mario had to endure the worst silence of that ill-timed leavetaking. Both Hermann and Paula tried to avoid looking at him, but their dissimulation made their rejection even more evident. Paula opened her enormous purse and took out a tiny, highly perfumed handkerchief to blot the abundant perspiration that always overcame her like a clammy curse. In order not to look at Mario, Hermann observed his daughter's movements in the kitchen through the sliding glass window separating it from the dining room. Unlike Paula, he avoided not only Mario but also that part of him that persisted in the suitcase, a few yards away.

When Eva returned with the *Kaffee mit Sahne* and handed it to Paula,

The Minister asked, as though he were presiding over a Cabinet session, "What's on the agenda?"

"Lorena's expulsion order," Eva replied in a steady voice despite the new well of tears in her reddened eyes.

"First I want to know what that suitcase is all about," said Paula, peremptorily.

"It means I'll be spending a few days with my children," Mario responded.

"Oh, yes? And where are your children?"

"In their house, of course."

"So you're going back to what always was your house," Paula concluded without intending the slightest irony.

"No. I'll just spend part of the time there, while Lorena's parents are here."

"It's strange that now that she has her parents' company, she needs yours too."

'And how long will they be in Berlin?" the Minister asked in a more neutral tone which nonetheless still held all the tension of the moment.

"A week or two."

"All right. That seems fine to me, if you two agree ..."

"But I don't agree!" Eva interrupted, at the edge of tears.

"*Dafür kann ich nichts*," the Minister said.

"You could cancel the expulsion order," Eva said, recovering her composure.

'I don't see what that has to do with the matter," the Minister said.

"I imagine this has been very hard for her. I feel obligated to be at her side," Mario said.

"Do her parents know you've been living with my daughter?" Paula asked.

A brief silence was sufficient for Paula to add, "Because if that's the problem, I don't see how Hermann ..."

"That's not the whole problem, mama. If such an unfair thing could be avoided ..."

"One moment, *bitte*, the Minister said abruptly. "Who has the right to decide if it's unfair? Who has all the background information? Who decides according to certain objectives, certain dangers, and certain information? You, or the agencies responsible?"

"That's just it! Papa, who has the right to decide it's unfair to expel a person who hasn't committed any crime and who has nowhere to go, besides?"

"First of all: she does have somewhere to go. She requested—in a very unorthodox manner, I might add—and received an exit visa, saying she wanted to live in Mexico. Second: our State has not only the right, but the duty to take measures in spheres that might affect its security."

"What security? And what State? This isn't just a state, papa. This is my country! I have no other place to live, and I want to love the country I live in. And it hurt me to see someone expelled from here who's been known for so many years as a *chilenische Patriotin.*"

"She's not here to judge our laws."

"But many others here are saying what she said."

"Who are these 'many others?' Dissidents, fringe elements, enemies of our State."

"No! I think the same thing! I'm part of those 'many others.' And I'm not a fringe element or an enemy of my country."

"I don't imagine you called me to tell me this," the Minister said, no longer able to control his vexation. And there was annoyance, but also a great deal of bitterness, in his voice.

"No. I didn't call you to tell you that, papa. Forgive me. I called you to ask you for something. And if I ask for it, it's because I can't believe that letter endangers my country's security."

"Any disregard of our socialist legal system is a danger to our State. What the enemy is waiting for is a sign of weakness on our part. From that point on, the very foundation of a legal system recognized by everyone will become undermined."

"Recognized? Or do you mean 'endured?'"

The Minister renewed his effort to remain calm. He decided not to answer. He waited a moment and turned to Mario.

"You Chileans are living in difficult times for our Party. Our duty is to support you. If we accept acts of dissidence by Chilean exiles, *we* won't be the ones affected, you understand. Our resolve is a gesture of solidarity with you. Our State is healthy. We don't want anything to happen here, among your people, that might end up affecting our Chilean comrades. There's a destructive virus out there. I suggest you speak with the Senator. He understood our arguments for solidarity very well."

*"Es ist schon fast drei, Hermann!"** said Paula, stuffing back into her purse the handkerchiefs which she had been using to mop up her interminable perspiration.

The Minister stood up, shook Mario's hand with a gesture that a photo would have captured as a model of courtesy, stopped in front of Eva, and after a silence in which he placed both hands on her shoulders, he kissed her affectionately.

"Take care of yourself, my child. I promise to forget about all the things you said to me." Then they walked toward the door. Hermann turned around to smile, but his face was distorted by a trace of bitterness. Paula found it necessary to make another display of revulsion toward the suitcase, and she even gave it an ill-concealed little kick with

*"It's almost three, Hermann!"

her silvery pumps.

From the open door, and so that the security guard wouldn't hear him, Hermann spoke as quietly as possible: "Solve your problems. Don't waste your youth. I believe in simplifying things. If she's not here, it'll be better for you both."

But Eva barely heard this, for she ran to lock herself in the bathroom.

Mario stuck his ear against the door and heard Eva's sobs, muffled by the noise of the water filling the tub.

The pealing of the bells accompanied the tiny sounds that came from the other side of the door: three o'clock!

At four his in-laws would be arriving at the Friedrichstrasse station. He had promised to be at Lorena's by two. He picked up his suitcase and stuck his ear against the door again. The sound of running water was no longer audible, just Eva's suffocated, continuous crying, weak but clear.

"Effa, listen to me. Effa? Effa, can you hear me? I've got to go now. But I'll be back tonight. And tomorrow. And the next day. I won't miss a single night. Believe me! Are you okay? Answer me, please! Say something, Effa. Effa? See you tonight. Effa? Please say something."

"Go away!"

The most urgent problem Lorena had to resolve that morning was how to get her parents settled in the apartment since she could no longer —thank goodness!— give them the master bedroom. She was thinking about this when the hourly signal from Radio Berlin announced three o'clock. Perhaps it would be better to reduce her terrible nervousness, that state of heightened anxiety, to the simple question of domestic space and options. That night she would sleep with Mario, and that would have to be in their double bed. Then the children could have the fold-out sofa-bed in the living room, and their grandparents could occupy the twin beds in the children's room, which were more comfortable than that convertible piece of furniture. Besides, in that room the old people would have a modicum of privacy, which they'd need during the next few days. That morning the children cheerfully accepted the idea, gaining a small advantage in addition to the excitement of the small change of venue: they could watch television until broadcasting ended.

On the nightstand that separated the beds her parents would occupy, she put the same photos that the children kept as a souvenir of old times: images of the family together in the Erzgebirge, their smiles concealed by brightly-colored scarves, and in the background, those Metallic Mountains. Not quite satisfied with that tangible evidence of uninterrupted happiness, she added other pictures of that vacation and testimony of even older moments of joy: she, younger and prettier; and he, with black hair and the equally black beard he wore until he was thirty-five, the day he discovered the first infiltrations of gray on his dark *chilenischer Patriot's* head. On the nightstand in the master bedroom, on the other hand, she put a faded photo of Santiago: the whole family together beneath the grape arbor at their house in Ñuñoa, at a Sunday lunch.

That morning her hairdressers understood what it meant to pick up one's parents who were arriving from Chile and whom one hadn't seen in twelve years. She didn't mention a word about that other visitor, who would arrive an hour before her parents did—who should have arrived already, Lorena thinks worriedly—and who was the hidden, but doubtless most important reason for her primping. Now she's sitting on the bed, looking at herself in the mirror over her dresser. Soon the bell will ring: first Mario, then *Tante* Ilse, who, on Mario's own recommendation was hired to prepare and serve the meal at the little party that night. Two enormous *Karpfen* in the refrigerator awaited *Tante* Ilse's gifted hands, as she was a specialist in fish—trout and carp—freshwater delights, a dish that brightened Christmas and New Year's celebrations in Berlin, and that were justifiable harbingers of the foreseeable festivities of that evening, only two days before Christmas.

Embrace notwithstanding, Mario arrived just as Lorena had been expecting him to for several days, ahead of *Tante* Ilse. Lorena greeted him with a kiss, but immediately noticed a shadow, like a veiled rebuke, in his serious expression and his gestures that awkwardly tried to convey naturalness, a sad imitation of indifference, Lorena thought. When he started to head for the living room, Lorena, with a gesture toward the suitcase, directed him to the bedroom, where, in addition to the old family photo, she had placed a few red carnations, about to open their splendid buds atop the long, narrow neck of their vase.

Mario put the suitcase on the bed without commenting on the conspicuous presence of the flowers. Then he sat down next to his suitcase, his eyes fixed on the pale designs adorning the wallpaper.

"Should I help you put your things away? We don't have much time."

"There's not much to put away. I'll do it myself."

"Are you tired?"

"Very tired."

"Don't you sleep well?" And she immediately regretted asking the question.

"No, no. I sleep well," Mario replied, and she heard something additional, something she didn't want to hear, something like "Don't delude yourself; I sleep fabulously well with Eva." Perhaps it was because Mario's tone allowed for this possibility, or because of her enormous fear of that shadow which had arrived along with Mario and his suitcase. Anything he might reply from now on to any of her questions—the spontaneous, inevitable ones and also the carefully prepared ones—would be cloaked in references to something which no longer was the world Mario had discovered on a sunny afternoon in Santiago, but rather to the Mario-Eva world, the world of abandonment and winter, the Eva-world, really—that alien world where, according to Lorena, Mario was trying to find a space, a crack, a hole where there was very little room for the impetuous, captivated (and therefore captivating) Mario; for the Santiago-Institute-Protest March-Miners-Prison-Dostoyevski-Indianapolis Cafe-Senator Mario. The last link in the series that would close that personal, intimate chain clinked casually in the bedroom at the end of Mario's sentence, which she barely heard:

" ...Don Carlos ..." and Mario paused.

"What's wrong with Don Carlos? I didn't hear you, darling."

"The old man's dying. But he's as stubborn as a mule. He doesn't want to go to the hospital."

"And what are they going to do?"

"The *Reigerung* spoke with the Bureau. They're going to take him tomorrow, regardless."

"So that's what you're worried about."

"Yes, because they asked me to go along to interpret for the medical team. A woman doctor and two male nurses, actually. In case he refuses! But, anyway,...what are you thinking about?"

"I was thinking about Don Carlos, really. I saw you there with that suitcase, and I remembered the afternoon he went to pick you up at the police station. Remember?"

"A little."

"Poor old man, " and she added to herself, quietly, engrossed in her discovery, "That explains last night, then."

"What?"

"Nothing, I'll tell you later. It's late."

"Where do you want me to put my things?" Mario asked, pointing vaguely toward the suitcase.

"In the usual place. In your drawers, on the right."

Mario would rather not have heard. The note of recovered intimacy which Lorena gave the phrase seemed heartbreakingly pathetic to him. He stood up and opened the suitcase, so he could turn his back to her, so Lorena wouldn't see his own pathos, that dampness in his eyes, at the edge of tears. Was he crying for Eva, as she cried in the tub? Or for the intimate tone with which Lorena pronounced such a simple, even prosaic, phrase: "In the usual place. In your drawers on the right"? And he still had to contend with the arrival of Lorena's parents, who would still treat him like a son-in-law; and the children's arrival, around seven; and having to tell Lorena that not even tonight, this first night, would he stop sleeping with Eva; and he still had to make Lorena understand that, even though he might put his things in the usual place, those drawers on the right had stopped being his a long time ago.

He was thinking about all this as he hid his face, squatting down lower than necessary to place his clothes in the drawers of the wardrobe, when the bell rang. He stood up with a little leap and a silent question in his eyes.

"It's *Tante* Ilse," Lorena said. She's come to cook and to celebrate with us."

Chapter Twelve

The arrival of Lorena's parents produced a tremor, like a magnitude three earthquake, in our community, a noticeable shaking of the ground that didn't cause any greater damage. By that time we had become so used to the comings and goings of our relatives that in many cases the departure of a permanent member of our community caused more commotion than the arrival of someone from the "interior," as we used to call it in a slang that was already becoming outmoded.

This visit, however, impressed us more than others. Perhaps because we felt so sorry for Lorena's loneliness that past year, perhaps because of the lie she had been constructing during that time, and of which we were already aware. All of us—some more than others—had cultivated that sort of merciful lie, thinking that we couldn't possibly inflict more harm on those who had suffered, so far away, as a consequence of our decisions.

What stirred up our murky emotions wasn't, therefore, the simple visit (even though a visit from such a distance and after so many years couldn't be called 'simple'), but rather the blundered circumstances surrounding it. When we found out at the last minute that Mario was part of the farce, our expectations of a happy ending to the intentional comedy of errors grew. We would monitor of the outcome to this charade, since if Lorena's parents returned to Chile without discovering what had occurred, not only would Lorena be happier, but so would many of us who had invented ideal situations, not thinking so much of the fulfillment of our own desires as of what was expected of us over there. If Lorena's parents went back as blissfully unaware as when they arrived, it would be possible to believe in the mollifying effect of our own compassionate inventions: interesting jobs, worthy salaries, doctorates, positions in international organizations, family harmony…in short, the thousand faces of a success that was more imaginary than real.

And so that afternoon we were all heedful of their time of arrival, and we calculated that if Lorena's parents lined up at the border gate at Friedrichstrasse around four, they'd arrive at Lorena's house shortly after five. Another pilgrimage from the end of the world to our little kingdom on Elli-Voigt-Strasse was about to end.

At six in the evening, when it had already grown dark and the city was all lights, shadow, and expectation, almost all of us were looking out our apartment windows, waiting for the taxi that finally stopped in front of the door to our building. Lorena got out first, then Mario, from the passenger's seat; then the driver, who went straight to the trunk and took out the old folks' luggage; and finally they themselves, assisted by Lorena while Mario paid the taxi driver. From our windows, the visitors looked like individuals who couldn't survive without help: two old people who could manage to support themselves only on Lorena's arms and who directed a blind gaze upwards when they heard our applause. We thought they must be exhausted and that's why they could hardly walk; they had traveled for more than twenty-four hours and tomorrow would be different. But deep down we knew it wouldn't be so different. And we thought about our own parents who were starting to die so far away, without even the possibility of reaching the heart of our ghetto to verify that our merciful lies might be true, and so go on living a bit more, here and there …

For our children, who had their whole lives before them (although we didn't know what kind of lives: that of exiles, like ours, or that of dark-haired native sons, as they imagined themselves to be), the arrival we were witnessing, leaning our elbows on our slightly opened windows, in spite of the cold, was the appearance of two almost mythical beings of whom the generation born here had no direct knowledge: grandparents. Our children went to school hearing about their classmates' Opa and Oma. Now Lorena's kids' Opa and Oma were arriving at our building. They were the first grandparents ever to be received in this building. Our younger children had never even met an older relative.

As we watched from the windows, the children who were waiting in the street for the taxi surrounded Lorena's parents as they got out of the car. They stared at them, surprised, drew near to touch them, thought of them as something of their own that they could just now discover.

"You can tell this is the children's room."

'I thought you were going to give them your bedroom."

"Shhh, Mario! They can hear everything."

"Is this how you imagined it, Elvira?"

"What?"

"The house, the grandchildren, everything ..."

"Let's hope they like it. Let's hope they don't notice anything."

"Why didn't you give them your bedroom? They'd be more comfortable."

"I thought everything would be bigger. Nicer."

"The kids too?"

"No. I thought *they* would be more affectionate. They hardly even spent two minutes with us and they left."

"They're children, Elvira. They have to play. They were nervous with all their friends there, looking at us. Even I was nervous."

"Because our bedroom is for us. That's why I put your things away in the drawers."

"I thought it was to make everything more believable. For them to see me take my things out of here every day. What's wrong? Are you tired?"

"I'm very tired, Elvira."

"Are you crying? Why are you crying, Lorena?"

"Didn't you see them? Wouldn't you cry too, seeing your parents like that?"

"How do you think they're doing, Arnaldo?"

"I think they're all right. It's a good building; the children look healthy; and Lorena's been to the beauty parlor. If you go to the beauty parlor, it's a sign things are all right, it seems to me."

"You're going to tell them."

"That's not what we decided.

"You tell them. It's your fault."

"Time passes for all of us, Lorena. I understand, but don't cry because they'll find out."

"Find out what?"

"That you've been crying. You can hear everything through the partition."

"Lower your voice, then."

"Lower your voice, Elvira. They might be in the room next door."

"You meant something else."

"No. What else?"

"That they'll find out about us."

"Do you think they found out, Arnaldo?"

"I don't think so. But if you keep on going like that, they'll find out for sure, this very night."

"Lower your voice!"

"If you don't eat, they'll find out! They'll notice that something is going on!"

"If they see you crying, of course they're going to think something is going on, Lorena."

"That's why I locked myself in here. If I locked myself in the bathroom or in the kitchen, they'd notice right away. This way they think I'm getting ready for dinner."

"Eat, Elvira, please. You want some chocolate?"

"No. Where'd you get that from?"

"They gave it out on the plane. It was on the tray."

"You were talking to yourself."

"What?"

"You were talking to yourself all through the trip. The flight attendant was laughing at you. I had to tell her you were crazy."

"What was I saying?"

"You were talking to everyone. You didn't want to sign the papers from the bank."

"I'm going to make a pisco sour for your folks."

"Did my dad bring pisco?"

"No. I'll make it with vodka, as usual."

"There's still time. Don't leave me alone, Mario. I hurt so. It's like I'm suffocating. I can't breathe."

" I can't sleep, that's all. If I slept better, everything I say would be part of a dream."

"But you say it out loud. That's called talking to yourself. It would be better if you told them the truth tonight."

"We said we'd wait a week. Let them have their illusions, anyway. We have to see if we like it here."

"What choice do we have? Beggars can't be choosers. You always said that; I learned it from you. And look how we end up. This room is so small. It's not my bed. I'm suffocating in here."

"You have to put up with it. And eat."

"I can't eat. I can't swallow. What do you want me to do?"

"There's not much time left. We'll die soon. At least let's try to be as little a burden as possible, Elvira."

"Don't cry, Lorena, please. Let's have a drink. Let me go look for something. You want the vodka straight or with orange juice?"

"I want to die. Yes…that's what I want. And for no one to find out. As if I never existed."

"…"

"What's the matter? What do you hear?"

"Sshhh."

"You have to tell them."

"Tell him or tell her?"

"Her. She's your daughter."

"But it's his house."

"Then tell both of them. But tonight!"

"Lower your voice, Elvira. You can hear everything here."

"…"

"What are they talking about, Lorena?"

"Oh, my God! How much longer, still?"

While these conversations managed to filter through the unguarded border formed by the partition, despite the hushed tones, another modulation, carefree and melodic, wafted into the bedrooms from the kitchen and then from the dining room as well, harmonizing with the tinkling of glasses and china. *Tante* Ilse was singing. She always sang. And sorrows, which other people hid so well, were no reason to stop doing so.

As she cooked the two lovely carp in the biggest pot she could find, she sang an ancient song from Saxony that she had learned when she was a very little girl, that is, just after the end of the First World War, when they most likely sang it to her to celebrate, if not victory, at least survival. When the carp were cooked, garnished with sauces and condiments that had been passed down from generation to generation like the song, she sprinkled just a few drops of white vinegar into the fish broth, and the fish immediately took on, as if by magic, a bluish color that spread throughout their brilliant skin, transforming them into two succulent blue whales trapped at the bottom of the pot.

Excited by this inexplicable (for her) metamorphosis, *Tante* Ilse switched repertory and began to sing Christmas carols in honor of the immediate reason for the party. *O Tannenbaum* accompanied the final touches as she set the table with a white cloth, adorned with a silver candelabra that belonged to her, a wedding gift that she rescued by accident from a black market negotiation six months after the war. It was, in fact, the only thing she retrieved from her house, which ended up as part of the rubble heap Dresden became after the North American air bombardment at the end of the war, when the articles of surrender were already being signed.

A certain mysterious relationship linked the existence of that salvaged candelabra with the Christmas festivities. It was as if the bombs and the rubble occupied one end of the story and the time period, while the Christmas carols, the candelabra and the blue carp which had symbolized Christmas celebrations in her country for generations occupied the other. *Tante* Ilse wasn't a Christian—she wasn't a believer who frequented churches—but she held her silver candelabra as though it were a cross that could exorcise some ever-threatening misfortune and the infinite brutality that had surrounded her on so many occasions. For that reason, whenever she was invited to cook her glorious carp and serve properly at dinner parties, *Tante* Ilse, who as we know had lost almost everything in the war, was careful not to forget (although she tended to it more often with the passing years) the silver candelabra that could alleviate other people's misfortune, as well.

From *Tante* Ilse's sideboard to our somewhat more primitive tables came not only her candelabra but also the long white tablecloth she inherited from her mother-in-law and some heavy napkins embroidered with her husband's initials—he who was introduced to the African desert in Rommel's offensive and was buried there—napkins embroidered with Gothic calligraphy in one corner, as heavy as a flag.

The third wonder that *Tante* Ilse brought to those houses which required her presence wasn't as tangible as the imposing candelabra and the ponderous napkins, but rather something impalpable, something like the infrequent blue sky on those winter days: her impressive will to be. And we're not talking here about the will to live or to hope. The will to live somehow presupposes a project of some kind, something like a program, which is dangerously connected to the fetish of success; while that trite word, hope, is the most common one in the mouths of exiles. No, the very will to be is what burned within *Tante* Ilse with its own light. That's it: to be herself, happily occupied with her blue carp; to keep on being in spite of all that was destroyed and killed around her; to exist at all times in a moment of plenitude, even when, as she used to say gaily on leaving our soirees: "I don't know if this will be my last party. I'm happier not knowing. *Gute Nacht, meine Herrschaften.*"

Tante Ilse spread the seven place settings around her candelabra like a fan, taking care that the spaces between them were even and that the embroidered initials were on the visible side of the napkins. The seven diners included the heads of the household (who, as we know, were no longer that), Lorena's parents (who weren't there for the reason everyone supposed), the children (who deserted before even coming to table), and who else but the selfsame *Tante* Ilse.

"What was the last thing you ate that tasted good, Doña Elvira?" Mario asks, trying to bring about a solution to her unavoidable fast.

"I don't remember any more."

"A biscuit during the flight," Don Arnaldo says, to mitigate his wife's abrupt answer.

"That? I hardly touched it," Doña Elvira insists in an even more brittle tone.

"But what was the last food you remember enjoying, mama?"

"A piece of meat. A slice of roast."

"Do we have any meat, *Tante* Ilse?"

"There's a piece in the freezer. I could cook it."

"Don't worry about it; it's not worth the bother. I can't eat anyway."

"A slice of roast, mama. Like that last one you ate."

"Do you remember that roast, Elvira?" Don Arnaldo asks, hopefully, trying to penetrate her stubbornness with his affectionate tone.

"Of course I remember. I was watching the river while I ate it. I still had the taste of that roast in my mouth when I saw our house pass by. Yes. I was watching the river and suddenly our house went floating by. It was moving away. It floated away on the river."

"*Tante* Ilse: cook it, please. Cook that piece of meat," said Lorena in a slightly annoyed tone of voice.

"No. I don't want that piece of meat," Doña Elvira insists, emphasizing '*that* piece of meat' disdainfully.

Tante Ilse gets up and goes to the kitchen, giving Lorena a look of complicity.

"Who is that person?" Doña Elvira asks as soon as *Tante* Ilse is gone.

"*Tante* Ilse. She helps us when we have guests. She's a marvelous cook; you'll see, mama."

"And why does she sit at the table?"

"Because she's like a member of the family."

"Of *your* family. In my house I never had a servant sitting at the table."

"She's not a servant, mama."

"What's she doing here, then?"

"She's helping me."

"And you pay her?"

"Naturally."

Doña Elvira pauses briefly to emphasize her conclusion and then says, in a somewhat indifferent voice, without taking her eyes off her husband's face, "Then she's a servant."

"She's a friend of the family. She's a widow, and we help her out. That's how she earns a living," Mario interjects in a conciliatory way.

"I wouldn't like to earn my living that way. I want to go back home."

"You will go back, mama. In two or three weeks you'll be back in your house," Lorena says, lightly caressing Doña Elvira's hand, which looks like a lifeless object, as pale as the tablecloth. And she adds in a jovial tone, "Don't you think we can take good care of you for a few days?"

"That's right," Don Arnaldo says supportively, and then, unable to avoid her reproach, he turns to his wife: "Why are you saying that? We talked about this already, didn't we?"

"Fine, I'll hold my tongue," Doña Elvira says, lowering her gaze.

"Yes, hold it, " Don Arnaldo says, as though he were saying, "Cut it off!"

"Some dessert? Would you like a chocolate dessert, mama?"

"Yes, I'd like that."

"Finally, mama. You're so thin." And she gets up to go to the kitchen.

"No, no. I'd like to, but I can't swallow it. And don't tell me I'm thin," she adds in a quavery voice. "I didn't say I don't want to eat. I said I *can't* eat."

"Leave her alone, please. She'll just get more nervous," Don Arnaldo pleads.

"Tell them why I'm nervous."

"Well, the trip…Seeing the grandchildren she never met ..."

"Tell them the truth."

"Elvira!"

"What's the truth?"

"What I was telling you. She's more nervous when she's away from home."

In a pathetically infantile outburst, Doña Elvira mocks him: "She's more nervous when she's away from home."

"Elvira, behave yourself. If you go on like this, I'll do what I said I would."

"What did you say you'd do, papa? What are you trying to tell us?"

"Nothing," Doña Elvira says, looking at Don Arnaldo.

"Nothing," Don Arnaldo confirms, looking at his wife.

And after a pause, Doña Elvira asks her son-in-law: "What time is the first mass?"

"The first mass? I don't really know."

"You don't know? I saw a church when we arrived. It's only a few blocks from here, surely."

"We'll find out what time mass is first thing in the morning," Lorena promises.

"The first one," Doña Elvira insists.

"Whichever one there is, mama. If there *is* one at that church."

"You don't go to mass. You already told me that. Nobody goes to mass here, " Doña Elvira says to herself, accentuating her reproachful tone.

"I told you not to mention that subject, Elvira."

"And what do you think of your grandchildren, mama?"

"They're indifferent."

"Have some salad, Don Arnaldo. I highly recommend these potatoes. They're seasoned with dill."

"What's that?"

"They've asked about their grandparents all these years."

"Dill is…how can I explain it? What's *dill* in Spanish, Lorena?"

"What?"

"What's dill? The stuff on the potatoes."

"*Eneldo.* So don't say they're indifferent, mama. They're children, that's all."

"But they left already."

"They're telling their friends in the building what their grandparents are like. They're nervous too, mama."

Back from the kitchen, *Tante* Ilse enters the dining room smiling, enthusiastically, like a tank at a parade.

"*Das ist aber ein wunderbarer Braten geworden!*"

Everyone is hanging on Doña Elvira, who keeps staring at the piece of juicy, fragrantly seasoned roast. Then she pushes it away gently without saying a word, looking at the air as if she were trying to track a fly buzzing slowly toward the ceiling.

"Does anyone want another piece of carp?" Mario asks.

No one answers.

"The taxis here belong to the government, I suppose?" Don Arnaldo asks.

"That's right," Mario answers.

"And if someone wanted to have a fleet of private taxis, nothing very big, let's say two or three taxis, what would he have to do?"

"Nothing. There are no private taxis."

"We had to wait in the cold for over an hour. I suppose you work for the government too."

"I teach classes at the university. I worked for the government in Chile, also."

"But now there are private universities. You'd earn a lot more."

"I don't think so."

"Do you earn enough working for the university?"

"Yes, I earn enough. And I'm doing what I like, Don Arnaldo."

'He published a book of short stories, papa. And he wrote a screen-play, as well as his doctoral dissertation."

"Then you're doing all right," Don Arnaldo concludes.

"Fine, papa. As you can see, we're fine. So tell us, how are Cecilia and Chepita?"

"Fine. Very well."

"Why did you say you saw the house floating in the river, mama?"

"Because that's what she saw in a dream," Don Arnaldo adds, hurriedly.

"Oh, it was a dream," Mario says, pouring more wine.

"A dream, a dream," Don Arnaldo repeats, holding out his glass.

"And how's the house, mama?"

"It's all right, isn't it?"

"I always think about the grape arbor. Were you able to expand it, like you wanted to?"

"Yes. It's larger now."

"Now I know what I could swallow."

"Tell us, mama!"

"I'd like to eat a little bit of *chirimoya*."

"But we don't have that here, mama. Wouldn't you like an apple?"

"No, not an apple. I can't swallow apples."

"Are hospitals very expensive here, Mario?"

"They're free here, Don Arnaldo."

"Free? And who pays for them?"

"The taxes everyone pays."

"And if someone isn't a permanent resident, how can he go to the hospital?"

"I don't know. But there are several Chilean doctors who could find out what's wrong with you, mama."

"I'm fine. I'd like them to examine Arnaldo."

"I feel fine."

"What's wrong with you, papa?"

"Tell them the truth."

"What's wrong with papa, mama?"

"He's sick in the head."

"One of Elvira's jokes. This is such good wine, Mario! Pour me a little bit more."

"It's Hungarian. I think it's wonderful myself."

"There are some very pretty places here. We should go to the Baltic and to Dresden. How many days are you planning to stay?" Lorena asks.

"Well, we have no firm plans. We can go wherever you like, sweetheart."

"We'll make a nice itinerary. One or two weeks would be enough to see the most interesting things."

"First I'd like Elvira to be examined."

"Let them examine *you*. You don't sleep. You go around talking to yourself."

"Don't talk nonsense."

"You talk all night long."

"Don't you sleep well, papa?"

"At my age people don't sleep much."

"And you, mama? Is it hard for you to sleep?"

"I prefer my own house."

"Well, you'll be in your own house in a matter of days."

"Would you like the chocolate dessert with whipped cream or with ice cream, *meine Herrschaften?*"

"With whipped cream. You're very kind," Don Arnaldo says in a comically chivalrous tone, almost flirtatious.

"Not me," Doña Elvira says, annoyed.

"With ice cream?" *Tante* Ilse asks, looking her right in the eyes.

"I can't swallow, but of course you didn't understand. It's not your fault," Doña Elvira replies, returning *Tante* Ilse's gaze with the same rancor.

"With ice cream, *Tante* Ilse," Lorena says.

"I'd like mine with a little brandy. Now you're going to try some Moldavian brandy, Don Arnaldo. And you're going to sleep like a log," Mario says, getting up to look for his Moldavian brandy, which he knows has been stored, for a year now, to the left of the sideboard.

Much later, almost at dawn—she can see the sky beginning to clear through the window—Lorena hears the noise of a key in the lock. She waits for the door to open, signalling Mario's return. Is he with Eva? Is he in the hospital at Don Carlos's deathbed? When the telephone rang, at the end of that interminable meal, she suspected the call was for Mario. And, in effect, the call had to do with his absence. Mario answered the phone in the bedroom, and when she left her parents with *Tante* Ilse and reached her bedroom, Mario had already removed his coat from the closet and was heading for the door.

"What's going on?"

"Don Carlos is in the hospital. It looks like he's dying."

"Who called?"

"Leni."

"Why did she call you?"

"Because she doesn't know anyone else to call."

"And what can you do?"

"I don't know. Go to the hospital; I suppose that's the first thing."

"Don't lie to me."

"What?"

"Don't lie to me. Not tonight. Don't you think I've had enough?"

"I don't get it."

"Who called you?"

"Leni."

"Not Eva?"

"No, of course not. I have to go, Lorena. Leni called from the hospital. I can't leave her alone with the old man."

'I'm going with you."

"Why?"

"Because I want to know what's going on with Don Carlos, too."

"Stay with your parents. It'll be better."

"When are you coming back?"

"Later, I guess. Explain to your folks."

"If she hadn't called you, would you have stayed with me?"

'I don't think so. I promised Eva I'd spend the nights with her."

"That's not what we agreed on."

"We agreed to invent a believable farce for your parents. They haven't noticed anything."

"And what if you don't come back?"

"They'll go to bed. Tomorrow night they'll see me again. Now the most important thing is Don Carlos. If it isn't too serious, I'll be back. But then I'll go to Eva's."

"That's not what you promised me."

"I promised you they wouldn't notice anything. You have to cooperate too. Go to them now. They must be finding this very strange."

She walked him to the door and watched him wait for the elevator. He didn't have his suitcase in his hand, but it was just like it was a year ago, only now she didn't know if he was going directly to Eva's house or if he was really running off to the hospital, fearing an imminent tragedy. Something that had begun with the phone call and ended with Mario's worried expression told her he wasn't lying. But after so many hours had gone by—her parents had gone to bed a while ago and the children were asleep on the rug in front of the television, which was still on—she imagined that even if the tragedy was legitimate, Mario had gone directly to Eva's from the hospital. Why didn't he call her? Didn't he realize what that night had meant to her?

She lit a cigarette, deciding to smoke it, as she usually did at that hour, on the balcony. Then she realized that if she didn't want to wake the children or her parents, she was limited to the tiny enclosure of her bedroom. Her space had been reduced and Mario wasn't with her. She opened the window, in spite of the cold, and stared at the multiplication of endless buildings, all of their windows darkened now; a concrete desert, the anticipation of a cemetery, a foreboding of the end. The silent snow was also part of this unwanted presage. She thought that if she couldn't hear a single sound, it would be have to do with Don Carlos's death. Or with Mario, ensconced in a different niche, perhaps less silent, having a drink with Eva before going to bed.

That's when she head the first noise.

It didn't come from the door, as she expected. It came from the children's room. It was the sound of a muted argument that grew louder and was painfully audible when she opened her bedroom door and approached the room her parents occupied. With her ear to the wood, she heard the sound of sheets, a violent quarrel that was contained in the suffocating limits of a whisper, some light steps on the floor. And then the voices, extremely clear:

"They already figured it all out. You're a chickenshit. You couldn't tell them. Go find a bed pan yourself."

"I can't move, Elvira. Please go for me. If I move I'm going to get the bed all dirty."

"I don't know my way around this house."

"Call Lorena."

"She's asleep."

"Wake her up!"

"Fat chance! You'll just have to put up with it."

"I can't."

"I've put up with lots of things."

"I can't! Go look for a bed pan."

"How am I supposed to know where it is? They probably don't even have one here. Go to the bathroom."

"You know what'll happen if I move. I can't wait any more."

"Go to the bathroom. Walk slowly."

As she went to look for a basin, a portable bidet, anything to solve the problem, Lorena heard the noise of sheets, some hurried steps, and then the sound of crying. When she opened the door she also heard a thundering that relieved her father's intestines and smelled a fetid odor she would never forget.

Surprised to be caught in these last few vestiges of intimacy, Don Arnaldo instinctively tried to take shelter behind the wardrobe. When Lorena opened the door and looked inside to see what was happening and to find out the reason for the argument, she saw her father in the shadows, trying to hide behind the only available piece of furniture, dragging his skinny humanity behind the wardrobe, while with his hands, which propelled him in this desperate attempt, he also tried to cover up the shameful result of the rumbling that had shaken his insides.

Lorena was assailed by the odor of her father's excrement at the same moment that the other indecency, even more terrible and painful, emerged from her mother's mouth:

"You shit yourself again, you old shit."

She also heard the old man's sobs, growing gradually louder, as though this had happened many times and the rhythm of its swell was a familiar thing.

"That's what you get for eating like that. The way they all eat around here, those pigs. Don't you want some chocolate dessert? Haven't you tried that brandy? Look how you're shitting now. You clean it up. I'm leaving. I don't know where. But I can leave. I'm clean. Tomorrow I'll go to mass and the priest will see what a saint I am."

"Hand me something, Elvira. Some paper, anything."

"There's nothing here. It's not my house."

"My handkerchief. In my pants pocket."

"Everyone says I'm skinny. But when you die, I'll meet the man who's been waiting for me all these years."

"You'll wake Lorena. Pass me my handkerchief."

"No. It was your fault we lost the house. Let them see you this way. And tell them we have nothing. Tell them we're here to stay, because even if we don't like it, we have nowhere else to live."

Lorena went to look for a bidet and some cloth to clean up her father, closing the door very carefully. She didn't want them to hear her; she didn't want them to feel obliged to explain everything she already knew from that very moment.

CHAPTER THIRTEEN

Lorena has just turned forty. She's crying; you can see some gray hairs; from a window in the hospital she's looking at the clear Berlin sky, stars crossing the night over the divided city; and party gaiety, fireworks in celebration of New Year's Eve. At her back, Don Carlos is dying. Her parents will die soon, too, and she'll be there. Her children will continue to grow, as will her dreams, and she knows she'll be there, closer to her children than to her dreams. Why me? she wonders, very quietly, and a second voice, one that floats from within her into her ear, replies: *Only you? You think it's only you?* She hears the old man's final death rattle and recalls how one night, lost in time and nagging at her memory, she wanted to kill him; she also recalls an ancient conversation at the Indianapolis Bar. The Senator radiated a magnetic attraction; he was good looking, nice; he promised every kind of freedom imaginable in the best of all possible worlds. He believed in the possibility of paradise on earth. She recalls one sunny Santiago afternoon, a beret, a libretto, some apples. She recalls a prison cell, a kiss from Mario, Sputnik lost among those same stars, seen that night from the door of her house.

Who was living in her house now?

She remembers an old song. Voices which always accompanied her and which echo on this New Year's Eve more loudly than the spectacular fireworks explosion:

> *Rosita, Rosita, to look at your toe,*
> *if this were allowed me,*
> *how far would I go?*

She saw Patricia hiding in the wings, winking, smiling at her, coaxing her to do what she didn't dare do. So much time had passed! As soon as she got home—a home that very soon would also cease to be hers—she'd send Patricia a telegram:

> *My parents have arrived.*
> *I'm staying in Berlin.*
> *Letter to follow.*
> *How far will this go?*

Go where? How will she explain to her that if she had to wait so many years for her own visa, it wouldn't make sense to request others for her parents now? It would be best to dilute everything in that ambiguous message: *Letter to follow.* The unexplainable part would be included in a letter that would never be sent. "I'm staying in Berlin." Even that wasn't the truth. Another friend, living in West Berlin—that part of the city Lorena isn't familiar with—told her that it was possible (possible, not certain) to get a job in a beef jerky factory. They always needed labor there, preferably foreigners. Most of them were Algerians, Turks, Portuguese. That was one possibility. If everything worked out, she could actually set herself up in West Berlin. Her friend offered her a place in her apartment for a couple of weeks, and after a while, everything would be arranged. She'd earn enough in the factory to support her parents. And by living on the other side of the Wall, she could visit her children a few times a week. She already knew they'd never receive permission to go with her. And she'd tell Patricia all that in the letter she promised. For now, she'd allow herself a little joke that would diminish the pathos of the telegram:

> *Rosita above, beef jerky below,*
> *If this were allowed you,*
> *How far could you go?*

Yes: she'd send it right away. She'd go straight from the hospital to the post office and she'd send the telegram. Three sentences. Sever the dream once and for all. A telegram has the advantage of clarifying everything with a single machete blow.

> *I'm staying in Berlin*

would be the first sentence. But that sentence led immediately to another which she imagined as she watched the shimmering fireworks still exploding on that New Year's Eve:

I'll die in Berlin.

She thought about her children, who would never stop needing her; about her parents, who could no longer go on living without her.

Then she heard the door opening, followed by a few steps, then silence; and after the silence, the steps of the nurse approaching.

"*Sind Sie die Tochter?*" ("Are you the daughter?")

"*Nein. Was ist los?*" ("No. What's the matter?")

"*Der Herr ist gerade gestorben.*" ("The gentleman just passed away.")

Don Carlos's demise confirmed a certainty for us which accompanied Lorena during the last days she lived in Elli-Voigt-Strasse. Far from the return we dreamed of, yet never close enough to the world that attempted to take us in, each departure only served to reinforce an experience that ultimately became part of our world view: life is continuous loss. We lost our hopes of returning; we lost those who nourished those hopes and brightened our memories—our only means of returning—and day by day, though we may not have noticed it, we lost our capacity to survive.

Shortly after the Senator's death, one of us received an invitation from the Bureau to the premiere of a Soviet film at the Cine Internacional. The invited guest did everything possible to interest others in those tickets,—and as he wasn't successful, he went to the premiere so the seats wouldn't all be empty. It turned out that the film had been banned for many years and had just premiered in Moscow as well. After seeing it, everyone thought it was something new, it was the truth. Three days later, there were endless lines in front of the Cine Internacional: block after block of people wanting to see that film, an occurrence that never happened with Soviet films, although, in compliance with official programming, they never ran for less than six weeks. This one, however, was withdrawn on the fifth day, which gave rise to a constant buzz in cafes and workplaces for weeks afterwards (at least for the six weeks it should have been playing), increasing public interest because of the mere fact that everything which might have been said about it had now passed into the realm of conjecture and, therefore, exaggeration. The significant thing is that it was the first time a movie showing in Moscow was ever taken off the boards in the GDR, one of those films with the image of the proletarian couple revolving with their hammer and sickle on high. How we laughed then, recalling Don Carlos's enthusiasm for the monumental sculpture which would outlive him *per secula seculorum!*

Because of this and other signs, there was some talk about certain changes in the orientation of the Soviet regime, but that was very hard to believe. And harder still to believe that the First Laborers' and Farmworkers' State on German Soil would adapt to those changes, even assuming they were to go into effect.

If the optimists insisted that something was beginning to change, the great majority disbelieved this with indifference, or imagined that they were merely subterfuges to placate those who were angry. Within our community there was the same degree of hope as that which our hosts displayed: none whatsoever.

Lorena visited us with her children from time to time. She used to cross the border at Freidrichstrasse two or three times a week to see them. Since she couldn't guarantee them a good existence beyond the Wall, she chose to accept the belief that they lived in a privileged world here. And the truth is that here the children, without knowing it, do live under the very strange conditions of privilege which history has granted them: nowhere else in the world is it sadder to stop being children.

But Lorena's children are still far from reaching that misfortune, and Lorena herself accepts their separation, aware that over there she couldn't offer them what the State – which separated her from them – can provide for them here. Whenever she visits, it hurts us to see her so reassured by the security the Big Bureau guarantees them, and at the same time so unhappy at having lost them.

Last night, after the big black Ministry car came to pick up the children, Lorena told us she had been with Mario that afternoon at the Espresso Cafe. This time she brought him José Donoso's *The Garden Next Door,* recently published in West Berlin. She was sure he would like it.